Two On Two Out

a novel by
Ryan M Blanck

ryan.blanck@gmail.com
805-990-5225

Two On Two Out
a novel by Ryan M Blanck

Cover art by Morgan Blanck.

Also by the author:

So, Yo Man, What's Your Story?
Rediscovering Middle C (cowritten with Robert Blanck)
#TheStruggleIsReal
Infinite LEGO
Supposedly Fun Things...
Engaging the Media 2.0
Engaging the Media

Acknowledgements:

I wish to acknowledge the contributions of the following people, without whom I don't think I could have written this novel.

Tanya, Emma, and Morgan. Thank you for your patience and encouragement through this long writing process.

John, Kurt, Meribeth, and Dad. Thank you for reading multiple drafts of this book and offering valuable feedback. This novel wouldn't be what it is without your help.

Mark, John, Rick, and Andy. Thank you for the many hours we spent talking about the game we love that inspired this story.

"We just don't recognize life's most significant moments while they're happening. Back then I thought, 'Well, there'll be other days'. I didn't realize that that was the only day."

-- Dr. Archibald "Moonlight" Graham
Field of Dreams

CHAPTER 1

September 26, 2002
The Ballpark in Arlington
Anaheim Angels (97-62) vs. Texas Rangers (72-87)

"Erstad takes ball four and jogs down to first base for the second time tonight, which gives the Halos two on with two out here in the top of the seventh. Hopefully the Angels haven't given up on this one yet. You never know what Mike Scioscia has up his sleeve," said Steve Physioc, the Anaheim Angels' television play-by-play announcer, as he shuffled the stack of papers on the table in front of him, papers containing every imaginable statistic on every player on both rosters.

"I think you're right, Steve, I wouldn't count the Halos out just yet. Alvarez appears to be struggling here despite having a two-run lead for the Rangers," said Rex Hudler, the Angels' color commentator. "He got those first two outs pretty quickly, but now he's having some trouble finding home plate. He's been giving up a lot of walks lately. And that has been the M.O. for the Rangers' bullpen lately. They're good at getting out the first couple of batters, but then they struggle to close out innings, especially this late in the game."

"Well, this is interesting, Rex. It looks like Mike is gonna pinch hit for Tim Salmon. Scioscia is calling him back into the dugout from the on-deck circle. We'll see who he decides to send to the plate."

"Right, it is an interesting move, Steve, pinch hitting for one of the best hitters in the lineup. But a week away from playoffs, I bet Scioscia just wants to give the guy a rest. It's a long season, man, and at this point in September, these guys are *ti-i-red*. But if things continue to go well, these Angels could be playing for another month. And the way they've been playing lately, I wouldn't be surprised if they go deep into October."

"You know, Rex, I've got a good feeling about this team. I'd put money on these Halos going all the way, and I'm not just saying that because they sign my paycheck..."

These two veteran announcers were experts at small talk. They both knew that the absolute worst thing about calling a baseball game was the dead air time when a manager made changes to the lineup or a catcher needed to chat with his pitcher. And they didn't always know if the break in the action would be long enough to necessitate going to a commercial. So, Steve Physioc and Rex Hudler just kept up the banter, waiting for Angels' manager Mike Scioscia to decide who would pinch hit for outfielder Tim Salmon, and waiting for the producers to decide whether to go to commercial or not.

"Would you like to bet your next paycheck on it, Steve? 'Cause I'd be willing to take that bet."

"Uhh... No... But I *would* bet you ten dollars..." Physioc paused, thinking he saw some movement down in the Angels' dugout. "It looks like Mike is still weighing his options. You know, Rex, even though the Angels are down by two, this is a great opportunity for some of those September call-ups to cut their teeth here in the Big Leagues, especially with a playoff spot already secured. Escobar had a good night last night with that double in the eighth off Vandermeer."

"You're right, Steve. That two-bagger definitely caught the attention of a few scouts in the stands. Escobar had a great season in Triple-A, which could earn him an invite to Spring Training next March. If he's given more opportunities like last night, and delivers like he did last night, then his name will definitely come up among the general managers during the Winter Meetings in December. If he's not the right fit for the Halos, I'm sure some other team will *make them an offer they can't refuse*." Rex

Hudler's voice went into a really bad Marlon Brando impression at the end there.

"I think you're right. But it doesn't look like Scioscia is sending Escobar to the plate again tonight, Rex. He's looking down to the *far* end of the bench. He's pointing at... uh... Mitchell... Henry Mitchell appears to be getting the nod. What can you tell us about this kid, Rex?"

Rex Hudler laughed. "Would you take a look at that, Steve? I think Mitchell is just as surprised as anyone that Scioscia is pointing at him. Would you look at that expression on his face!"

"Let's see what the producers were able to pull on Mitchell. Henry Aaron Mitchell..."

There was much scrambling taking place at the producers' table behind the two announcers. It would seem that nobody - in the dugout or in the booth - expected Henry Mitchell to make an appearance today.

Rex Hudler continued as he looked at the fact sheet handed to him, "Wow, *Henry Aaron* Mitchell? I wonder what it was like for this kid from the suburbs of Kansas City to grow up with the same name as the greatest homerun hitter in history. No pressure, I'm sure."

"Oh yeah... no pressure at all. His dad must have been a pretty big baseball fan," Steve Physioc began reading aloud. "Let's see... name: Henry Aaron Mitchell. Born on December 9, 1974, making him... 28 years old. He played AAA ball at Salt Lake this past year, and came to the Angels organization last winter in the trade that sent Mo Vaughn to the Mets. He just barely made the 40-man roster expansion this year. I think the Angels were planning to bring up Jason Rockwell, but he's still nursing a hamstring injury from earlier in the season. It seems that Mitchell did not have a lot of notice before he had to get on the plane to meet the team out in Orange County."

"Well, Steve, it looks like Henry is having trouble finding a bat that suits him." Hudler paused, then let out a little laugh as he called out. "You can't be too picky there, Hank..."

"You know, Rex, with the short notice that Mitchell received, he likely didn't have time to pack all of his equipment. He was probably lucky to show up with his glove, cleats, and jockstrap, and now he has to rely on the team for the rest. So, he's gonna have to borrow a bat from one of the regulars."

"Well, ladies and gentlemen, I have a feeling we are in store for something special here in Arlington tonight. Making his Major League debut with the Anaheim Angels, number 10, Henry Aaron Mitchell..."

"Harry... Harrison..." Angels' Manager Mike Scioscia shouted from his perch near the dugout steps to the group of players at the opposite end of the bench. Scioscia adjusted his cap as he waited for a response.

"It's Henry, Mike. Henry Mitchell," said bench coach Joe Maddon.

"Right... Henry!" Still no response from the other end of the bench, even when Scioscia did call out the correct name. Henry Mitchell was deep in conversation with a few of the other September call-ups, his teammates in Triple-A Salt Lake. They had joined the team some three weeks ago, but they mostly kept to themselves. They were all too intimidated by the Big Leaguers to approach them. Not that the guys were unapproachable, but the newbies didn't feel comfortable approaching them on their home turf.

"Yo, Mitchell," shouted one of the Big Leaguers leaning against the dugout fence. Henry finally looked up.

"Coach is calling you," the Big Leaguer said as he spit out a sunflower seed shell.

Henry broke away from his conversation and made his way across the dugout toward Mike Scioscia, nervously adjusting his cap.

"Grab a bat, kid; you're up," said Scioscia.

"Go get 'em, kid."

"You got this."

Words of encouragement came with pats on the back as Henry reached into his back pocket for his batting gloves. His quickening pulse caused his hands to start trembling, making it more difficult to put his gloves on. He'd been in this moment a thousand times or more. How many times had he put on those batting gloves, grabbed a bat, and stepped into the batter's box? But this time was different. This was the Big Leagues. This was the dream. This was the moment he imagined as he fell asleep almost every night since his first Little League t-ball practice.

He continued walking toward the dugout steps, his teammates' words slowly fading into the background. When he would look back on this moment and tell this story twenty years from now, he'd like to be able to say that he was entering "the zone," tuning out all of the distractions around him and becoming one with the game. But it was his nerves, plain and simple. Henry started taking slow, deep breaths. This breathing technique had served him well throughout his career as he would walk from the dugout to the on-deck circle in high-pressure situations. And one's Major League debut is probably one of the highest of high-pressure situations.

As his foot touched the first dugout step, Henry felt yanked back into reality by a firm hand on his shoulder. It was hitting coach Mickey Hatcher.

"Hey, kid, forgetting something?" Mickey asked. He could see that Henry was nervous, and he hoped a friendly smile would help ease the pressure.

"Huh?" Henry said.

"Grab a bat and helmet, kid," Mickey said. "Just relax, kid. Get up there and take your swings and see what you can do with that curveball of his."

Henry stepped back into the dugout and grabbed his batting helmet. As he put it on, one of the veteran players grabbed his bat and offered it to Henry.

"Here you go, kid. It's my lucky bat... Just don't crack it," said the left fielder. Henry took the bat from him. It felt a little heavier than the bats he usually played with, but - as they say - beggars can't be choosers.

Henry gripped the bat tightly with both hands, took a deep breath, and started up the steps. On the second step, he felt his foot slip ever so slightly. A sharp pain shot up his leg from his ankle - the one he injured his freshman year in high school. That moment came shooting back to him as the pain shot up his leg. He was a cocky young player, thinking he was a bigshot for making the varsity team as a ninth grader. He knew he should have listened to his coach and stayed at first when he hit the ball to the right field fence. But no, he had to show off and go for extra bases. He barely beat the throw, but his foot hit the third base bag hard, severely injuring his ankle.

It'll be fine, he thought.

"Your attention please," boomed the voice of the public address announcer. "Now batting for number 15, Tim Salmon, and making his Major League debut is number 10, Henry Mitchell."

To say that the crowd of Rangers fans roared with enthusiasm would be a gross overstatement. Some fans applauded. A few whooped and hollered. There was even a whistle or two. But not much beyond that on this warm September evening. The Rangers had a losing record and the heat of late summer kept many fans away from the stadium that night. So even a frenzied crowd of this size wouldn't make much noise. And, besides, what more would you expect when a rookie makes his debut for the visiting team?

When Henry got to the on-deck circle, he reached for the pine tar rag. Ever since he witnessed the infamous George Brett pine tar incident as a kid, Henry liked to use a lot of pine tar on his bat. It didn't do much to help his grip or swing, but Henry started the habit in Little League. As he was about to apply the tar to the handle, a loud "Hey, hey, hey!" came from the dugout. The owner of the bat did not approve. Henry tipped his helmet respectfully and let the rag fall back to the ground.

Henry tightened his grip on the bat and took a couple of practice swings in the on-deck circle. He twisted his torso once or twice to stretch out his back a little. His muscles had grown stiff standing at the dugout fence watching the game with his teammates. Then another practice swing.

The Rangers' catcher was growing impatient.

"Come on, rookie," he said as he lifted the bottom of his facemask and spat on the ground in front of him. "Let's get a move on. I've got a hot date with your sister after the game."

The home plate umpire smiled behind his mask at the catcher's comment and motioned to Henry to tell him to hurry up, then checked his wristwatch to see what time it was. You know it's been a long, slow game when the umpire is anxious to get home.

Henry hurried to the left-handed batter's box. He looked down to the third base coach for the signs as he dug his back foot into the dirt.

"Alvarez settles in on the mound, glancing at the runners on first and second," Steve Physioc said. "Mitchell glances at the third base coach again to make sure he's got the signs right."

"The rookie looks pretty nervous down there, Steve," Rex Hudler chimed in.

"Alvarez from the stretch… and a *huge* swing and a miss from Mitchell." Steve Physioc's description was a gross understatement. Henry Aaron Mitchell swung at the ball like he was trying to knock it into the middle of next week. But he swung so early that his body had almost made

14

a complete rotation before the ball made it to the catcher's mitt. Even the umpire chuckled a bit at Mitchell's nervous enthusiasm.

"Man, oh man. He was *way* out in front of that one!" Rex Hudler said.

"Mitchell steps out again. It looks like Mickey Hatcher is shouting something to him from the dugout steps."

"Probably just telling the kid to calm down. He's got way too much adrenaline. Mix that with the nerves of his first Big League at bat, and you've got a recipe for a three-pitch strikeout," Hudler paused and then continued, turning the conversation away from Henry Mitchell's nervousness. "You know, Steve, Mitchell's in the ideal situation here. The Halos may be behind on the scoreboard, but they have their playoff spot secured, so this game really doesn't matter in the grand scheme of things. Mitchell's got nothing to lose here. If I were Hatcher, I'd tell him just get in a few good swings and hope for the best."

Steve Physioc took a sip of water before continuing the play-by-play.

"Alvarez sets for the 0-1 pitch. Delivers from the stretch... Mitchell gets a piece of it and fouls it down the right field line, bringing the count to no balls and two strikes," Physioc paused as the players on the field got ready for the action to resume. Henry adjusted the Velcro straps on his batting gloves before stepping back into the batter's box, and the Rangers' pitcher rubbed the shine off the new baseball with his bare hands, his mitt tucked under his arm.

"Alvarez on the mound. He looks at the runner on second, who's got quite a lead from the bag."

"You're right, Steve, that is quite a lead, but Ramirez is not much of a threat to steal," Rex Hudler chimed in. "I think he is just trying to get into Alvarez's head to give the rookie at the plate a chance to swing at a bad pitch."

"Alvarez doesn't like the lead that Ramirez is taking at second. He steps off the rubber, and Ramirez retreats back to the bag."

"You know, Steve, looking over Mitchell's AAA stats here, he's not a bad hitter in these situations. We might just see a little hit-and-run action here, even with two outs."

"Alvarez delivers the 0-2 pitch... A big swing by Mitchell... It's a high fly ball down the right field line. It's got the distance, it's just a matter of if it stays in fair territory..." The entire Angels dugout was waving their arms as if trying to create a strong enough wind to keep the ball from going foul.

"The right fielder is at the wall in the corner...and the ball lands... *just* foul and into the seats."

A mighty groan went up from the dwindling crowd. This was the most excited these fans had been all game, even with their home team holding onto a two-run lead.

Henry had made it around first base and was halfway to second by the time he saw that his monstrous fly ball was nothing but a really long foul ball. He hung his head in disappointment as he trotted back toward home plate. The baserunners returned to their places as the pitcher rubbed the shine off another new ball.

"Man, that's about the closest I've seen a ball come to being a homerun in a long time," Rex Hudler said. "Look at the replay, Steve. From this angle, it looks like only a matter of *inches*."

They, along with their television audience, watched the replay several times, each time a little slower than the last. It truly was a matter of inches separating the foul ball from the home run that it could have been. It seems that all that arm-waving from the dugout had not quite done the job.

"You're right, Rex," his partner in the booth replied. "But take a look at Mitchell; look at the confidence on his face now."

As Henry took his place in the batter's box, he did have a newfound confidence. He pin-wheeled the bat around a few times, now with the posture of a ten-year veteran.

"Right, Steve. The butterflies seem to have settled down and he's ready to hit. Man, look at the smile on Mitchell's face. He's a totally different batter than the one we saw step into the batter's box a moment ago."

Steve Physioc called the next pitch. "Alvarez from the stretch..."

"What the..." Rex interjected.

"Alvarez throws high and way outside! Luckily the catcher got a good read on it, otherwise that ball bounces to the backstop and the tying run moves ninety feet closer to home plate."

"That's right, Steve. Great defense behind the plate... What's happening down there? Do you see that, Steve? Alvarez is walking toward home... looks like he's got a thing or two to say to Henry Mitchell."

"I can't quite tell what's happening, Rex... Now both managers are on the top steps of their respective dugouts. The Rangers' catcher is jogging to intercept Alvarez, who looks really upset about something."

Down on the field, Alvarez was pointing at Mitchell and shouting expletives at him. Henry took a few steps in the direction and safety of the home plate umpire, who had his facemask off and was warning Alvarez not to come any closer. The Rangers' catcher met Alvarez on the infield grass and attempted to walk him back to the mound.

In the stands, there was a delayed reaction. Fans saw that something was happening, but no one seemed to know what. Even the home plate umpire, who was trying to calm everyone down, didn't seem to know. The only people who did know were Alvarez, his catcher, and Henry Mitchell.

Up in the announcers' booth, Steve Physioc and Rex Hudler were also trying to make sense of the nonsense happening on the field down below.

Physioc, recognizing that silence is the worst thing to broadcast on live television, did his best to narrate the action. "Alvarez is back on the mound and is fuming at Mitchell. Maybe Mitchell said something as he went into his delivery? It's hard to say. Mitchell is a few steps up the third base line now, talking things over with the base coach. And the home plate umpire is standing in the middle of the infield making sure no one gets any closer to each other."

"You know, Steve, our producers are reviewing the tape, and you're not going to believe this..."

"What'd they find, Rex?"

"Check out this footage from the camera on the third base side. Watch Mitchell's face. He's waiting for the pitch. Look. Right there. He gets that little smirk on his face... And right there... Look... Did you see it? He *winked* at Alvarez."

Steve Physioc chuckled as they watched the footage again in even slower motion.

"Well, look at that," Steve said. "It's just like that 'Moonlight' Graham character in *Field of Dreams.*"

"I think every ballplayer who ever watched *Field of Dreams* as a kid wishes he had the guts to stare down a Major League pitcher and wink at him."

"And Henry Aaron Mitchell from Kansas City, Missouri, had the guts to do it, Steve. Can you believe it?"

CHAPTER 2

December 9, 1974
St. Louis, MO

"Excuse me, Mr. Mitchell," the chief buyer's secretary said as she peeked her head into the conference room. "I have a message for you. They said it's urgent."

She smiled as she handed him the note, and then smiled again as she left the room.

Jack Mitchell was in the middle of his sales presentation to the chief buyer for this very important client, and he was on fire. He had the buyer right where he wanted him and was about to "go in for the kill," so to speak, when he was interrupted by the note from the secretary. Jack was about to shove the note into his pants pocket, but it was obvious by the looks from the chief buyer and his assistant that they weren't going to let him ignore an "urgent" note.

The phone message was from Jack's mother-in-law. It read: "Diane went into labor. Taking her to the hospital. Hurry home."

The baby was not due to be born for another ten days, but Diane had a hunch it might come sooner. She begged Jack not to go on this sales trip, even though he was only going to be a few hours away. All these thoughts screamed at him as he stared at those eleven words on the slip of paper.

An awkward silence now hung in the conference room that everyone but Jack noticed. The assistant buyer cleared his throat and Jack finally realized that all eyes were on him and he gave the room a sheepish grin.

"My... uh... my wife is in labor... She's... uh... on her way to the hospital..." he stammered as his eyes went from the note in his hand to his briefcase and other belongings on the table in front of him.

The chief buyer spoke up, "Well, what the hell are you still doing here? Go!"

Jack just stood there as if unable to move.

"Look, I'll have my secretary clean up your stuff and we will have it sent to your office," the buyer said in a calm, reassuring voice. Jack had several poster boards set up on easels around the conference room, along with copies of his firm's latest product catalog in front of each member of the buying team.

"And, yes, we would like to renew our contact, and increase our monthly orders by 3%," the chief buyer said. "And congratulations. Now go. Be with your wife."

One of his assistants came around to Jack's side of the table to help him to the door.

"Th... thank you," was all that Jack could say.

When Jack got into his car out in the parking lot, his head finally began to clear. He had a nearly four-hour long drive across the state of Missouri from St. Louis to Kansas City ahead of him. As he made his way to the freeway, Jack kept hearing his wife's voice over and over, asking him not to go on this sales trip. Yes, he was only a few hours away. And yes, Baby Mitchell was not due for another week and a half. And yes, Jack would only be gone for three days. But Diane had not been feeling well during the past week, and she really didn't like the idea of him being away from home so close to her due date.

But Jack insisted that his boss really wanted *him* on this sales trip. He told Diane that he was the only person his boss trusted in handling this particular client. This sales meeting could mean one of the biggest contracts in the firm's history. Even though Jack knew deep down that there were other salesmen who could have done as good a job, he *really* wanted to be the one to make the sale. He knew that the promotion his boss had been dangling in front of him would be his for sure if he was successful.

Now he had a huge lump in his stomach. Would she ever let him live this down? The silver lining was that he had made the sale, and that promotion was his for sure. But the likelihood of missing the birth of his firstborn was still a pretty dark cloud.

The traffic gods smiled on Jack Mitchell as he drove across the "Show Me" state toward his wife and soon-to-be-born child. He maintained a cruising speed of about 65 miles per hour, and he only had to stop for gas and a bathroom break once. He hadn't eaten since that bagel and coffee he had for breakfast, but the guilty, anxious lump in his stomach left no room for food.

As mile after mile of Interstate 70 passed under his car, Jack found himself recalling the memory of when Diane first told him that she was pregnant.

This pregnancy wasn't planned, but it certainly was a welcomed surprise. Jack and Diane wanted kids, but they wanted to wait until he was in a better position with the firm and until she had finished her schooling to become a dental hygienist. But as the Scottish poet Robert Burns once wrote, "The best laid plans of mice and men often go awry." Despite being careful, one of Jack's swimmers had plans of its own.

Back in April, Jack found out that Diane was pregnant while he was away on another sales trip, this time to Atlanta. At the time, he had been with the firm for a little over a year and this was his first big solo trip. His boss saw a lot of potential in Jack, and wanted to see how he would do with this particular client in Atlanta. This client had a pretty substantial account with the firm, and they were a very loyal customer, so there was little chance of Jack truly screwing things up. Jack's boss wanted to see if he could get the buyer to increase their monthly purchases.

Jack's sales pitch went better than anyone could have expected, thanks to the fact that he had been up until 1:00am the night before rehearsing the presentation. Getting the client to renew the contract was a given, but no one expected them to increase their order by four percent each year for the next three years. And to top things off, Jack was invited to a fancy dinner and to that night's Atlanta Braves game by the company's vice president in charge of purchasing. No one in Jack's firm had ever received this kind of treatment from the client.

The date of this magnificent sales pitch and fancy dinner and evening in the company suite at Atlanta Stadium just happened to be April 8, 1974. That's right, the day Henry Aaron hit home run number 715, breaking Babe Ruth's nearly forty-year-old record.

Jack Mitchell could not believe his good fortune. He was tempted to hop on the next plane to Las Vegas after the game to try his newfound luck at the craps table. But receiving a phone message at the front desk when he got back to the hotel snapped him back to reality. The message was from his wife, Diane. Jack was almost in a panic by the time he got up to his room and started dialing the rotary phone next to the bed. They couldn't afford the long-distance calls when he was on the road, so they agreed she would only call in an emergency. And besides, he had a ticket for the 6:00 flight back to Kansas City the next morning.

His feelings of panic were quickly assuaged when Diane spoke six words during that short phone call: "You're going to be a daddy."

First, the amazing sales pitch. Then witnessing baseball history. Then finding out he was going to be a father. April 8, 1974, turned out to be a perfect day for Jack Mitchell.

Jack was so caught up in the memory that he nearly missed his exit. Luckily there was no one in the right-hand lane when he swerved onto the offramp. The hospital was just a few blocks away.

He parked the car on the third level of the hospital parking structure, not bothering to lock the doors. He ran down the stairs, along the sidewalk, through the main entrance, and into the hospital lobby. Out of breath, he asked the receptionist how to get to the maternity ward. Jack and Diane had been to the hospital for the "new parents" tour that her doctor had arranged, but with all the excitement and stress of the day, Jack had no clue of where to go.

"Down that hall," she pointed to her left without even lifting her head to look at him. "Take the elevator to the seventh floor, then turn left and down that hallway."

"Thank you," Jack said as he hurried off in the direction she pointed to. He considered taking the stairs instead, but seven flights was a bit more than he thought he could handle under the circumstances. He pressed the call button.

Exiting the elevator on the seventh floor, he turned left and jogged over to the nurses' station. Before the nurse on duty could even say "may I help you?" Jack asked, "Mitchell? Diane Mitchell?"

The nurse checked the chart on the desk for Diane's name while Jack paced back and forth. Echoing through the hallway were the sounds of childbirth and newborn babies' first cries.

"Here it is, room 715," the nurse said.

"Thank you," Jack said as he headed down the hall in the wrong direction toward the labor and delivery rooms. The nurse, seeing his mistake, called out to get his attention. He spun around to see her pointing in the opposite direction toward the recovery rooms. Jack jogged back toward the nurses' station and then passed it with an embarrassed half smile on his way to the correct room.

When he reached room 715, he was disappointed not to hear his wife crying out in the pains of childbirth; either he had the wrong room, or he had missed the delivery. There was no sound coming from the room, actually. He hesitated a moment, then knocked softly as he pushed open the door.

Sitting there in the bed, with a look of utter sweaty exhaustion, was Diane, holding the baby to her breast. Jack's shoulders sank a bit when he realized he had arrived too late. Baby Boy Mitchell had been born about an hour before Jack's arrival, so given the drivetime between St. Louis and Kansas City, there was no way he would have made it on for the birth.

"Oh my god, I'm so sorry... I can't..." he stammered.

"Shut up and come meet your son," Diane said with a smile. Most of her long, dark hair was pulled back in a ponytail, but the hair around her face was plastered to her skin with sweat.

Jack walked over to the bed and Diane scooted over a few inches to make room for him to sit down. He kissed her still damp forehead as he sat. He reached out and stroked the top of his son's head, which was covered with a pale blue cap. Jack leaned over and kissed his wife's cheek. She rested her weary head on his shoulder.

The baby finished feeding and Diane covered herself with the flap of her hospital gown. She lifted the baby to her shoulder and gently patted his back to try to induce a burp. There was no burp, but he did spit up a little. Diane had forgotten to put a burp cloth on her shoulder, so the spit up started to soak into her shirt.

"Look, I am so sorry about..." Jack tried to apologize again, but Diane cut him off.

"I know, but I'm sure you earned a huge commission to make up for it," she said.

He nodded and smiled at his exhausted wife. They sat in silence for a moment before she continued, "So I've been thinking about this little guy's name..."

"Yeah?" Jack said hesitantly.

"He just doesn't look like a Roger to me," she said. "Look at that face. Is that the face of a Roger?"

Jack studied his son's face. He had to agree with his wife. That was not the face of a Roger.

"I agree," he said. "So, what did you have in mind?"

"Well, I know Roger is your dad's name, but what if we named him after my dad?"

"Henry?"

Diane nodded, smiling an exhausted smile. Jack took another long look at his son.

"Henry?" he said again. "Henry? Do you think he looks like a Henry?"

"Yeah, I do."

"Henry?" he said a fourth time. The name was starting to grow on him. "I kinda like it... So, what about his middle name? I don't think my mom will be too happy since she was hoping we would name him after my dad."

Jack's father had passed away suddenly from a heart attack shortly after Jack and Diane had gotten married. And it wasn't long before Jack's mother was dropping hints about wanting a grandchild, as well as dropping hints about naming that grandchild - if it was a boy - after Jack's father: Roger Mitchell.

"Well, what about your dad's middle name?" Diane asked. "It's Aaron, right?"

"*Henry Aaron* Mitchell?" Jack asked.

"Yeah. It's got a nice ring to it."

Jack just smiled and shook his head.

"What?" Diane asked. The *other* significance of the name was lost on her at the moment.

"I love it," Jack said. For the second time that afternoon, he was visited by the memory of April 8, 1974. "But he'd better be one helluva ballplayer."

Chapter 3

April 5, 1980
Flora Park
Gladstone, Missouri

"Come on, Henry. It's time to go. You don't want to be late for your first day of baseball, do you?" Jack Mitchell shouted down the hallway to his son as he waited by the front door.

"But Dad, I can't find my glove! Where's my glove?" Little Henry was frantically tearing his room apart looking for his brand-new baseball mitt. He and his dad had spent about three hours the other night going to five different sporting goods stores to find the perfect glove. Sure, they found at least half a dozen perfectly good baseball mitts, but little Henry just had to have one with Hank Aaron's signature printed on it.

"It's right here, Hammer." Jack called out. Based on the sounds of Henry's things hitting the floor and the walls, Jack knew that Henry was well on his way to full-blown panic mode. He would get this way sometimes when he thought something important had been lost. Just a week ago, Henry thought he had lost his brand-new Boba Fett action figure. He had saved up his allowance and then begged his mother for two days to take him to Toys R Us to get the coveted toy. Not two hours after he had freed it from its cardboard and plastic packaging, Henry thought he had lost the toy forever. But, of course, it was on the top shelf of his bookcase, exactly where he had put it for safekeeping.

Jack hurried down the hall to cut off the madness.

"Hammer... Hammer... Henry!" Little Henry jumped and finally turned around to face his father, surrounded by a growing pile of clothes and toys in the middle of the floor.

"I've got your glove right here, buddy," Jack said reassuringly. Jack held out the reddish-brown baseball mitt. It had a baseball wedged into the pocket and a heavy-duty rubber band wrapped around it to help break it in. That's how the big leaguers do it, his father told him. Fortunately, Jack was able to convince Henry that he did not need a brand-new ball to break in his brand-new glove. The Hank Aaron-endorsed glove was almost twice the price of similar gloves at other athletic stores, so Jack didn't have enough cash to buy the glove *and* a new ball. Henry would have to settle for one of the many baseballs that sat in a five-gallon bucket in the garage.

"Remember, buddy? We put it right over there by the front door so we wouldn't forget to take it to practice." Jack pointed to the spot on the entryway table that could actually be seen from Henry's bedroom. "Now come on, let's go play some baseball."

Henry looked up at his father rather sheepishly. Jack, crouching down to look Henry in the eye, handed the mitt to his son. Henry took it, snapping the rubber band on his glove and smiling at his dad. He put his hand in his father's, and the two walked toward the front door. Jack grabbed the car keys and knew that Diane would not be happy to see the mess in Henry's room when she got home from work. But they would be late for t-ball practice if they didn't leave right away, so the mess would have to wait until later.

The drive to the park was only about ten minutes, but those ten short minutes were filled with conversation all about baseball. Little Henry, not quite five-and-a-half years, loved to talk and talk and talk with his dad about baseball. Most dads told their sons stories about brave knights fighting dragons or about Old West sheriffs driving the bad guy out of town, but not Jack Mitchell. He told stories of no-hitters and walk-off home runs.

28

Ever since Henry was old enough to sit still and listen to a story, Jack had filled his head with the legends from baseball's mythical history. Lou Gehrig's seemingly unbreakable games-played streak. "Shoeless" Joe Jackson and the 1919 Black Sox scandal. Even stories from the Negro Leagues, like Satchell Page's knack for not only talking trash, but for backing it up as one of the greatest pitchers to ever play the game. It helped that Jack was one hell of a storyteller, able to turn even the most trivial event in baseball history into the most heroic of deeds.

"Daddy... tell me about the Babe again... about him callin' his shot," Henry said from the backseat, a gleeful smile covering his face. Of all the stories that Jack had told his son, the one about Babe Ruth calling his home run shot was by far Henry's favorite.

Jack rolled his eyes, but Henry didn't notice because he was too distracted counting the birds perched the electrical line running alongside the road.

"That story again? You *always* want me to tell you that story," Jack said.

"Come on, Daddy. Tell me about the Babe." Henry's voice took on a playful, whiny tone. He knew his father was only feigning protest. Jack was never one to say "no" to a baseball story request.

"Alright, alright... I'll tell you the story... *again*."

"Yay!" said Henry as he snapped the big rubber band wrapped around his new baseball mitt.

Then, as if he had flipped a switch, Jack launched into storyteller mode.

"It all happened way back in 1932. Game 3 of the World Series... Yankees versus Cubs... Wrigley Field." Jack's voice deepened and he enunciated every syllable of every word, just like the sports announcers that Jack and Henry watched on television and listened to on the radio.

"It was the top of the fifth inning and the game was tied at 4-4, and George... Herman... Ruth..."

"The Great Bambino!" Henry chimed in, right on cue.

"Yes, Henry, George Herman Ruth, the Great Bambino, stepped into the batter's box. The Cubs fans were booing the Babe, and the Cubs players on the bench weren't being much nicer. The Babe had already hit one home run that game, and nobody rooting for the Cubbies that day wanted to see him hit another one.

"Cubs pitcher Charlie Root wound up and threw the first pitch to the Babe."

"Strike one!" Henry said, raising the index finger on his left hand.

Jack continued the story as he glanced at Hammer in the rearview mirror. "The crowd booed louder and the Cubs' bench yelled louder, but the Babe just stood there. Root threw strike two, and the crowd booed even LOUDER and the bench yelled even LOUDER. But the Babe just stood there.

"Then the Babe did something no one had ever seen before. Standing there in the batter's box, he raised his hand and pointed toward the fence in the deepest, farthest part of center field." Right on cue, Henry pointed his finger at some distant object outside the back-seat window as his father continued the story. "Nobody could figure out what he was doing, but the Babe knew exactly what he was doing.

"The next pitch was a hanging curveball. The Babe swung his bat at that hanging curveball and..."

A loud WAH-POW sounded from the back seat as little Henry swung his arms like he was hitting a baseball.

"The Babe swung his bat and that hanging curveball flew right over the outfield fence, landing in the exact spot that he pointed to. The Sultan of Swat rounded the bases for his second time that afternoon. George... Herman... Ruth..."

"The Great Bambino!" once again sounded from the back seat.

"Yes, the Great Bambino had called his shot!"

Henry lifted his hands in exaltation. He'd heard this story so many times that he could practically recite the damn thing himself, but he got sucked into his father's theatrics every time he heard it. Jack looked at Henry in the back seat and smiled. His first and only son, the one he found out about after watching Hank Aaron break Babe Ruth's home run record, the one who shared a name with the home run king, had fallen in love with the game that Jack loved so much.

Jack entered the parking lot and pulled into a spot under the shade of a tree. After shutting off the rattling engine, Jack came around to the passenger side of the car and opened Henry's backseat door. Henry adjusted his Kansas City Monarchs cap as he slid off the seat and started running down the sidewalk toward the baseball diamond.

"Hey, Hammer!" Jack shouted after his son. Henry, who was about thirty feet down the sidewalk already, turned around to face his father. When Henry saw Jack holding the brand-new baseball glove, he smacked his forehead with the palm of his hand. Jack smiled and shook his head as little Henry came running back. He snatched the glove out of his father's hand and ran off back toward the field. Jack chuckled as he grabbed his own Kansas City Monarchs cap from the passenger seat, putting it on his head as he walked after Henry. Henry's mother had bought Jack and Henry matching Monarchs hats for Father's Day last year.

Near the end of the team's hour-long practice, Henry got his first chance to take batting practice. He selected his bat from the ones leaning against the dugout fence, totally disregarding the length or weight of the bat and choosing the bright orange one leaning all alone away from the rest of them. Orange had always been Henry's favorite color. From the nearby bleachers, Jack noticed this and made a mental note. He would have to take little Henry out this weekend to buy a bat – a bright orange bat, of course – that was an appropriate size for him.

Henry stopped a few steps away from the dugout, making sure he was far enough away so as not to hit anyone, and swung the bright orange bat a few times before walking over to home plate. He dug his brand-new cleats into the left-hander's batter's box and pinwheeled that too-heavy orange bat a few times - like he'd seen some of his favorite big leaguers do on TV - before sizing up the ball on the tee. He took a huge swing at the ball, one that would have sent the ball soaring into the parking lot... if he had actually made contact.

Jack winced when he saw Henry's epic whiff. "Come on, Hammer! You've got this!" he shouted toward his son standing at home plate. Jack wiped away the sweat from his brow with his shirt sleeve and adjusted the well-worn Monarchs cap on his head. It was a warm spring day and the bleachers were in the afternoon sun. But the perspiration was caused just as much by nervousness as it was by the warm weather. He really wanted Henry to hit that ball.

Henry stepped out of the batter's box and looked over his left shoulder at his dad as he adjusted his batting helmet. Jack gave him a big thumbs up and a reassuring smile. Henry smiled back and returned the thumbs up gesture to his dad, then turned around and dug into the batter's box again.

Henry went through the same routine: pinwheeling the bat around twice, then staring down the ball with a look of pure determination. Then, as if an actual light bulb switched on above his oversized batting helmet, Henry shifted the bat into his left hand, letting it rest momentarily on his shoulder, and extended his right arm and pointed his finger at the deep centerfield fence. A chuckle ran through the parents in the bleachers behind the dugout, followed by a loud cheer by Hammer's dad. "That's right, Hammer! You call your shot!"

Henry choked up his grip a little and took another monstrous swing at the stationary ball on the tee.

PING!

Hammer made solid contact with the red-laced leather ball. It flew off the tee, high into the air toward the centerfield fence. But, alas, little Henry Aaron Mitchell was no George Herman Ruth.

The ball landed somewhere behind the pitcher's mound on the infield grass, and the middle infielders just stared at it as the ball rolled toward the second base bag. The ball had barely made it beyond the pitcher's mound, but the mighty Henry Aaron Mitchell had indeed called his shot.

Chapter 4

July 24, 1983
Yankees Stadium
Kansas City Royals vs. New York Yankees

Kansas City Royals All-Star third baseman George Brett trotted triumphantly around the bases as the ball he had just hit soared over the right field fence, giving the Royals a 5-4 lead over the Bronx Bombers in the top of the ninth inning. Up in the nosebleed seats behind home plate, eight-year-old Henry Mitchell recorded in the Scorebook the run scored by U L Washington - the base runner who was on first when Brett hit the dinger - and then recorded the home run by Brett.

The Scorebook was a sacred object in the Mitchell household. Back when Jack was about eight years old, his father took him to his first Major League Baseball game. Jack's father had bought a brand new faux leather-bound scorebook to keep score during the contest between the Detroit Tigers and Cleveland Indians. He taught his son how to keep score that day, and a tradition was born. From that day forward, every time Jack and his father went to a game, they kept score in that Scorebook. And now, Jack was passing on this beloved tradition to his son.

Henry looked up at his dad for approval, but it took Jack a second to notice Henry pulling at his pant leg. Jack was on his feet applauding and cheering for George Brett's two-run homer. He drew dirty looks from the Yankees fans in the seats around him. But Jack Mitchell didn't care; dammit, he was at Yankees Stadium watching George Brett hit the potentially game-winning home run. It was a thrill just to watch a game at Yankees Stadium, but to see his hometown Royals actually beat the Yankees – if they could hold onto the win - in such dramatic fashion would be a story he would be telling his friends and coworkers for years.

"Good job, Hammer, you're gettin' it," said Jack Mitchell as he looked down at the Scorebook, paying no attention to all the eraser marks and corrections all over the pages spread out on little Henry's lap. "That's why we do it in pencil," Jack remembered his father always telling him.

All throughout the game, Jack patiently explained the ins and outs of scorekeeping. The tally marks to keep track of pitch count. The defensive position numbers to record each out (Jack had stuck a Post-It note on the top of the page to help Henry out). Tracing a runner's path around the bases. Henry caught on pretty quickly, more quickly than Jack had caught on when his father taught him.

This trip to New York, and specifically to this Yankees/Royals game, had been months in the planning. Jack had saved up his vacation time all year for this trip, and he and Diane had spent hours planning the trip with her brother, Steve, who worked as a travel agent. They had saved up plenty of money to do New York right – it helped that Jack had been bringing home a fat commission almost every month – but Jack could not stand paying what he thought was too much for things. He wasn't cheap, but he made sure to get the most bang for his buck. Hence the hours spent with Steve looking for the best deals on flights, hotels, and sightseeing attractions. And even though he could have splurged on better seats, Jack got some of the cheaper ones available for their trip to Yankees' Stadium here on July 24. Besides, the upper deck behind home plate was his favorite place to take in a game; it provided the perfect view of all the action.

In the week leading up to the game, Jack and Diane and Henry took in all the sights of NYC. They snapped lots of pictures from the tops of the Empire State Building and the World Trade Center. They went to Ellis Island to see the Statue of Liberty. Jack and Henry took the stairs up to the

34

top of the Statue of Liberty to take in the view from Lady Liberty's crown. They ate hot dogs from a vender's cart in Times Square and rode bikes in Central Park. It was the perfect big city vacation for this suburban family from the Midwest. All of Jack and Diane's research and planning had certainly paid off.

And this perfect week spent in a nonstop blitz of the Big Apple culminated with a trip to the hallowed grounds of the House that Ruth Built. Watching a game at Yankees Stadium is akin to going to Easter Mass at St. Peter's Basilica. Or a personal audience with the Dalai Lama. Or sharing a meal with the Reverend Billy Graham. And the events of the ninth inning of this game would make sure that neither of them would ever forget it.

George Brett's two-run home run in the top of the ninth inning put the visiting Royals ahead and seemed to deflate the hometown crowd that day at Yankees Stadium. Typically, these Yankee fans would stay to the bitter end to watch their team cruise to a victory, but many fans started for the exits, hoping to beat the foot traffic to the nearby subway station. With most of these fair-weather fans facing toward the exits, it took many of them a few moments to realize that something was now happening behind them down on the field.

Henry was in the middle of asking a question about scorekeeping, but Jack was no longer listening to him. Jack, who was already on his feet after cheering Brett's homer, could see that trouble was brewing down on the field at home plate. He stretched out his hand toward Henry to shush him so that he could focus on what was happening down on the field. But Henry kept right on talking, oblivious to what was happening around him.

George Brett headed toward his cheering teammates in the visitors' dugout, receiving high fives and pats on the head and shoulders. Meanwhile, Yankee manager Billy Martin exited the dugout on the other side of the infield and strolled calmly and confidently toward the home plate umpire. The Royals were oblivious to Martin's antics until it was too late. A brief conversation ensued between the calm and cool Martin and the ump, the content of which was unclear until crew chief Tim McClellan walked toward the Royals' dugout and signaled for Brett's bat to be brought back onto the field from the dugout.

"Oh no. What in the damn hell?" Jack began muttering under his breath. He never swore in front of Henry, except when he got really upset while watching baseball. The first time Henry had ever heard PG-13 language from his father was when the Phillies beat the Royals in the 1980 World Series. Diane first had a long, stern talk with her husband, then she had to have a talk with little Henry to explain why he was not to use those words, no matter how upset he was watching his hometown Royals lose or how upset he was at the boy who lived three doors down. This was also when Diane first put "The Jar" on the kitchen counter. Anytime someone, namely Jack, swore in the house, that person had to put a quarter in the Jar. This helped to curb Jack's colorful language, and provided the family money for the occasional treat of ice cream sundaes.

"What, Dad? What's going on?" Most of the remaining crowd was now on their feet, and those in the row in front of them were blocking Henry's view of the action down there on the field. The once-silent fans started clapping and cheering as the bat in question was brought out to home plate. Very few of the fans really knew what was going on exactly, but if manager Billy Martin was behind it, then so were they.

"Dad, I can't see. What's going on?" Jack's attention was finally broken away from the field as he turned to the child tugging at his pant leg. Jack took Henry's hand to help him balance as he stepped up onto his seat.

"I'm not sure, Henry. Looks like there's something wrong with George Brett's bat..." Jack's said, his attention focused on the field down below. He was witnessing what would become a legendary moment in baseball history, and had perhaps the best view in the stadium. This is why he loved these seats.

Down on the field, the umpire crew, led by Tim McClellan, was examining George Brett's bat, more specifically the amount of pine tar on his bat and how far up the handle of the bat the pine tar covered. The Major League Baseball rulebook states that a bat may not be covered with a foreign substance more than eighteen inches from the knob of the handle. Any more than that disrupts the weight distribution of the bat, adding extra force to the swing, and giving an unfair advantage to the batter. At Billy Martin's request, the umpires were trying to determine if Brett's pine tar-covered bat was in violation of this rule.

"This is total BS," Jack muttered under his breath as he began to put things together. "He's been using that bat the whole damn game. And *now* Martin decides to say something?! Bullshit!" His voice grew louder as he finished articulating the thought, drawing annoyed looks from the

36

cheerful Yankee fans standing near him. But it was the surprised look from little Henry that caused Jack to be embarrassed. Henry had not heard his father swear since the infamous 1980 World Series. He gave Henry a sheepishly apologetic look as he knew he would owe money to the Jar when they got home.

The umpires stood huddled in the infield between the pitcher's mound and home plate, continuing to examine the bat in question as they were surrounded at a short distance by Yankee coaches and players. After several minutes of conferring, the home plate umpire walked back toward the plate with Brett's bat in hand. He laid the bat down across the front of home plate, using it to measure the amount of pine tar on the bat. The front edge of the plate is seventeen inches across, so it provides a good impromptu ruler for measuring how far up the handle of the bat is covered in pine tar.

"What's going on, Dad?" Henry asked, barely able to see what was happening on the field below. "What are they doing with the bat?"

"It looks like they're measuring the pine tar," Jack said, rubbing his forehead after taking off his Kansas City Monarchs cap. This was not his original Monarchs cap. It was actually his third; the other two had gotten worn out and dirty from wearing them to Henry's Little League games every weekend and Diane had made him throw them away.

"What's pine tar, Dad?"

"It's this sticky stuff that hitters put on their bats so they can get a better grip. But you're not allowed to put too much on your bat..."

"How come, Dad?"

Jack was not able to answer Henry's question; things started to intensify down on the field, whipping the crowd into a growing frenzy. If the umpires ruled in favor of the Yankees' complaint about the bat, Brett would be called out, ending the inning and the game; the two runs wouldn't count, and the Yankees would win the ballgame. If they ruled against the Yankees by saying that Brett's bat had not exceeded the pine tar limit, the two-run homer would stand, play would continue, and the Royals would likely go on to win the game.

"Hold on, Hammer. Looks like they've come to a decision."

The home plate umpire, still holding the bat, walked away from the huddle and toward the Royals' dugout. He scanned the anxious players, looking for Brett. He found Brett amongst all the light blue uniforms, pointed at him with the end of the bat, and motioned him "out" with his other hand. George Brett charged out of the dugout toward the umpires like a running back breaking through the defensive line. Before being hauled back into the dugout by his teammates, Brett managed to give the umpires quite an earful. Meanwhile Billy Martin and the Yankees looked on from a safe distance with smug satisfaction.

The crowd began cheering and applauding. Their hometown team had won the ball game on a virtually unheard-of technicality. The official scorekeeper took back the two runs from the Royals and recorded the game-winning out on the big scoreboard above the outfield bleachers. Meanwhile, George Brett and his teammates continued screaming at the umpires.

Jack could not believe what he was seeing. He began booing loudly, but was very careful with his word choice. He knew he was already going to be in trouble when they met up with Diane at the hotel for the swear words he had said earlier; he didn't need to push his luck.

"What happened, Dad? What happened?" Henry kept asking.

"They called him out! I can't believe it; they fu... called him out!"

"Called who out, Dad?" Henry asked.

"George Brett. They called him out for having too much pine tar on his bat."

The scene on the field was dying down as Brett's teammates wrestled him back toward the dugout. The umpires were on their way off the field, and the Yankees had all but cleared out their bench. Many were probably already in the showers. It wasn't a pretty win for the Yankees, but it was a win nonetheless.

Jack's attention finally came back to Henry, who was staring at him in confusion. Fortunately, Henry had been holding the Scorebook all this time, otherwise Jack might have thrown this prized possession toward the field in angry protest.

Jack and Henry sat back down as other spectators tried to squeeze past them on their way to the exit. Both of them hated getting stuck in large crowds, so Jack didn't mind just waiting until the aisles were clear before they left. He did his best to explain to his son what had happened down on the field, that Billy Martin knew all along that Brett's bat had too much pine tar on it. Hell, everyone in the whole damn league knew that Brett's bat *always* had too much pine tar on it. But no one ever bothered to say anything until he hit a potentially game-winning home run with it. The more Jack explained, the more indignant little Henry became.

Some ten minutes later, Jack had finished explaining the situation, and Henry had finished asking his questions. Jack stood up and took Henry's hand as the two started walking down the steep stairs of the upper deck seats toward the nearest exit. Henry was quiet the whole way out of the stadium and to the nearby subway station, still processing the overwhelming amount of information he had received at the end of the game. When they found a seat on the train that would take them to their hotel a few miles away, Henry looked up at his father and said, "You know, Dad, they really did bullshit to George Brett back there."

Jack did his best to keep a stern face even though he was dying laughing on the inside. He knew he shouldn't have been thinking this, but there is nothing cuter than an eight-year-old using profanity... and using it incorrectly. Henry never seemed to gain a knack for swearing; he knew all the words at a young age - from both his dad and the kids on the playground - but could rarely use them correctly. He stifled his smile and said, "Henry Aaron Mitchell..."

Henry looked up at his father. He knew it was serious if Jack referred to him by his full name.

"I don't want you using that kind of language... even if it is true."

"But you said it, Dad."

There was no arguing that.

"Ok, I'll tell you what." Ten years of haggling sales with penny-pinching buyers had made Jack quite the master negotiator. "I won't tell your mom on you if you don't tell on me... And instead of putting money in the Jar, we can go get ice cream after dinner at that place down the street from the hotel."

Jack winked at his son, knowing he had made Henry an offer he couldn't refuse. Henry held out his left hand with his pinky extended. Jack did the same and they interlocked their pinkies, shaking their hands up and down three times to seal the deal with an official pinkie promise.

Chapter 5

September 6, 1983
Meadowbrook Elementary School
Gladstone, Missouri

"Good morning, boys and girls. Welcome back to school, and welcome to the third grade," said Mrs. DeYoung after the 8:15 bell finished ringing in the hallway just outside the door of Room 17. All thirty students sat attentively at their assigned seats. The desks were arranged in horizontal rows across the classroom; five rows of six desks each. And each desk had that student's name neatly written in cursive on a laminated nameplate.

Henry Mitchell sat in the third row from the front of the room. With a last name smack in the middle of the alphabet, he had come to expect a desk in the middle of the room at the start of each school year. Not in the front, right under the teacher's nose, and not in the back, the inevitable magnet for troublemakers. Henry had grown to like his spot in the middle of the room and the lack of attention it brought.

Henry recognized most of the kids in Mrs. DeYoung's class. About half of the thirty students had been together since kindergarten. The other half - mostly the "rowdy" kids and the "low" kids - got shuffled around among the teachers at each new grade level. There were groups of kids that needed to be split and re-split because they were too much trouble when placed together in the same classroom. And the "low" kids were distributed according to the students' academic needs and particular teachers' strengths. So, there were very few faces that Henry didn't recognize in Mrs. DeYoung's classroom.

Seated next to Henry was one of those new kids; not just new to his cohort of students, but new to the school. Henry looked over at the nameplate taped to the top of the desk; it read "Jackie" in large, black cursive letters.

My dad's name is Jack, Henry thought about saying this to the skinny Black kid seated next to him. But the teacher was still talking, and he didn't dare speak when the teacher was talking in the front of the class. And besides, Henry was also pretty shy around people he didn't know.

Jackie must have sensed that Henry was looking in his direction because he turned to look at Henry. Caught off guard, Henry offered a shy, embarrassed smile. Jackie smiled back.

"Now that you know a little bit about me, it's time for me to get to know you," Mrs. DeYoung said. Both Henry and Jackie turned their heads so that they were looking at the teacher again. Neither had heard a single word she had said in the last few minutes.

"... and it's important that you get to know each other as well," Mrs. DeYoung continued. "So, turn to the person next to you and ask each other the questions that are written up here on the board... eyes and ears up here, please... and then you will stand up at your seat and introduce your partner to the rest of the class."

The girl who - based on the seating arrangement - should have been Jackie's partner for this activity shot him a sideways look and turned to the girl on the other side of her and started chatting away. Henry didn't see the look, but did see that Jackie didn't have a partner. Henry raised his hand to get Mrs. DeYoung's attention and asked if Jackie could join him and his partner, Melody, a shy blonde-haired girl whom Henry had known since kindergarten. Mrs. DeYoung, privately thrilled that Henry so readily asked Jackie - the only Black student in the class - to be a part of his group, quickly agreed.

Henry learned all about the new kid in class in the ten minutes that Mrs. DeYoung gave the class to get to know each other or, in the case of most of the students, get reacquainted after their summer vacation.

Jackie Roosevelt Marcus's dad was the new pastor at Good Shepherd United Methodist Church; the family had moved to Gladstone from St. Louis just a few weeks before the school year started. Jackie had two older brothers and a younger sister. And, most important to Henry, Jackie loved baseball.

Chapter 6

April 18, 1984
Mitchell Home
Gladstone, Missouri

"Mom... Mom... I'm bored," Nine-year-old Henry whined as he emerged from his bedroom and walked down the hall into the kitchen, his footsteps heavy on the carpeted floor. His exasperated mother had sent him there not that long ago to play by himself to give herself a few moments of quiet. She thought the new LEGO set she bought would keep him occupied for at least half an hour. No such luck; he had built the set based on the instructions, then rebuilt it as something else in about twenty minutes, and now he was headed back into the kitchen to complain a little more.

Spring break wasn't even half over, and Henry was already driving his mother crazy. She had taken him to the park every day so far, but the rare mid-April heat and humidity made these visits rather short. He had watched his favorite movie on VHS tape about six times in the past three days. Diane was afraid he would wear out the tape or the VCR, and then what would she do? They had been to the grocery story - twice - to pick out his favorite snacks. Diane had officially run out of ideas of ways to entertain her son.

It didn't help that Jack was out of town on a business trip. Jack typically tried to work from the office during Henry's breaks from school, but his boss was called out of town for a family emergency. Jack's boss couldn't go on the trip to the firm's main office in Chicago, so he sent his top salesman, Jack Mitchell. Jack was disappointed by this last-minute change in plans, but not nearly as disappointed as Diane was.

The 1984 baseball season was only a few weeks old, but the hometown Royals were playing at home that week, so their games were blacked out on the local television network, and the AM radio station that broadcasted the games had very spotty reception in their neighborhood. The Mitchells seemed to live right on the border of the sports station from Kansas City and the Spanish language station from nearby Independence. It was mostly static mixed with mariachi music and, occasionally, the baseball announcer if you held the antenna in just the right spot. And because of the Easter holiday at the end of the week, Little League did not hold practices or games that week.

"Well..." said Diane, trying not to express her exasperation and really wishing that Jack wasn't on a business trip to Chicago. "Do you want to invite a friend over to play?"

Henry was intrigued by the idea.

"What about Ryan? Or Andy? Maybe one of them can come over. Go get your class directory from your school binder."

Henry ran off to his room. Diane could hear him making quite a mess as he searched for the class directory that the room mom had sent home back in September. She was mentally adding "clean room" to Henry's to-do list for later that afternoon.

"Found it!" Henry shouted from his room. He came running back to the kitchen with the piece of paper in his hand.

"Great! Why don't you give Andy a call?" Diane asked, motioning toward the wall-mounted phone.

The smile slowly slid off Henry's face. He hated talking on the phone. He never answered the phone, even when his mother specifically asked him to. And he never, ever called other people... except for calling his dad when he was on the road.

46

"Can you call? Please, Mom?" Henry pleaded with his mother. She had tried to break him of this lately, but with little luck. When he was younger, sure, she would call his friends' moms to set up playdates. But now that he was nine years old, he needed to start doing these things for himself.

"Henry... Hammer..." Diane could see that Henry was not just pulling his normal I-don't-want-to-do-this bit. He appeared genuinely upset at the prospect of calling one of his friends to invite him over to play. But she didn't want to back down, either.

"Henry, if you want your friend to come over, you need to call him yourself... you can do this."

"But I... I... I can't," Henry whimpered.

Diane still didn't want to give in, but she could see how desperately Henry did not want to make the phone call. This wasn't just Henry being stubborn, but right now was not the time to get into it.

"Henry," she said as she put the class directory on the kitchen counter. "What about the new boy in class, the one who sits next to you?"

"You mean Jackie?"

"Yeah, doesn't he live just a few blocks away? We could walk over to his house and see if he wants to come over and play."

Henry's eyes began to light up. He loved the idea. Diane felt rather proud of herself for coming up with this compromise. Henry would get to (hopefully) play with his friend - and stop whining about being bored - but she wouldn't have to give in and make the call for him.

Knock, knock, knock. Henry looked back at his mother standing on the sidewalk. She made him walk up the driveway to the front door by himself. He opened his mouth to ask her to come stand with him but, before he could say anything, the door opened. Standing there inside the door, wondering why this little white kid was on the front step was Jackie's mother, Victoria.

"May I help you?" she asked.

"Hello, m...m...ma'am. My name is... is Henry Mitchell," he began to repeat the speech that his mother helped him rehearse as they walked over here. He stared at his feet, never making eye contact with Mrs. Marcus. "I am in Jackie's class at school..."

Hearing the familiar voice at the door, Jackie came running from the nearby living room to stand next to his mother. When Henry caught sight

47

of his friend's smile, he began to relax and finally made actual eye contact with Mrs. Marcus.

"... and I was wondering if Jackie can come over to my house to play."

Jackie's eyes lit up as both he and Henry looked longingly into at Victoria. It would seem that another thing that Henry and Jackie had in common was their similar ability to make irresistible puppy dog eyes.

Seeing that things were going well for Henry, Diane walked up the driveway to join the crowd at the door. Victoria's eyes met Diane's and they gave each other a look of sympathetic exasperation. It had been a long half a week for both of them. It was that shared feeling between them that sealed the deal for the boys. Victoria nodded and smiled at the boys, who went racing off to Jackie's room to gather a few things. Diane walked up to the stoop, extending her hand to shake Victoria's.

"Hi, I'm Diane Mitchell," she said.

"Oh, I'm a hugger," said Victoria as she hugged Diane. Diane was caught off guard, but she just went with it, hugging Victoria back. "My name's Victoria. Victoria Marcus."

"So, what brought you and your family to Gladstone?" Diane asked.

"My husband's job. He's a Methodist minister and was transferred to Good Shepherd back in July. We moved down here from Maryville last summer."

"Oh, wow. That's great! Well, welcome to Gladstone, and welcome to the neighborhood. How do you like it here?"

Before Victoria could answer, Jackie and Henry came running back down the hall, squeezing past their mothers. Jackie had a Kansas City Monarchs hat on, just like Henry's, and had his well-used baseball glove on his left hand. Before either mom could say anything, they were running down the driveway toward the sidewalk, and then toward the Mitchell house.

"I guess I'd better chase after them," Diane chuckled. "What time would you like Jackie home?"

"Oh, keep him as long as you like," Victoria laughed as she waved her hand.

"Well, he's welcomed to stay for dinner."

"Oh, no, no, no... I was only kidding!"

"It's really no trouble at all. Henry's dad is out of town on business, so it would be nice for Henry to have some company," Diane said.

48

"Well, thank you so much. I really do appreciate it." Victoria said, and they both turned to see that the boys were already halfway down the block.

"I'd better get going. Here's my number in case you need to get a hold of us. So nice to meet you, Victoria." Diane handed Victoria a slip of paper and turned to walk back down the driveway. She quickened her pace when she saw how far down the street the boys were already.

"Bye, bye." Victoria waved as she went back inside and closed the door, tucking the phone number into her pocket.

As Diane reached her own front porch, Henry and Jackie raced past her, back out into the front yard. Both had their baseball gloves and matching Monarchs caps on, and Henry had a ball in his hand. Jackie stayed near the driveway and Henry ran to the far end of the yard. Diane smiled a smile of freedom as she went into the house. She made her way into the living room, sat on the couch, and put her feet up as she watched her son and his friend play catch through the large front window. A slow, deep breath released the past three days of stress caused by being cooped up in the house with her very bored son.

She sat there for a while, maybe fifteen minutes or so, just waiting for Henry and Jackie to come running back into the house, complaining they are bored already. But nope. They just kept tossing the ball back and forth, back and forth. Their conversation - she couldn't make out what they were saying - was punctuated only by occasional laughter and the THWAP! THWAP! THWAP! of the ball hitting their gloves.

Diane closed her eyes - just for a minute - enjoying this moment of tranquility. But the tranquility quickly lulled her into a deep sleep, a sleep she had not enjoyed since her husband left to go on his business trip.

But this momentary tranquility only lasted about half an hour. The boys came running into the house, slamming the door behind them and rousing Diane from her much-needed and much-deserved rest.

"Is there any Kool-Aid, Mom?" Henry shouted from the kitchen.

"Huh... what... yeah, there's some in the fridge." Diane thought she remembered making some the day before.

Before she could even get off the couch after a few long stretches to wake herself up, she heard the crash of empty plastic cups in the sink and the CLOMP! CLOMP! CLOMP! of the boys running back toward the front door.

About an hour later, Diane hadn't moved from the couch and would not be ashamed to admit it to anyone, and the boys came back in, all sweaty and a little smelly. She wasn't sleeping this time, but rather had just been staring out the window watching Henry having so much fun with his friend.

She was so happy that this desperate suggestion had worked out so well. She was thrilled that Henry was able to spend time with his friend doing something he loved: playing baseball. Even though Diane was not much of a baseball fan, she loved watching her son play the game he loved so much. Give that kid a ball and a bat and he transformed into a totally different kid. Henry was a happy kid, but he was also shy and timid and quiet. But put him on a baseball diamond, and he came to life.

"Can we go back to Jackie's house? He wants to get his baseball cards so we can trade before dinner tonight," Henry asked. He paused a moment, looking at Jackie then back at his mom. Jackie gave him a hesitant nod. Henry nodded back, then asked his mom, "And if it's ok with his mom, can Jackie spend the night tonight?"

Diane couldn't help but smile. She had not seen Henry this excited since his dad took him to Yankees' Stadium last summer. She was happy that he had found a new friend, and even more happy that she would not be expected to join Henry in attempting to listen to tonight's Royals' game on the radio. Really, it was a win-win situation. She might not get as much sleep as she'd like since the boys were bound to stay up into the wee hours of the night, but it would be worth it.

"If it's ok with his mom, then yes, Jackie can stay the night."

Henry gave his mom a hug, as did Jackie... much to Diane's surprise. She patted each boy on their sweaty back and gently tried to free herself from their grasp. They let go and raced out the front door, then down the sidewalk toward the Marcus home.

There was an early knock at the front door, waking Henry from a dream that he was in the batter's box against the great Nolan Ryan. He looked around the room in the early morning sunlight and saw Jackie sound asleep on the floor. *Should I go get Mom? Should I answer the door?* Henry quickly got lost in indecision. Before Henry could decide what to do, he heard his mom's door open and footsteps coming down the hallway. Diane paused outside Henry's door and peeked inside. Henry quickly closed his eyes and pretended to be asleep. The knock came again and Diane hurried to answer the door before the boys woke up.

Henry heard a familiar voice; it was Jackie's mom at the door. *Why would she come so early to bring him home?* Henry focused his ears on the voices coming from the entryway.

"What's the matter?" Diane asked, her voice muffled by the distance and the partially closed bedroom door.

Henry heard Victoria say, "It's George... my husband... he... he was arrested early this morning. I have to go pick him up from the police station... Can Jackie stay here with you until I get back?"

What the...? Henry thought. He looked down at Jackie to see if he had heard any of this but, no, Jackie was still asleep. *Why would Jackie's dad get arrested?* Henry's anxious mind started racing. He rolled over to face the wall and pulled his Kansas City Royals comforter up to his chin.

A long hour later, Jackie finally started to stir and wake up. Henry rolled back over and tried to act cool.

"How'd you sleep?" Henry asked. "I know the floor can be kinda hard."

Jackie yawned. "Nah, I slept fine. But man, am I hungry."

"Me too," Henry said. "Smells like my mom is making breakfast."

The boys staggered down the hallway toward the kitchen. The scent of pancakes got stronger with each step. Diane had not gone back to bed and started making her famous pancakes when she heard the boys waking up. It was a very simple recipe, taken from the back of the Bisquick box, but she added a pinch of nutmeg which made them Henry's absolute favorite breakfast food.

Later that morning - at about 10:30, while the boys were in Henry's room talking baseball and trading baseball cards - there was another knock at the door. When they heard Jackie's mom's voice, Jackie started gathering his baseball cards but Henry just froze. The yummy pancakes and the past hour or so of trading baseball cards had caused him to forget about Mrs. Marcus's earlier visit. He tried to listen intently to the conversation between his mom and Jackie's mom, but Jackie just continued putting his baseball cards away, pretending not to hear.

"Thank you so much for keeping Jackie a little longer this morning. I hope he wasn't any trouble," Victoria said.

"Oh, no, no, no... he was no trouble at all," Diane replied.

Henry could hear their footsteps travel from the entryway to the kitchen, followed by the sound of his mom pouring two cups of coffee. By this time, Jackie had all his things packed up and was ready to go. But when he saw the concerned look on Henry's face, he decided not to get up off the floor.

"What's wrong?" Jackie asked.

How do I tell Jackie that his dad got arrested? Henry thought. Fortunately, he didn't need to say anything because Jackie's mother was about to tell the story herself.

"So, what happened... if you don't mind me asking?" Diane's voice was clearer now that the conversation had moved to the kitchen.

"Oh no, no, it's ok. It's really stupid... really," Victoria replied.

Jackie shot Henry a puzzled look. Henry's eyes darted from the bedroom door to Jackie and back to the door.

Victoria continued her story.

"Early this morning, George realized he forgot his briefcase and wallet at the church. He had a late meeting at church last night, and he was in a hurry to get home, and he forgot them on his desk. I tell you, that man would leave his own head at his office if it wasn't attached.

"So, he went over to the church at about 5:00 this morning to get his things before his breakfast meeting with the District Superintendent in KC. But the lock on his office door always sticks and while he's fiddling with the lock, a cop drives by."

Jackie finally looked up at Henry, who was sitting on the bed. Henry's eyes got really big.

Victoria continued her story. "It was still dark, mind you, and the cop sees George fiddling with the lock to the office door, and assumes he is trying to break in."

"Oh my god," Diane couldn't believe what she was hearing and neither could Henry in the other room. He shot Jackie a puzzled look, but Jackie wouldn't make eye contact.

"The cop tells George to put his hands against the wall," Victoria went on. "But George turns around and tries to tell the cop that he is the pastor of this church. But the cop's not listening and he pulls his gun and tells George to get on the ground."

Henry let out an audible gasp, then covered his mouth for fear that their moms could hear him from the kitchen. Jackie gave him a funny look.

52

"And while he's laying there like a two-bit thug, George keeps trying to tell the cop that he is just trying to use his busted-ass key - pardon my French..."

"No, no... it's ok..." replied Diane. "The boys are in the other room."

Victoria kept going, "Right, right. At this point, the cop isn't even listening to him. He decides he's had enough and tells George to put his hands behind his head, then he approaches George all cautious-like... with his gun drawn... and slaps his cuffs on my George's wrists and drags him back to the squad car."

At this, Henry had so many questions but didn't have the words to ask them. He just stared at Jackie, who was looking down at the floor.

"So, what happened after that?" Diane asked.

"Well this is where the story gets good..." The boys could hear a dramatic change in Victoria's tone. Jackie perked up and looked at Henry.

"So, they get to the police station, and this cop drags my George down the hall to be booked, and guess who happened to be working the, uh... *reception desk*."

The boys gave each other puzzled looks as Victoria paused in her story.

"Sitting there behind the desk, ready to fingerprint my George was none other than Mrs. Jeanine Henderson, the wife of *Deacon* David Henderson."

Jackie's worried look turned into a slight smile, which gave Henry a feeling of relief. His heart had been racing all through Jackie's mom's story. He was so confused. *Why on earth wouldn't that police officer listen to Rev. Marcus? Why would he tell him to get on the ground, and then arrest him? There's no way Rev. Marcus looked like a criminal.*

With all these questions rolling around his head, Henry had stopped listening to the story for a moment.

"Jeanine recognizes George right away, but then she sees the handcuffs, and she hands the cop a clipboard with the standard booking paperwork and tells my George to have a seat on a nearby bench. While the cop is filling out the forms, she makes a quick phone call to this cop's commanding officer who shows up a few minutes later."

Jackie's smile got bigger, and Henry's heart rate slowed down to closer to normal.

"So, when the commanding officer shows up, he relieves that cop of the chore of filling out all those forms. He hands the clipboard back to Mrs. Henderson and says, 'Be sure Reverend Marcus gets home safely to his family.' Then he says to my George, 'I'm so sorry for this misunderstanding.' And then he takes that cop into his office and uh... chastises him for his error."

Henry was relieved that the story had a happy ending, but he was still so confused by what had happened. He was working up the courage to ask Jackie, but Jackie was standing up with his belongings and turning around toward the bedroom door. Henry followed him out the door and into the kitchen.

When the boys got into the kitchen, Diane walked over and mussed Henry's hair. "What were you two up to back there," she asked. "It's been awfully quiet."

Henry was afraid his mom knew that they had been eavesdropping on their conversation. "Just trading baseball cards."

Diane nodded, then grabbed the coffee pot and held it up, offering to top off Victoria's cup.

"No, thank you," Victoria said. "We really need to get going. We've got a lot to do at home."

Chapter 7

June 14, 1986
Flora Park
Gladstone, MO

It was the 1986 Gladstone Under-12 Little League city championship game, and the crowds in the stands were going wild as the Pirates took the field for the final three outs against the Reds. The Pirates fans were hoping the defense could hold onto their one-run lead, while the Reds fans were all wearing their rally caps and stomping on the metal bleachers to get the offense going.

Henry Aaron Mitchell adjusted his Pirates cap and then threw his warm-up pitches from the mound, while first baseman Jackie Roosevelt Marcus tossed the ball to his fellow infielders who threw it back to him. Henry had pitched in a few high-pressure games in his Little League career, but never in a situation this difficult. Both the Pirates and the Reds had records of twelve wins and one loss; the Pirates beat the Reds the first time they played each other, while the Reds won the second time. Both games had been decided by only one run.

Henry was hitting his spots with every warm-up pitch. Inside corner. Outside corner. High and inside. He'd never felt so good on the mound. Meanwhile, his coach's word echoed in his head, "Just throw strikes, son, and let your defense do the work."

Making quick work of the first two batters, Henry walked a slow lap around the mound as the next batter settled into the batter's box. The two sides of the crowd grew louder and louder, trying to drown out the other. Jackie jogged over to his friend, patted him on the back, and said, "You got this, Hammer!"

But "got this" he did not. Henry walked the next batter, who easily stole second due to the catcher's weak throwing arm. He advanced to third on a base hit by the next batter. This hitter then stole second without even a throw from the catcher. The no-throw was intentional; the catcher knew not to throw to second with a runner standing on third base.

With runners on second and third with two outs, and a very flustered pitcher on the mound, the Pirates coach gathered Henry and the infielders just behind the pitcher's mound. The players leaned in close, straining to hear their coach over the roar of the crowd.

"Hammer, just throw strikes, ok?" The coach said. Henry's teammates chimed in with words of support and encouragement as the coach continued, "You've got a great defense behind you. You do your job, and trust them to do theirs."

What those players didn't know was that these weren't just empty words, but words of desperation. There was no one else, on the bench or in the field, who could close out this game for the Pirates. Henry was quite literally the team's only hope.

The boys clapped and cheered. Jackie gave Henry another pat on the back as he went back to his spot near first base. As the coach made his way back to the dugout, the crowd grew louder and louder. Henry, game ball in his left hand, took his place on the mound. He scanned the crowd behind his team's dugout and found his parents a few rows back. They were on their feet cheering their star pitcher. Jack gave Henry a thumbs up, and Henry returned the gesture.

Henry Aaron Mitchell had had a stellar season on the mound, at the plate, and in the field. He led his team - and the city league - in almost every offensive and pitching category. Batting average. Hits. Doubles. RBI's. Wins. ERA. Strikeouts. He had already earned a spot on the League's

All-Star team that would represent Gladstone in the regional playoffs. And a win in relief today would ensure that his name would be on that league MVP trophy.

Henry peered in to get the sign from the catcher. Outside fastball. Working from the stretch, he threw his fastball just off the outside corner of home plate for ball one. The Reds' fans cheered as Henry took a slow walk around the mound.

Henry took his spot on the mound, pushing against the rubber with his left heel. He got the sign from the catcher. Inside fastball. Henry reared back and flung the ball as hard and as fast as he could toward home plate. He totally overthrew it, trying to make up for the shortcomings of the previous pitch. But this pitch was even higher and even more outside than the last one. Henry knew from the moment the ball left his hand that it was a bad pitch, and watching the catcher have to overextend to prevent the ball from going to the backstop only confirmed it. Fortunately, the catcher had a quick glove.

After that second pitch, Jackie could see that his best friend was rattled. Henry didn't get like this often, but when he did, there was little that could be done to pull him back. But luckily, Jackie had seen Henry like this before, and he was pretty good at helping his friend out of a jam.

Jackie asked the home plate umpire for a time out and jogged over to the pitching mound. He could see that Henry was on the verge of tears. Jackie reached out his hand and placed it on Henry's chest; he could feel Henry's heart pounding.

"Hammer, Hammer. Look at me, man… Hey, look at me." Henry finally raised his head to meet Jackie's gaze. Jackie looked deep into Henry's eyes.

"Hey, man. Get this guy out. You drag this game out any longer, and tonight's pizza is gonna get cold." Jackie was referring to that evening's end-of-the-season pizza party. "And I know you don't want to be responsible for cold pizza."

Henry cracked a smile.

"Now, come on, man. Get this guy out. Nice and easy, over the plate." Jackie could feel Henry's heart rate slowing down and knew he had done his job. As he jogged back to first, he hollered over his shoulder, "No cold pizza!"

Henry once again took his spot on the mound. He focused in on the catcher's fingers giving him the sign. He shook off the first sign, another inside fastball. The next sign was for a fastball down the middle. Hammer nodded. He focused on each movement in his wind up and delivery. Everything felt perfect as he delivered the pitch, a medium-speed fastball right down the center of the plate.

PING!

The batter connected with the pitch and hit a ground ball right at Jackie at first base. It was a slow grounder, slower than the ones Jackie and his teammates had practiced fielding at least fifty times each and every practice. Jackie squared his shoulders to the ball as it approached. He crouched down, bending at the knees, his weight on his toes as the ball got closer. All he had to do was to scoop up the ball with two hands - the way his coach had taught him to - and take a few quick steps to the bag to his left. The hitter was slow getting out of the batter's box and was only jogging down the first base line. The slow jog of a runner who knew that the game and the season would end in defeat.

Even though it had been drilled into them to run on contact when there are two outs, the runners on second and third jogged toward home plate and third base as they watched the ball roll toward Jackie. They knew it was an easy out, so why bother going all out.

But nobody saw the little clump of red clay on the ground about two feet in front of Jackie. A clump no bigger than a marble, but just big enough to redirect the ball before Jackie was able to gobble it up in his mitt. The ball hit the clump of clay and took a wonky bounce away from Jackie's perfectly placed glove. The ball bounced right between his legs and rolled past him, coming to a stop in short right field.

Jackie went through the motions of scooping up the ball, covering it with his other hand, and had taken about a step and a half toward the bag before he realized he didn't have the ball. His head swung back and forth as he looked for the ball. It took him a very long split second to see that the ball was about forty feet behind him in the outfield grass. He ran toward it as quickly as he could.

When the Reds' coach realized what had happened, he yelled and screamed at his baserunners to move, move, move! But they were slow to process the fact that the game was not over, that the ball was still in play, and that they had the chance to score the tying and winning runs.

The runner on second was the first to realize this, and he sprinted toward third base. The runner on third was a little slower to put all the confusing pieces of this puzzle together. The runner behind him had to slam on the brakes so as not to pass the runner on third. He yelled at his teammate to move, move, move! The runner on third finally realized what was happening and started sprinting toward home plate.

When Jackie finally got to the ball, pandemonium had broken loose on the infield. The Reds' base runners were in danger of passing each other on the base paths. Coaches on both benches were yelling unintelligibly. The infielders were running all over the infield; the second baseman ran out toward Jackie to position himself as the relay man. The shortstop jogged toward third base, following the Reds' baserunner. The third baseman did a sort of sideways slide step down the third base line as the lead base runner sprinted home. The catcher tried to take charge and bark orders at the infielders, but no one was listening and everything coming out of his mouth was nothing more than half sentences that made no sense anyway.

Meanwhile, Henry just stood there on the mound, frozen in the confusion.

Jackie grabbed the ball and threw it toward home plate, but his throw was way off line. Fortunately, the third baseman just happened to be in the right place to cut off the throw and prevent it from going into the Reds' dugout. But it was too late. The lead baserunner was already going into a headfirst slide into home plate, and the second runner was only a few steps behind him. The third baseman didn't even attempt a throw. Instead, he threw the ball at the ground, then threw his glove and hat to the ground.

The Reds' bench cleared as the tying and go-ahead runs crossed the plate. The baserunners were mobbed by their teammates. Parents and siblings poured out of the stands to join the celebratory mob. So much jumping and hugging and cheering.

On the other side of the infield, the Pirates' coach congratulated each of the players on their efforts as they shuffled into the dugout, heads hung low in defeat. "Keep your heads up, boys. You fought hard. Nothing to be ashamed of, boys."

The coach knew these were empty words. What do you say to a group of boys who played their hearts out all season, only to have it end like this? He was so proud of what his team had accomplished this season, but he was still in shock over what had just happened. And he knew the team was disappointed. He knew not to blame Jackie; he saw the wonky bounce the ball had taken. It was a fluke, a simple stroke of bad luck.

Meanwhile, in short right field, Jackie crumpled under the weight of his error. He flung his glove to the ground and pulled his cap down over his face to hide his shame and the tears beginning to well up in his big brown eyes. By the time Henry got to him, Jackie was kneeling in the grass, trying to will the outfield grass to swallow him whole. Henry sat down next to his friend, flung his glove in the direction of the dugout, and put his arm around his friend. Just a few minutes ago, Jackie had had the right words to pull Henry out of his near-meltdown. But now, Henry had no idea what to say to his friend.

"Look, Jackie, it's not your fault. It took a bad bounce. I saw it. I don't think even Wally Joyner could have fielded that one," Henry said, trying his best to comfort his friend after a long silence.

"Wally who?" Jackie asked as he slowly pulled his cap away from his face.

"Wally Joyner. Angels' first baseman. That rookie who started in the All-Star Game."

Jackie just shrugged his shoulders and wiped a tear from his cheek.

After the customary handshakes and high fives between the teams that follow every game, the newly crowned Gladstone Little League champion Reds and their elated fans slowly cleared the field, their coach holding the championship trophy high over his head.

The Pirates' coach gathered his team together in the dugout to give them the customary "that-was-a-tough-loss-but-I-am-so-proud-of-you" speech. Several were in tears. As he looked at his downtrodden players, he noticed that Henry and Jackie were not there. He looked back out to right field, and saw them sitting there still. Henry had his arm around Jackie, trying to console his friend. The coach decided to let them stay there for a moment.

Later that evening, during the Pirates' end-of-the-season pizza party at Tony's Pizzeria, the mood was similar to that in a dentist's office waiting room. The team members only ate about half the amount that they normally would have, so there was lots of pizza getting cold on the tables. The arcade in the back room of the provided some distraction from their sorrows over the hard-fought loss. Jackie and Henry sat at the far end of the table; their teammates were not very interested in talking to them.

As the party was beginning to wind down, the coach gathered the team back at the tables to hand out the runner-up trophies and to deliver his end-of-the-season speech. Most of the team sat together listening to the coach, but Jackie and Henry were still on the outs with their teammates, sitting about ten feet away from the rest of the boys.

As the coach's long-winded speech was coming to an end, the team mom brought a small brown paper bag to him and whispered something in his ear. She appeared out of breath, having just run back into the restaurant from the parking lot. After she said what she had to say, she handed him the bag and returned to her seat. The coach paused for a second before he shifted gears in his speech.

"I know that our season did not end the way we hoped it would, but we have a lot to celebrate. And despite the fact that Hammer... uh, Henry... got the loss in today's game, I just got word," the coach nodded to the team mom, "I just got word that Henry was voted... uh, unanimously... by all the coaches in the league, the Most Valuable Player of the Gladstone Under-12 Little League!"

Cheers erupted as the coach pulled the MVP trophy from the brown bag and as Henry sat in stunned silence. Jackie, who was sitting next to him, was the first to congratulate his best friend by giving him a big pat on the back.

"Hammer, come on up here and accept this award," the coach said over the cheers and applause.

Six months later...

"But Mom, the game's not over yet. You said I could stay up and watch it," Henry whined, not taking his eyes off the TV. Game 6 of the 1986 World Series between the Boston Red Sox and the New York Mets was going into extra innings, forcing Henry to stay up past his bedtime, causing his mother Diane to be rather annoyed.

"Oh, let him stay up, Diane," Jack chimed in. "It's Game 6 of the World Series."

"Yeah, it's Game 6, Mrs. Mitchell." Even Jackie was joining in on this one.

"Alright, fine," Diane conceded with a roll of the eyes.

In the top of the tenth inning, the Red Sox scored two runs, and going into the commercial break it looked like Boston was finally going to break the decades-old Curse of the Bambino. Henry took advantage of the short break in the game to run to the bathroom. As the television coverage returned to the game, Henry, Jackie, and Jack could sense that they were about to witness history. The Boston Red Sox were a mere three outs away from bringing an end to the 66-year Curse.

But the Mets weren't going to go down without a fight, sending their number 2, 3, and 4 batters to the plate in the bottom of the 10th. Catcher Gary Carter singled to left field. Pinch hitter Kevin Mitchell also singled. Then Ray Knight singled, scoring Gary Carter and sending Kevin Mitchell - the tying run - to third.

This brought Mookie Wilson to the plate. Wilson dueled with Red Sox relief pitcher Bob Stanley, passing on and fouling off half a dozen pitches. Stanley threw an inside breaking ball in the dirt in front of Wilson, causing him to fall out of the batter's box. He signaled to Mitchell to take home as the catcher scrambled to retrieve the loose ball. Knight moved into scoring position on the play.

The roar of the crowd became deafening as the Curse of the Bambino sucked the hope out of the Red Sox dugout. Just a few minutes ago, it appeared that the Sox were finally going to do it; they were finally going to end the drought. But in only a matter of minutes, the possibility of winning a World Series had begun to slip through their fingers.

Then it happened.

After ten pitches, Mookie Wilson put the ball in play, an easy ground ball to Red Sox first baseman, Bill Buckner. Buckner moved to his left and set himself to field the ball cleanly, but the ball rolled right between his legs. By the time he retrieved the ball from shallow right field, the game was over. Knight had had a suicide lead at second, and when he saw what happened, he rounded third and broke for home with reckless abandon, and scored the game-winning run.

On the other side of the television screen - in the Mitchells' living room - the three guys sat there speechless. They'd been pulling for the Red Sox to win, not because they were actually Red Sox fans, but because they wanted to be able to say they had witnessed history on that October evening.

Even the television announcer, the legendary Vin Scully, was stunned into silence. After an excruciatingly long three minutes of saying nothing, Scully finally said, "If a picture is worth a thousand words, you have seen about a million words, but more than that, you have seen an absolutely bizarre finish to Game 6 of the 1986 World Series. The Mets are not only alive, they are well, and they will play the Red Sox in Game 7 tomorrow!"

The silence in the living room was broken by Henry. "He pulled a Jackie. Bill Buckner pulled a Jackie!"

"Shut up, man!" Jackie said as he punched Henry in the arm.

Chapter 8

Summer 1989
Meadowbrook Elementary School
Gladstone, MO

"Mom, me and Jackie are going over to Meadowbrook to throw the ball around," Henry yelled from the entryway of his home as he dumped his backpack by the door, grabbed his glove from the nearby table, and ran back outside.

"Be home by dinner!" she yelled from the kitchen as she heard the front door slam shut.

"And don't slam that damn door," she muttered. Diane took another drink of her iced tea and went back to mopping the floor. Diane wanted to savor these last few hours of personal tranquility and a clean house before Henry's summer vacation began. She loved her only son, but the house was a lot cleaner and more peaceful when he was in school.

Henry's birth had sidelined her plans to finish her courses to be a dental assistant. She took time off to take care of Henry. Money was tight with the family being supported only on Jack's income. But Jack quickly proved himself as a salesman. By the time Henry was a year old, Jack had received a substantial raise in his base salary and was being given more important clients, which meant larger sales and bigger commissions. When Henry was old enough for Diane to resume her studies, Jack was making enough money to provide a comfortable life for his family. So, Diane never went back to school. She worked odd jobs here and there, mostly for something to do while Henry was in school.

In addition, Henry turned out to be their only child, but it wasn't for a lack of trying. Jack and Diane wanted to have more kids, but they just couldn't get his swimmers to connect with her eggs. So, they happily settled on being a family of three.

Today was the last day of the school year for Henry; his last day of 8th grade. But more importantly, it was the first day of summer vacation. This meant staying up late, watching lots of daytime game shows, and most importantly, lots of baseball.

Henry and Jackie hopped on their bikes and rode to the elementary school where they met nearly six years ago. This had become their after-school routine, which they gladly continued now that it was summer vacation. They would walk home from school together, drop off their backpacks, and then ride their bikes to the schoolyard where they would play catch or pepper, or just hang out on the playground equipment and talk baseball until it was time to go home for dinner.

They'd stay there for an hour and a half, maybe two hours, then sometimes stop at 7-Eleven on their way home for a treat that they bought with money they earned from mowing their neighbors' lawns. They thought they were being so sneaky by buying candy that their parents didn't know about. But the truth was, they were really bad at hiding it. They'd come home with brightly colored tongues or chocolate around their lips. If only they'd stopped and looked at themselves in a mirror, they might have gotten away with it. Even though their parents knew, they never said anything. If buying candy without permission was the worst offense these boys had committed, then their parents didn't see any reason to make an issue of it.

Henry and Jackie coasted their bikes through the gate and onto the grass of the expansive field next to the playgrounds. On weekends, the field was used for youth soccer games. But on most weekday afternoons, it was pretty empty.

Except today. Today, there was a group of older boys hanging out under the tree where Jackie and Henry would usually park their bikes while they played catch on the grass. Henry and Jackie recognized the boys, by reputation more than anything else. They were known to knock over trash cans, steal people's mail, and torment local cats. They were bad news.

Seeing the older, bigger, stronger boys in their usual spot, Jackie and Henry decided to set their bikes down under a different tree about 100 feet away. It was no big deal, they figured. Better safe than sorry, they thought. They put on their baseball mitts and started tossing the ball back and forth. These soon-to-be high school freshmen had not a care in the world; school was out for summer vacation and they were doing one of their favorite things in the world.

They planned out their entire summer vacation as they threw the ball back and forth. Their plans consisted of playing catch here or at the park in the mornings, swimming at the community pool in the hot afternoons, and watching baseball games on TV or listening to them on the radio while trading baseball cards in the evenings. It was going to be a great summer.

Their moment of bliss did not last long. Henry threw the ball in the dirt, and it took a bad hop and got past Jackie, rolling toward the group of older boys who were standing around and smoking cigarettes.

"Man, come on, Hammer!" Jackie yelled back over his shoulder as he chased down the ball. But one of the older boys – the apparent ringleader - got to the ball first. He grabbed it and held it up to show his buddies. This obviously wasn't going to be the first time they bullied some younger kids, so it only took a glance and a smile circulating the group to hatch a plan.

Henry saw the looks the older boys were giving each other, and had a pretty good idea of what was about to go down. Or at least he thought he did. Actually, Henry was pretty bad at reading confrontational situations like the one he was about to find himself in the middle of.

The older boys walked toward Jackie, shoulder to shoulder with that "tough guy" swagger. The one who first picked up the ball tossed it up in the air and caught it again. He did this repeatedly, like one of those 1920s mobsters flipping a coin over and over as he took a drag from his cigarette. He snuffed it out on the bottom of his shoe and flicked it into the grass. The other boys followed suit, flicking away their cigarettes and exhaling the last of the smoke they had just inhaled.

Jackie walked toward them. He instinctively took off his cap and wiped the sweat from his brow before putting his cap back on.

"Hey, can we have our ball back?" he asked. He glanced back to see that Henry was slowly approaching.

"Is this your ball?" the boy holding the ball asked, smiling at the other boys. "This is *your* ball?"

He held the ball in front of Jackie, just out of reach.

Henry continued stepping toward Jackie, ready to come to his friend's aid, if necessary.

Jackie stood his ground. He didn't want trouble, but he did want the ball back. He held out his hand.

The older boy - the largest and obviously the strongest of the bunch - dangled the ball in front of Jackie's face. But Jackie wasn't going to play this game. He just stood there, holding out his hand, waiting for the boy to give it to him.

"This ball? You want this ball?" He held the ball closer to Jackie's face. "But this is my ball. It just rolled right up to me, like a little lost puppy. I think the ball is much happier with me than it would ever be with you."

The boys nudged and elbowed each other and laughed. Henry stepped closer. Jackie stood firm, hand outstretched.

The boy holding the ball went back to tossing the ball in the air, but did so right in Jackie's face, thinking that Jackie might try to grab the ball out of the air. But Jackie just stood there with his hand out. Jackie knew what these bullies were up to, and he wasn't about to go along with it. By now, Henry was just a step or two behind his friend.

After about the fifth toss of the ball in front of Jackie's face, Henry had had enough. He wasn't going to let these bullies pick on his friend like this. He pushed his way past Jackie and got in the guy's face.

"Give him the ball, you stupid son of a bastard!" Swearing had never come naturally to Henry. Actually, he was really bad at it.

The older boys chuckled at Henry's weak attempt at being tough. Jackie took a step back. Henry's fists clenched as he stepped closer to the tough guy. He wanted to get right up in the guy's face, but Henry's eyes were at about the guy's collarbone level.

"Come on, Hammer, let it go." Jackie tugged at Henry's sleeve, urging him to back away from the obvious ass-kicking he was about to receive. Jackie knew they didn't stand a chance against these bullies. But Henry

68

wasn't listening. Jackie wanted the ball back, but he wasn't interested in fighting. Not over this. His dad had taught him to punch back to defend himself but to never pick a fight with a bully. "Always end the fight, son, but never start it."

"Yeah, listen to your little friend," the tough guy said. His friends snickered, angering Henry even further. "Just turn around and walk away, if you know what's best for you."

Henry turned to Jackie, handing him his baseball mitt.

"Hold this," Henry said.

Jackie gave Henry a quick look that said, "What the hell are you doing? Don't be stupid."

Henry just stared back at his friend with determination. He was not going to let these chumps steal their ball *and* make a fool of his friend.

The problem was that Henry Mitchell had never been in a real fight in his life. He and his dad would wrestle in the living room - mostly when his mother wasn't home - but that was just messing around. And there were those three months of martial arts classes he took the summer after *The Karate Kid* was released. But the most he did there was punch and kick some targets and break a ¼-inch thick piece of balsa wood to "earn" his white belt. So, if Henry went through with this, he was certainly in for his first real ass-kicking. Henry was strong from playing baseball for years, but swinging a bat and throwing a ball are very different from a street fight.

Henry's only thought as Jackie reluctantly took the glove from him was to try to sucker-punch the bully. He whipped around quickly, fist flying toward his opponent's face, trying to catch him off guard. Unfortunately, Henry totally telegraphed his move. Before Henry was even facing him, the older, bigger guy had stepped to the side. As Henry punched the air where the guy had just been standing, the bully landed a punch to Henry's gut, knocking the wind out of him.

Henry crumpled to the ground. Jackie stepped toward him and knelt beside him to be sure he was okay. And the older boys just stood there laughing their asses off.

"Come on, man, let's just go home," Jackie said to his friend. Jackie thought this was the end of it. The older, bigger boys had won. They got to keep the ball they had stolen and they had made Henry look like a chump. Jackie knew exactly how Henry was feeling. He had once gotten into a real fistfight with his older brother and got sucker punched just like Henry had. "I'll go get the bikes while you catch your breath." Jackie looked up at the bullies, who were laughing at Henry and high-fiving each other for their victory. His look conceded the loss.

Henry went down a lot harder than he should have, trying to play a little mind game with the bully. Henry was caught off guard by the punch, and it was a solid punch, but it was not that hard of one. At that moment, he remembered that Daniel LaRusso had done something similar in his first run-in with Johnny and his gang in *The Karate Kid*. Daniel stayed down for a moment, then when Johnny stepped closer, he jumped up and gave Johnny a bloody nose. But what Henry forgot about that scene was that even though he bloodied Johnny's nose, Daniel still got the crap beaten out of him.

Jackie turned his back and walked toward the bikes under the nearby tree. The group of bullies stepped closer to get one last look at Henry, who was still in fetal position on the ground. Then Henry sprang into action. He jumped to his feet, this time looking before punching, and hit the bully square in the nose.

"Shit, man!" the bully said, startled by this new development in the action. The bully's friends jumped back as well. Henry stood there, fists raised, ready to finish the fight. A small trickle of blood dripped from the bully's nose.

The bully wiped his nose and handed the stolen ball to one of his buddies.

"Come on, man!" Henry yelled. "Come on!"

Jackie was about ten yards away when Henry decided that he did, in fact, want to get his ass kicked that afternoon. He turned around and stood in shock as he watched what was about to unfold.

"You had to go there, you little bitch. You just had to go there," said the bully as he laughed at little Henry Mitchell. The bully wiped away the slow trickle of blood coming from his nose.

The fight was over before Henry even had the chance to throw another punch. A left punch to the stomach followed by a right uppercut to Henry's left cheek just below his eye, and Henry was once again back on the ground in a crumpled heap. This time it was for real; he was not getting back up. The gang of bullies stood over him laughing for a moment before turning around to walk away. The one holding the ball dropped it on the back of Henry's head. It hit with a dull thud before it rolled onto the ground.

The group of older boys were gone by the time Jackie arrived at Henry's side. They exited the ball field, lit up another round of cigarettes, and headed down the sidewalk to find more trouble to get into. Jackie helped his beaten and bruised friend get up and onto his feet. He could already see a black eye forming under Henry's left eye, but he could not see the much more painful bruise developing on Henry's ribs.

"You okay, Hammer?" Jackie asked as he offered Henry a hand. Henry reached out and used the help to get back to his feet. Henry took a moment to steady himself again. He walked around in small circles, slightly hunched over and holding his side. It hurt to breathe. His left eye was swelling shut.

"Can you ride?" Jackie asked as he held both bikes. Henry grabbed the handlebars of his bike and attempted to throw his right leg over the seat, wincing in pain before he was able to do so.

"No, we'd better walk home," Henry was barely able to get the words out as he tried to catch his breath. He lifted up his shirt with one hand to assess the damage. There were two big red spots on his torso, one on his gut and the other next to it on the bottom of his rib cage. Henry knew he would be feeling these for a few days.

Jackie stood a few steps away from his broken friend, his hands on the handlebars of his bike, and waited for Henry to catch up. Aside from Henry's sighs and groans, they walked their bikes back home in silence. They both knew that, in addition to the black eye and potentially bruised ribs, Henry was likely to be in big trouble with his parents.

When they reached Henry's house, Jackie said, "That's quite a shiner you've got there," pointing at Henry's eye that was almost completely swollen shut. It was the first thing either of them said since they left the schoolyard. Henry reached up and gingerly touched his swollen cheek and nodded.

"I'll call you later tonight, if that's ok," Jackie said. He was sure Henry would be grounded for at least a week for picking a fight, so he wasn't sure if Henry would be allowed to take the phone call.

Henry just nodded and turned up the driveway to park his bike in the side yard next to the garage. Jackie just stood there, watching. *It's been nice knowing ya*, he thought. Jackie was a few houses down the street when he heard the sound of Henry's front door thudding shut, followed by the muffled sounds of Henry's mother getting hysterical about his injuries. Jackie could almost make out the words, "Wait until your father gets home."

Jackie picked up the phone receiver and put it to his ear... for the fourth time. It had been about four hours since he heard Henry's mother yelling at Henry as Jackie walked down the street to his own house. Jackie was too nervous to call his best friend, knowing that Henry was probably in deep doo-doo with his parents for getting in a fight earlier that day. Jackie was afraid that Henry's parents would be equally mad at him for being involved, so he wasn't sure how welcome his call would be. He had picked up the phone several times, but always hung up the receiver before he dialed more than two digits.

But this time, after a deep breath, Jackie began punching digits into the phone. Like ripping off a Band-Aid, he knew he had to just dial the numbers and get it over with. The phone began to ring. No turning back now.

Diane answered the phone after about two rings.

"Hello?"

"Hi, Mrs. Mitchell," Jackie said timidly. "Can I talk to Henry?"

There was a brief pause, followed by a sigh of exasperation from her.

"Hold on, Jackie." Jackie could hear her pull the phone away from her ear and say to Henry, who was obviously nearby, "Five minutes."

Yup, Henry was grounded, which meant his phone privileges had been taken away. But sometimes he was still allowed to talk to Jackie for very short periods of time. Diane had developed quite a soft spot in her heart for Jackie. And the fact that Jackie was allowed to talk to Henry meant that Henry's parents weren't angry with Jackie for his involvement - although, in actuality, he had been only a spectator - in the altercation that afternoon.

"Hey Jackie," Henry said when he took the phone from his mother.

"Hey Hammer," Jackie replied. "Grounded?"

"Yup."

"How long?"

"A week." Jackie could sense a bit of pride in Henry's voice, like he considered himself a martyr or something.

"Not too bad, I guess," Jackie said. "How's the eye?"

"It's pretty bruised and swollen." Again, that smugness was creeping into Henry's voice, like he was talking about a war wound he received while saving the rest of his platoon.

"That stinks. I guess no baseball for a while."

"Nah, I guess not."

There was a moment of silence between them. Jackie didn't really know what to say. He was happy he would be getting his friend back in a week, and there were only so many ways he could offer his sympathies with phrases like 'That's too bad" or "That stinks." But it kind of seemed like Henry was waiting for Jackie to say something, even though Jackie had no idea what that could be.

"Well... uh... I guess I'll see you around." Jackie wasn't sure what to say and he knew that their time on the phone was limited, even though they had been talking for maybe a minute at the most.

"Yeah... I guess."

The tone in Henry's voice changed. He now sounded disappointed. There was another pause. Jackie figured the conversation was over, so he pulled the phone away from his ear. But before he could actually hang up, he heard Henry speak up.

"Well..."

"Well, what?" Jackie asked.

"Aren't you going to thank me?"

"*Thank you?* For what?" Jackie began to get defensive. What had Henry done that deserved his thanks?

"Um... for standing up to those guys! For saving your butt!" Henry would have used the word "ass," but his parents were in the room, no doubt listening to the phone conversation.

"What are you talking about?" Jackie's defensiveness was turning to anger.

"The guys who stole the ball. They were taunting you, and I wasn't going to let them get the best of my best friend. Aren't you going to thank me for that?!"

"Why? I didn't ask you to do *any* of that!"

"Oh, I see how it is," Henry had obviously been rehearsing this speech for quite a while. He had expected Jackie to call and thank him for standing

73

up to the bullies, for coming to his rescue, and for getting beat up and getting into trouble for doing so.

"What's that supposed to mean?" Why was Henry attacking him, Jackie wondered.

"Um, let's see. Those guys at the park were making you look like a fool, and if I hadn't stepped in, you would be the one with the black eye and bruised ribs… or worse!"

"Like I said, I didn't ask you to do anything. You were the one who jumped in and got your ass kicked," Jackie's parents were not within earshot of the call, so he could swear all he wanted. "Those guys were jerks, but they weren't going to do anything other than steal our baseball. I didn't ask you to fight that guy."

"Oh, you think they were just going to walk away with our ball? They weren't going to do anything else?"

"No, they weren't."

"Yes, they were. You're dumb if you don't think they would've done something to *you*." Jackie could hear the obvious emphasis that Henry was putting on that last word.

"Why would they do something to me?"

"Because you're…" Henry cut himself off, afraid to actually say it.

"What? Because I'm what?" Another long pause before Jackie asked the next question. "Because I'm *Black*? You think this was all because I'm *Black*? And you said I'm the dumb one."

At this point, Jackie and Henry were past the five-minute mark of their conversation. Henry's father was about to get up and end the conversation, but Diane stopped him. She knew that Henry would learn much more from this conversation than he would from the black eye, bruised ribs, and grounding combined.

Jackie finally composed himself enough to lecture his friend.

"Look," Jackie began. "First of all, what happened at the schoolyard had nothing to do with me being Black…"

"But…"

Jackie wasn't going to let Henry interrupt him.

"Those guys were just a bunch of stupid jerks who were picking on a couple of younger kids. They would have done that if I was white, brown, or aquamarine."

Jackie paused a moment to let his first point sink in. He had been listening to his father's sermons all his life and had become quite an eloquent orator himself, once he got going. And he was going.

"Second, I didn't ask you to fight for me. I don't need you to rescue me. It's not your job to save me and fight my fights for me. If it came to blows, I could have handled myself. But I wasn't going to pick a fight with those guys over a stupid baseball. What you did out there was just plain dumb."

Jackie felt the urge to slam the phone down as an exclamation point to his little soapbox speech. But he resisted that urge, keeping the phone to his ear, trying to catch his breath as he waited for Henry to respond. This was the first real fight that Jackie and Henry had had in their years of friendship. Sure, they argued over silly things, but nothing like this; nothing real.

"I'd better get going. I think my five minutes is up," was all that Henry could say. But Jackie understood that it was his friend's way of apologizing for his stupidity this afternoon.

"Alright, I'll see you around."

"Yeah. See ya."

And they both hung up the phone.

Chapter 9

July 16, 1989
Oak Tree Community Pool
Gladstone, MO

It wasn't long after Henry's grounding that he and Jackie were back to their old ways. There was about a day and a half of awkwardness between them, but Henry's assumptions and misunderstandings were not enough to keep these best friends apart. There was no formal apology; all it took was a baseball and their mitts, and things were basically back to normal. Soon they were playing catch at the elementary school, swimming at the local community pool, and trading baseball cards in one of their bedrooms as they listened to Kansas City Royals games on the radio.

The summer weather in Gladstone is a bitch, plain and simple. Temperatures can get up into the 90s, and the humidity tends to hover around 65%. So, for most of July and August, it feels an awful lot like living in someone's armpit. Most of the homes in the Mitchells' mostly working-class neighborhood were built in the 1950s, so very few had air conditioning, and even fewer had in-ground swimming pools. This meant that the community pool was typically quite crowded with teenagers trying to escape the midsummer heat.

And on this particular day in mid-July between their eighth grade and ninth grade years, Henry and Jackie were at the pool earlier than normal. They had gotten in maybe half an hour of playing catch at the nearby park before calling it quits at about 10:30am to go for a swim. They hurried home in the heat to change into their swimsuits and rode their bikes to the nearby pool.

Henry and Jackie locked up their bikes at the very crowded bike rack outside the pool gate, and ran into the pool area. Their timing was perfect as a couple of younger boys gathered their things from a reclining lounge chair on the pool deck; it was the only deck chair available. They had worn their swim trunks as they rode to the pool, so they threw their towels down on the chair to claim it as theirs, then tore off their shirts and shoes. Within seconds, they were submerged in the coolness of the heavily chlorinated water.

They chased each other around the pool, jumped off the high dive, and got into a big game of Marco Polo with some of their friends from Little League. Within about an hour, they had worn themselves out and returned to their lounge chair on the deck. Fortunately, the chair next to theirs became available as many of the "morning shift" kids left the pool to go home for lunch and the afternoon crowd had not yet arrived, so they didn't have to try to share the one chair as they sunned themselves dry. In the heat of the day, it didn't take long for their swim trunks to dry. It was still hot and muggy, but much more bearable after having soaked in the pool until their fingers and toes were all pruny.

One thing they couldn't help but notice was their female classmates at the pool, sporting their bikinis and attracting attention from some of the older boys at the pool. Even though Henry and Jackie had a one-track mind - and that track was baseball - they weren't blind, and they certainly noticed that Mother Nature had worked her magic on the fairer sex that summer.

It was sort of an unspoken rule – at least for the younger kids – that the boys stick to one side of the pool deck and the girls stay on the opposite side. The older kids, however, tended to comingle on the far side of the deck, mostly out of view of the lifeguards. There tended to be a lot of kissing and petting going on over in that part of the pool deck.

Henry was in the middle of recapping last night's Royals' game when he noticed that Jackie was not at all paying attention. He followed his friend's gaze to see him gawking - and nearly drooling - at the pool hunnies who were lying out on the other side of the pool from them.

"And then Bo Jackson hit the ball 734 feet, landing in the parking lot behind right field..." Henry was trying to see just how smitten Jackie was with the girls across the way.

"The parking lot? Wow..." Jackie mumbled, never averting his gaze.

"Dude! What's your deal?"

Jackie snapped out of it finally and looked at his rather angry friend. He had no words to defend himself. Instead, he stood up, walked around to the back of Henry's lounge chair, cupped the sides of Henry's head in his hands, and turned him so his friend could see the babes lying out on the lounge chairs a mere hundred feet or so in front of them.

"Look," was all Jackie could get out.

Henry stopped thinking about baseball for just a moment to see what Jackie thought was more interesting than talking about the Royals' game.

And there she was.

Molly Jacobs.

Molly Jacobs was the girl who always sat directly in front of Henry every year in school since her family moved to Gladstone when she was in second grade. It never failed. For some unknown reason, every teacher Henry ever had would start the school year by putting students in an alphabetical-order seating chart that started in the front right corner of the room and zig-zagged back and forth across the rows of desks to the back-left corner of the room. Even though there were never the same students in their class every year, there always seemed to be the same number of students between Molly Jacobs and Henry Mitchell, so that Molly always sat right in front of him.

Molly was not the prettiest girl in class, nor was she very popular. She wore glasses all throughout elementary and middle school, glasses that were typically too big for her face. Her clothes were often last year's fashions, hand-me-downs from her older cousin. She had mousy brown hair that sometimes looked like she had gone to bed with wet hair the night before and hadn't done much to try to tame it that morning.

But she was really smart. And really funny. And she had this crooked little smile that she sometimes flashed at Henry if he said something funny. And there was the adorable way she would always tuck her hair behind her ear when she was concentrating really hard on her seat work. And she was left-handed, just like Henry was.

It might have been the fact that he spent every day for the past six years sitting right behind her, but Henry had developed a little bit of a crush on Molly Jacobs. Nothing too serious. He would never admit to this crush and certainly would never actually ask her out; he was just too damn scared. In elementary school, he was very careful in selecting just the right Valentine card for her; a card that professed his feelings for her, but in a cryptic, rhyming sort of way. But she never figured it out, and there was no way in heaven or on earth that he was going to say something to her - or to anyone else - about this. He had not even told Jackie about his crush on Molly, and he told Jackie everything. But Jackie was no fool; he knew Henry liked her even before Henry knew it himself. It was pretty obvious by the way Henry would stare at Molly in class, or the way he managed to sit by her in reading circles, or the way he would pick her to read after him when the class was "popcorn" reading from the textbook.

This was the first time since the end-of-the-year pool party in fourth grade that Henry had seen her in a bathing suit, and never had he seen her in a bikini. At school, Molly tended to wear loose-fitting shirts and jeans; sort of a tomboy look, which Henry also found quite attractive. So, until now, Henry had no idea how nicely she had "matured" over the past year or so.

Henry's chin literally dropped when he saw the girl Jackie was pointing his head at, and then dropped even further when he realized it was Molly Jacobs who was now making him feel kind of tingly all over. After a seconds-long eternity, Henry turned and looked at Jackie, who had returned to his lounge chair and was giving him a "see what I mean?" look. Then they both turned their attention back to Molly and her friend, who was just as nice to look at.

After almost a minute, Molly and her friend realized they had some fans sitting and staring at them from across the pool. When Molly realized who these fans were, she waved and smiled with that crooked little smile that made Henry feel so happy.

Henry instinctively turned around to see who was behind him, too quickly to be able to actually articulate the thought "she couldn't possibly be waving at *me*." This made Molly chuckle, which Henry saw once he turned back around and realized that she was waving and smiling - and now laughing - at him. Henry waved sheepishly back to her. He leaned back in his chair. The prettiest girl at the pool, and the girl he'd had a crush on since second grade, waved *and* smiled at *him*. A big smile crept across his face. Could it be that she actually noticed him... really noticed him... in *that* way?

"So, dude, you gonna go talk to her?" Jackie asked, bringing Henry back to reality.

"Huh? What?"

"You should go ask her out. Haven't you been crushing on Molly since... like... forever?"

"What?? No," Henry said bashfully.

"Dude, you've totally had the hots for her!"

"Man, shut up!" Henry said as he gave his friend a shove.

Jackie gave Henry a "seriously?" look. He wasn't going to let this one slide. See, it was a win-win situation for Jackie. Either he got the satisfaction of helping his best friend land the girl of his dreams, or he got the satisfaction of teasing said best friend for a couple hours that afternoon.

"Well, I mean, I guess I sort of think she's kinda cute..." Henry replied, turning a shade of red about as bright as the stitching on a brand-new baseball. He knew the jig was up. He now knew that Jackie knew. There was no more denying it. It was just a matter of damage control. How could he prevent Jackie from embarrassing him too badly?

"Well, from where I'm sitting, it looks like she's totally crushing on you right now..." Jackie said with a big grin.

"No, she just waved. I mean, we haven't seen each other since school got out a few weeks ago... she's just... being nice."

Jackie just laughed.

"All I know," Jackie said, "is that if a girl who looked like *that* was waving and smiling at me, I certainly would not be sitting here talking to my friend. I would be over there, scoring some digits."

Henry looked the other way. There was no way he was going to walk over there and talk to the Molly Jacobs.

When it came to self-confidence, Henry was something of an enigma. On the baseball diamond, he was unstoppable; as a pitcher, he wasn't

81

afraid to throw high and tight and even less afraid to challenge hitters by throwing right down the middle of the plate. And as a hitter, he was just plain fierce.

But this confidence did not translate in any way whatsoever to approaching and talking to girls... especially Molly Jacobs. It wasn't until almost February of second grade before Henry worked up the courage to simply ask her if he could borrow a pencil, and that was only after asking every boy in class who sat within a three-desk radius.

Henry and Molly had been paired up for group projects and other assignments quite a few times over the years. But, for the most part, Henry was strictly business. Very little talk of personal things. And it wasn't for lack of trying - on Molly's part. She would ask him questions, mostly about baseball because she knew how much he loved baseball. But Henry was oblivious to her tactics. He just figured she was one of those cool chicks who was into baseball. And baseball was the one thing that Henry was willing to talk to anyone about, even if he had a crush on her.

Henry had certainly fantasized about asking Molly Jacobs out... someday... in the undetermined future. He had planned it all out; in fact, there were quite a few scenarios that he had meticulously thought through in which he would ask her out. Asking her to be his date for the school dance. Asking her to go get ice cream after attending a high school football game. Asking her to meet him at the arcade (he'd heard she liked video games, too). He just had no intention of *actually* following through on any of them. After all, if he never actually asked her out, then she could never actually reject him. Better safe than sorry.

And now, here at the pool on a hot and humid July afternoon, was neither the time nor the place to cross that line. He hadn't thought through this scenario before. This scenario had never crossed his mind. And he especially was not going to go talk to her when she was wearing that brightly colored bikini that covered a little too little.

Jackie sat staring at his friend. He couldn't believe that Henry was just going to pass up this opportunity to make his years-long dream come true. Well, knowing Henry as well as he did, he actually could believe it. Jackie gave Henry a shove in the shoulder and shook his head in resignation. Henry wouldn't make eye contact with him, and didn't want to look over toward Molly Jacobs either, because - heaven forbid - she just might get some idea that he actually likes her. He just stared over at the diving boards, not actually watching the divers plunge gracefully into the pool.

Jackie finally broke the awkward silence. "I'm hungry. Wanna go to 7-11 on the way home?"

"Yeah. Sure," Henry said, still avoiding eye contact.

Henry finally glanced back in the direction of where Molly had been sitting as he gathered his towel and t-shirt, and slipped on his sandals. Molly and her friend were gone. They had left unnoticed in the few moments that Henry had spent purposely avoiding looking at her.

Henry felt a mix of relief and regret. Relief because he was off the hook for actually having to talk to Molly Jacobs. He no longer needed to worry about finding the right words, or hearing her response. But he was also disappointed with himself. How many opportunities to talk with her had he passed up already? And how many more would he let slip by before he would actually talk to her? And surely, she wouldn't wait forever. Eventually, she might meet some other guy and fall in love with him, and any feelings she had for Henry would be a distant memory. He didn't want that to happen either.

"I gotta pee before we go," Jackie said, sounding impatient. Henry was lost in thought about Molly and was taking more time than normal gathering his things. He took another long, regretful look over at the chairs that were once occupied by Molly and her friend. Jackie started walking off toward the restrooms with Henry following at a distance.

A few moments later, when they exited the restroom and turned toward the bike rack a few yards away, Henry was fumbling with the zipper on his backpack and bumped right into someone.

"Sorry," he said without yet looking up. Then he heard a familiar giggle and looked up. His eyes got big, his heart started racing, and his palms got sweaty all at once when he realized he had just run into Molly Jacobs.

"That's ok. I was hoping to bump into you again... just not so literally." She continued that familiar giggle while Henry smiled awkwardly, barely able to make eye contact with her, but also careful not to be caught looking down at her body. It was a difficult balancing act, avoiding eye contact and avoiding gawking at her chest. Jackie and Molly's friend Tisha both rolled their eyes, as if in unison, at the cheesiness of Molly's attempted flirting. Molly looked up at Henry, forcing eye contact for a second, then looked over to her friend, then looked back at Henry. Henry diverted his eyes again as his fight-or-flight impulses started rising within him. It took every ounce of willpower he had not to jump on his bike that was only ten yards away and ride home.

Then in a moment of premeditated recklessness, Molly Jacobs put her hands on Henry's cheeks, lifting his face ever so slightly so that his eyes met hers. She closed her eyes and planted a big ol' kiss on Henry's unsuspecting lips. This was Henry's first kiss, but he was too nervous and was too caught off guard to be able to actually enjoy it. In fact, it wasn't until this whole episode was over and he was halfway home that he even realized that he'd just had his very first kiss.

Molly took a step back; she too could not believe that what just happened had actually just happened. Then she held out her hand and Tisha gave her a folded-up piece of paper, which she shoved into Henry's hand. She gave him a little peck on the cheek, and whispered, "Call me" into his ear. With that, she grabbed her friend's hand and the two ran off toward the parking lot giggling all the way. Henry just stood there; that was way too much to process in the eight seconds that it took for all of it to unfold.

"Come on, Hammer, just call her. She *wants* you to call her. She *told* you to call her," Jackie said. He and Henry were seated on the floor in Jackie's room. The door was shut. The handheld cordless phone receiver was on the floor between them. And Molly Jacobs' number was in Jackie's hand just a few inches in front of Henry's face. They had been sitting like this for about the last forty minutes since they had finished eating dinner.

Henry had picked up the phone at least sixteen times. He even started to dial a few times. But he always chickened out. His heart was racing. His mouth and throat were bone dry. His palms were sweaty and his hands were trembling ever so slightly. He desperately wanted to call Molly Jacobs and ask her out but he was scared. Scared of rejection, even though she told him to call her. Scared of saying something foolish. Scared of not being able to say anything at all.

Jackie - for whom it should be noted had never had a girlfriend - had come up with a great plan for Henry. The Gladstone Parks & Rec was doing a summer "movies in the park" series, and the following Wednesday they were showing *The Karate Kid* at Flora Park, a film that Jackie was pretty sure Molly liked (he remembered seeing a hand-drawn Cobra Kai logo on her Pee Chee folder that she used in math class). All Henry had to do was invite her to go to the movie in the park with him. They could even meet at the park, which could be more convenient for Molly and less awkward for Henry. And Jackie had even volunteered his mom to make her famous oatmeal-chocolate chip cookies for them to take to the movie night. Seriously, it was a foolproof plan. There was no way that Molly was going to say "no."

All that was needed for this plan to work was for Henry to get up the courage to pick up the damn phone and make the damn phone call.

There was a knock at the door, which startled both Henry and Jackie. Jackie quickly crumpled up the slip of paper with Molly's number on it, slipped the paper under his rear end, and sat back down on it.

The door didn't open, but Jackie's dad could be heard from the other side of the door.

"Boys, dessert is almost ready. Your mom made Grandma's famous peach pie. It will be ready in about ten minutes, ok? Oh, and hurry up with the phone, wouldya?"

The boys smiled wide at each other. "Ok," they said in unison.

After hearing Jackie's dad go back down the hall to the living room, Jackie said, "Ok, this is it. It's now or never."

He uncrumpled the paper with the phone number, then grabbed the phone and forced it into Henry's hand.

"You've got like five minutes, dude," Jackie said. "You gotta do it."

There was a look of sheer panic in Henry's eyes, but Jackie was too frustrated to notice it. Finally, Jackie decided he'd had enough, and with a "shit, man" muttered under his breath, he swiped the phone away from Henry. He turned on the receiver, made sure there was a dial tone, dialed Molly's number, and then shoved the phone into Henry's hands. Before Henry could do or say anything, it started ringing. His shaking hand raised it to his ear as he shot Jackie a look of death. Jackie just looked back at him with smug satisfaction.

The phone rang twice before a middle-aged man's voice came on the line.

"Hello?" the voice said. "Hello?"

All the man on the other end could hear was Henry's anxious breathing.

"Hello, m-may I speak to M-m-molly, please?" was all Henry could get out after far too long of a pause.

"Just a moment," said the voice.

The voice - apparently Molly Jacobs' father - seemed to pull the phone away from his mouth, but Henry could still hear what was being said. "There's some guy on the phone asking for Molly. He sounds like he's about 20."

During this past school year, Henry went through all the awkwardness of puberty just like his peers - the acne, the funky smell, and the squeaky voice - but he came out the other side just fine, especially vocally. Once the hormones settled down, Henry ended up as a full-bodied baritone. If his dream of becoming a professional baseball player didn't come true, then he could always pursue a career as a play-by-play announcer. So, it would have been easy for someone who did not know Henry to mistake him, over the phone, for someone much older than the fourteen-year-old that he was.

Henry waited anxiously for Molly to come to the phone. Jackie moved closer, trying to listen in on the call. Then he heard the voice again, speaking away from the phone, "Who is this guy? Since when did 20-year-old guys start calling my daughter?"

Henry turned to look at Jackie, whose mouth was agape. *What the hell is going on?* They both thought. They could hear someone - presumably Molly - grab the phone and put it to their ear. The voice could still be heard in the background, but what the voice was actually saying was now unintelligible. But whatever the voice was saying, it certainly wasn't happy.

"Hello?" said Molly. It was reassuring to hear her familiar voice, but her voice sounded almost as nervous and scared of the voice as Henry was.

"Hi, Molly. It's... It's Henry... Henry Mitchell."

"Hi Henry," Molly said hesitantly. "Thanks for calling, but I... I can't really talk right now."

"But... But..." was all Henry could say.

"I have to go," Molly said. Then she added, optimistically, "But I'll see you around. Sorry. Bye."

The other end of the line clicked off and Henry just sat there speechless. Jackie gingerly took the phone receiver from Henry's hand and set it down. Henry had finally worked up the courage to call a girl to ask her out, and he got shot down on a technicality. *Damn you, puberty!*

After about a minute or two of very uncomfortable silence in Jackie's room, Jackie said, "Hey, let's go get some pie."

As delicious as Victoria Marcus's peach pie was, Henry just wasn't very hungry.

Chapter 10

July 26, 1989
Royals Stadium
Kansas City, MO

July 26 was another hot, muggy day in the Midwest. Storm clouds were building over the farms and fields not far from Royals Stadium. The concessions vendors assigned to the stands had side bets going as to when the game would be called due to rain.

"Ice Cream! Chocolate Malted Ice Cream!" The nearby concessions vendor momentarily distracted Henry from his conversation with Jackie about George Brett's recent hitting slump. Henry, still holding a half-eaten hot dog in his hand and a huge bite of hot dog in his mouth, looked at the ice cream vendor and then gave his dad a longing look.

"No, Henry," Jack Mitchell said. "You know the rule: no ice cream until the fifth inning."

Henry nodded as he finished his bite of hot dog, remembering the incident that prompted the no-ice-cream-before-the-fifth-inning rule. Several years ago, Henry and his dad were at a Sunday afternoon Royals game. They bought their hot dogs and sodas before the game started, and were each a few bites into their foot-longs when they had to pause their lunch for the National Anthem. Then after maybe four pitches in the top of the first inning, Henry saw the ice cream vendor a few aisles over from where they were sitting. With a mouth full of hot dog, Henry asked his dad if he could have a chocolate malted ice cream, his absolute favorite ballpark treat. Jack said Henry could have one after he finished his lunch: the hot dog he was currently working on, the small order of nachos that he insisted on getting, and the paper cup of semi-flat Dr. Pepper.

What Henry's father meant was, "Take your time and eat your lunch and you can have ice cream later in the game."

What Henry heard was, "If you can finish all this food before the ice cream guy gets over here to us, then yes, you can have a treat." It never even crossed little Henry's mind that there would be more opportunities to buy an ice cream later in the game.

This misinterpretation proved to be costly for both Henry's father's wallet and Henry's gastrointestinal system. In approximately six minutes, Henry scarfed down the entire hot dog and finished off almost the entire plate of nachos. Right as the ice cream vendor started his way up the steep stairs of the nearby aisle, Henry got a funny look on his face; a look that said everyone around him would be seeing his lunch again soon. Like REALLY soon.

The ice cream vendor never saw it coming. Before he could say the words "Chocolate Malted Ice Cream," his brand-new walking shoes and the cuffs of his black Dickies pants were covered in a partially digested hot dog, nachos, and Dr. Pepper.

When Jack heard the sound of his son's explosive vomiting, he was caught between helping his son and apologizing profusely to the ice cream vendor. Henry and his dad were on the way to the car before the second batter had even stepped into the batter's box. It was the only time they had ever left a game early.

And that was the reason for the "no-ice-cream-before-the-fifth-inning" rule.

Henry looked at the half-eaten hot dog in his hand, remembering just how awful that day was. He could almost taste that mix of hot dog, mustard, nacho cheese, Dr. Pepper, and stomach acid. Jackie just laughed at Mr. Mitchell's reminder as he took another bite of his ketchup-covered hot dog; he wasn't with the Mitchells on that fateful day, but he'd heard the story plenty of times. Hell, Jackie had told this story plenty of times, usually when Henry was getting a little too cocky in the dugout of one of their Little League games. Telling the other boys on the team this story was a good way to put Henry in his place.

Once Henry had finished his hot dog - eating at a reasonable pace, of course - his father handed him the Scorebook. His dad had filled in the box score for the top of the first inning, and now it was Henry's job to track the progress of the game. This job had been unofficially passed down to Henry when he turned 13. The Jewish boy living two houses down had gotten a Bar-Mitzvah and several hundred dollars in savings bonds; Henry had received scorekeeping duties at the ever-increasing number of baseball games he attended with his father. If he was ever asked, Henry would say he got the better coming-of-age gift.

The Royals were retired in order in the bottom of the first, and Henry recorded the details of each out: the strike out, and the two fly balls to left-center field.

About an hour and a half later, in the top of the fifth inning, Cal Ripken, Jr. was set to lead off the inning for the Orioles. Henry, his father, and Jackie all peered down intently from the upper deck to get a glimpse of the All-Star shortstop as he took a few practice swings just outside the batter's box. Even though Henry would have to say that Royals infielder George Brett was his favorite player, deep down Henry really admired Cal Ripken, Jr. Henry studied his moves in the field and at the plate, trying to emulate the grace with which Ripken fielded a ground ball and the smoothness of his swing. Henry's dream since the first time he watched Ripken play was to travel to Baltimore to watch him play on his home field of Memorial Stadium.

As Henry recorded ball two in the Scorebook, Jackie gave Henry a little nudge. Ice cream vendor 130 was making his way toward them. All Henry and Jackie noticed were the big insulated bag the guy was carrying over his right shoulder and the wad of cash in his left hand. But Henry's father could see the weariness in the vendor's eyes and the sweat dripping down his face. It was a look that Henry's father could identify with, having spent many long days on the road making sales calls. Henry's father knew all too well the physical and emotional toll that this Midwestern heat can take on a person. He couldn't imagine being made to walk up and down these flights of stairs with that bag of ice cream slung over his shoulder.

Vendor 130 drew closer to where they were sitting, his shouts of "Ice Cream!" and "Chocolate Malted!" growing much harsher, as if he were commanding those in the stands to take heed and buy some damn ice cream. Henry's father raised his hand to get the vendor's attention when he looked his way. When he made eye contact with the vendor, Henry's father gave him a sympathetic little smile, as if to say, "I feel ya, buddy."

The vendor either didn't see the smile or wasn't amused by it because he scowled as he began marching up the aisle toward Jack and the boys. He was hot and tired, and his feet ached badly. Sweat beaded at the tips of his hair at the back of his head and dripped down the back of his shirt. He could see the storm clouds brewing as he took a quick glance at the field behind and below him. *Would you just hurry up and start raining already?!* He thought to himself.

Henry's dad raised two fingers, indicating how many chocolate malted ice cream cups he wanted, one for each of the boys.

"Six dollars," Vendor 130 said sternly as he stood at eye level with Henry's father. Henry's father took the money out of his wallet and handed it to the vendor. The vendor grabbed the ice cream and spoons and handed it all to Henry's dad. If Henry's dad wasn't so distracted by the obvious pissed-offness exuding from Vendor 130, he might have been in awe at how the vendor could grab two ice cream cups and exactly two spoons with one hand while sorting the bills he was given and counting back change with the other hand. This was multitasking at its finest; too bad no one was paying attention.

Once the transaction was complete, the vendor continued his journey into the stratosphere of the stadium's upper deck.

Henry and Jackie were too enthralled with the battle going on between Cal Ripken, Jr. and the Kansas City pitcher, Luis Aquino. Jack could see that the boys were "in the zone" and decided to wave the ice cream in front of their faces to get their attention. But just as he did so, Ripken hit a sharp line drive between Kurt Stillwell at short and Kevin Seitzer at third base. Seitzer dove to his left, going completely airborne, the length of his body almost parallel to the ground beneath him, snagging the ball out of midair before it went into left field, ending the inning right there.

Collectively, the 30,000-plus fans erupted into cheering when Seitzer made the diving catch that was sure to be on that night's sports highlights reel on the 11:00 news. But the boys missed the play because Henry's father was dangling chocolate malted ice cream cups in front of their faces. Fortunately, they showed the play about six times, from different angles, on the jumbotron out in center field, so the boys quickly forgave Jack for distracting them. He took the Scorebook off of Henry's lap as the boys dived in to their ice cream.

As the Royals got ready to bat in the bottom of the fifth, the first rolls of thunder could be heard in the distance. Vendor 130, who was now several aisles away from Jack and Henry and Jackie, cracked the ever-so-slightest smile knowing he stood a good chance winning the vendors' pool. It would only be a matter of minutes before the game would be officially rained out, and Vendor 130 knew it.

The thunder grew louder and the breeze became more of a wind as the public address announcer introduced the next Royals batter in the bottom of the fifth inning. The latest and loudest thunderclap caused Henry and Jackie to jump a little. They were used to Midwestern summer thunderstorms, but the acoustics in the stadium made the echoes of the thunder especially loud. Over the next few minutes, as the Royals batter dug into the batter's box and awaited the first pitch, the thunder got louder and more frequent; the wind got cooler and stronger; and the crowd got a bit antsy as they knew the rapidly approaching storm was about to unleash. Was it going to be a bad enough storm to cancel the rest of the game? Or would the crowd merely be wet and miserable for the next two hours?

Experience had taught Henry that these summer storms are anything but predictable. It could be blustery with cracks of thunder one minute, then pouring rain the next, then partly sunny a few minutes after that. Or, it could rain for hours. So, this looming storm could mean a short rain delay, or it could mean an early drive home. There was simply no way to know for sure.

The first drops of rain were big and fell hard, causing many of the spectators in the field-level seats to work their way to the shelter of the seats that sat under the upper decks. Some simply headed for the exits. Those in the upper decks, like Henry, his father, and Jackie, were shielded from the rain by the large metal coverings above their seats. Say what you will about the cheap seats, at least you don't get drenched when it starts raining.

Henry's father closed the Scorebook and tucked it under his shirt to protect it from the falling rain. Henry and Jackie sat unfazed, enjoying their ice cream and anxiously hoping that this would be a short delay in the game.

The home plate umpire - the crew chief - called an indefinite time-out and collected the game ball from Baltimore's pitcher. The Royals' batter and base coaches headed for the dugout as the Orioles' defense cleared the field. With the score currently tied at two runs apiece, everyone on the field below and in the stands above was hoping this storm would pass quickly.

But pass quickly it did not. The hard rain did not let up and the thunder increased in volume as the storm cell decided to park itself right over Royals Stadium. The umpires weren't quite ready to officially call the game, but the crowds were. The spectators crammed into the aisles and pushed their way toward the exits. Most of the spectators anyway. Henry wasn't anxious to leave, just in case the storm did let up, and his father wasn't too keen having the boys navigate the crowds and the stairs and the exit ramps while finishing their chocolate malted ice creams. They were still shielded from most of the falling rain, but with the wind picking up, they were starting to get wet. He told them that they would leave as soon as they finished the treat if the game hadn't restarted. So, they began eating as slowly as humanly possible.

When they finally finished, there were maybe forty spectators in the entire stadium; most of them were other kids eating their ice cream while their impatient parents looked on trying to get their children to just hurry up already. Henry's father reminded the boys to gather up their trash as he led the way down the stairs toward the exit tunnel. Jack Mitchell had spent two years while in college working as a custodian at the elementary school near the campus, so he was appreciative of the hard work put in by those who maintained the stadium. He made an extra effort to instill this appreciation in his son.

By this time, the game had been put on hold and would be finished at a date and time to be determined later that evening. The PA announcer told the few remaining that they would be receiving a voucher to attend a game later in the season as they exited the stadium. The rain had let up a little bit, but had already done its damage; the field down below was too drenched to even think of continuing the game.

Henry, his dad, and Jackie made it to the concourse under the shelter of the upper deck bleacher seats. They walked toward the ramps that would take them to the exits on the ground level. The concession stands were all closing up shop and the custodians were emptying trash cans and servicing the restrooms. Never had they stayed so late after the end of a game, even though the game had only been called about fifteen minutes ago. But it was obvious that everyone had kicked it into high gear in hopes of getting out of there as quickly as possible. Traffic at this time of day was a bitch anyway, but was especially bad on a rainy afternoon.

After walking down the ramp that wound around and around, they arrived on the field-level concourse that went right past the visiting team's clubhouse exit. It was blocked off, of course, but the door was still in full view of where the ramp met the concourse. As they approached the area, Henry and Jackie slowed their pace in hopes of seeing a big leaguer, no matter how obscure a player he would be. Henry's dad continued his regular pace and was quickly several yards ahead of them before he turned around to see the boys lingering near the temporary fencing that separated them from the clubhouse door. He called out to them, "Come on, guys. The team is probably already on the bus back to their hotel. Let's go."

Henry pretended to ignore his dad's call, but Jackie tugged on his shirt sleeve to get Henry to go with him. Jackie held on to that shirt sleeve as Henry dragged his feet behind him. Just as they caught up to Henry's dad, they both heard the very distinct sound of the clubhouse door behind them opening and slamming shut. Henry spun around to see who it might be. Jackie turned a bit more slowly, and Henry's father walked a few more steps before he realized the boys were no longer at his heels.

It was difficult to see because the hallway was not well lit, but they could see a rather tall figure walking away from the door. Henry's and Jackie's eyes were able to adjust to the darkness, and they realized who it was that was exiting the visitors' clubhouse: the one and only Cal Ripken, Jr.

When the boys realized it was him, they stopped in their tracks; both of them staring toward the clubhouse door with jaws dropped open. Jackie once again grabbed Henry's shirt sleeve, but this time to walk with him back toward where Cal Ripken, Jr. now stood.

Only about four seconds had passed since that door had opened and closed, and Jack Mitchell - tired and just wanting to get to the car and get home - had backtracked to where the boys were standing.

"Come on, guys, let's go," Jack said impatiently. But then he looked up toward the clubhouse door to see who had snatched the boys' attention. Once his eyes adjusted, Jack could see him too; Cal Ripken, Jr. was standing there on the concourse, looking around like he had made a wrong turn and walked through the wrong door.

"Oh my god," Jack said under his breath. He looked down at Henry and Jackie and nudged them both on the shoulder and said, "Go talk to him. Get his autograph."

Jackie turned and looked at Henry who was still staring at one of his heroes. "Come on, Hammer. Let's go talk to him," he said.

Henry just stood there as if his shoes were filled with lead. His heart started pounding and his palms started sweating. His brain was trying to force his body to move - and move quickly as it appeared that Ripken had figured out where he needed to go and was starting to walk in the opposite direction of where the boys stood - but his anxiety-ridden body was not cooperating. The thump-thump-thumping of his pulse was drowning out the pleading of his best friend.

"Dude, come on Hammer," Jackie said. "Look, he's walking away."

Sure enough, Cal Ripken, Jr. was walking off toward one of his teammates standing in the distance. And Henry was frozen where he stood.

Jack looked down at his son. He could only imagine the conflict raging inside Henry. He had seen Henry freeze up like this before, but he hated to think that he would miss an opportunity to shake the hand of one of his heroes. He gave Henry another nudge as Jackie continued pleading with him. But Henry didn't budge.

"Hey Mr. Ripken!" Jackie shouted as the future Hall of Famer walked away. "Cal! Mr. Ripken!" But it was no use. He was out of earshot in the echoey concourse of Royals Stadium. Cal Ripken, Jr. stopped a moment as if he heard something, but then kept walking away.

Jackie threw up his arms in frustration, wishing he had just run over to meet the Baltimore third baseman. He started walking away toward the exit gate. Jack moved a little closer to Henry and put an understanding arm around his son's shoulder. He gave a gentle squeeze as he turned

Henry around and walked with him to meet up with Jackie and head to the parking lot.

Jack and Henry dropped Jackie off at his house before heading home. Jack pulled the car into the driveway and turned off the engine. Henry unbuckled his seatbelt and reached for the door handle, but saw that his dad wasn't going anywhere, so he put his hands in his lap and looked out the passenger side window. He knew he had a serious "talking to" coming from his dad. It wasn't often that they had these little driveway chats, and they were rarely good chats.

"Got a little stage fright back there, huh?" Jack asked, trying to sound as understanding and sympathetic as he could.

Henry just shrugged his shoulders and continued looking out the window.

"Look," Jack said, then paused for a second to be sure he chose the right words. "You're not in trouble and I'm not upset or anything like that. I... I just want you to know you can talk to me about it if you want."

The truth was, Henry really didn't know what had happened back there, and he had been beating himself up the entire drive home over the situation. He had the once-in-a-lifetime opportunity to meet a demigod of the baseball diamond and he blew it; he goddamn blew it.

Jack didn't want to push things with Henry, but he also didn't want Henry to just shut down, which he was prone to do in instances like this. He decided to give his son a minute and see if he would open up.

"I... I don't know... I guess I..." Henry started, but didn't know where he was headed with this. Jack knew better than to say anything. He just sat there and waited for his son to finish.

"I... I just... I froze. I mean, what if he's a jerk?" Henry stammered. "What if I walked up to him and he just blew me off?... I don't know..."

Father and son sat in silence for a good minute or more. Jack looked at his watch.

"You hungry?" he asked Henry.

Henry shrugged his shoulders. "Maybe a little."

"Let me go get some cash from your mom, and then we'll go grab a bite. Sound good?"

Henry nodded as his dad opened the car door.

Chapter 11

September 5, 1989
Winnetonka High School
Gladstone, MO

"You have everything? Your notebook? Your lunch?" Diane knew that Henry was anxious about starting high school; he always was on the first day of school. She couldn't believe her baby was now a freshman in high school. Henry nodded his head, eager to step onto the campus of Winnetonka High School as a Griffin.

"Have a good day, Henry. Love you."

"Love you, Mom," he said as he closed the car door. He watched his mom exit the drop-off area before turning around to face his freshman year. Henry was looking forward to this new adventure. A new campus. New friends. And the chance to play high school baseball. His most recent Little League coach was friends with the head varsity coach here at Winnetonka, and he told Henry that he had a shot at making the varsity squad, even as a freshman.

As he turned toward the main gate, he heard a familiar voice calling his name. Henry saw Jackie walking toward him. Henry was relieved that

Jackie remembered to wear his Kansas City Monarchs hat like they agreed to do last week. Not that Henry would have been embarrassed if he was the only one to wear the hat, but it would have been awkward if only one of them had remembered.

When Jackie walked up to Henry, he extended his hand to do their "secret" handshake: a regular handshake grip that went up and down twice, then a fist bump, then they pressed their thumbs together, raised their hand up to eye level and slammed them down toward the ground. Jackie always batted just ahead of Henry when they played Little League; Jackie had a knack for getting on base and Henry had a knack for driving him home to score a run. Several years ago, they made up this handshake for this oft-celebrated occasion. They still did it every now and then, just for kicks. The beginning of their high school careers seemed like a good time for the handshake, no matter how dorky the upperclassmen thought they were.

The boys had received their class schedules in the mail about a week ago. Unfortunately, they only had two classes together, one of them being first period English / Homeroom with Mrs. Abbott. Had it not been for the freshman orientation a few days ago, Henry and Jackie would have had no idea where to go. Even though that orientation day did give them the lay of the land, it in no way prepared them for the sea of humanity that awaited their arrival.

Henry paused at the main gate for a moment and took a deep breath. The nervous butterflies that kept him up part of the previous night had returned. Jackie saw Henry's hesitation and tugged at his sleeve, "Come on, man, let's do this."

Jackie led the way as they walked past several "Welcome Griffins" banners that hung on the front gates to the school. They had about ten minutes before homeroom began, and it would probably take most of that time to play the giant game of "Red Rover" to get to the classroom on the other side of campus.

The boys made it to room A-7 with only a few minutes to spare. Their teacher, Mrs. Abbott, was one of those teachers who stood at the door on the first day of class and greeted each student with a handshake or high five and an unnaturally large smile. Jackie and Henry arrived at the same time as about five other classmates. Henry hoped to dodge Mrs. Abbott's greeting by slipping into the herd, but no such luck. She was like the Black Knight from Monty Python - "None shall pass" - but a whole lot cheerier.

"And what is your name, young man?" she asked Henry as she stood in the doorway, extending her hand to shake his. Henry glanced past her to Jackie who was looking at him from inside the classroom. He knew full well that Henry just wanted to sneak on by without all the hullabaloo, thank you very much. Jackie just smiled at his friend, looking for some sign of awkwardness that he could tease Henry about later.

"Henry... Henry Mitchell," he said, trying his best to avoid eye contact with his teacher. There were very few things that Henry hated more than meeting new people.

"Well, good morning Henry, Henry Mitchell," Mrs. Abbott said with a big smile, giving Henry a firm handshake. "I see you've got a Monarch's hat on like Jackie over there." *How could she possibly know his name already?* "I guess you're a baseball fan."

She was still shaking his hand. "Yes, ma'am."

Mrs. Abbott finally let go of his hand when she saw that the line of students was backing up down the hallway. "You may choose your own seat, and it looks like your friend Jackie has saved you one over there."

"Thank you, ma'am." Henry walked over to where Jackie was seated near the window. Jackie was chuckling. Henry slugged him in the arm as he sat down and put his backpack under his desk. He instinctively adjusted his Monarch's cap as he surveyed the room.

So, this is high school, Henry thought as he looked around. To be honest, the classroom didn't look much different from his junior high English classrooms. Same posters with witty grammar puns and inspirational quotes. One poster caught his attention from the back of the room, featuring William Shakespeare in hip-hop regalia: gold chain with a big medallion around his neck, sunglasses, and were those dreadlocks? The caption read "Prose before Hoes." Henry didn't really get the joke in the caption, but he thought the picture was funny.

About half of the thirty desks were occupied already as the rest of the students filed past Mrs. Abbott – but not without a personal introduction and a handshake – and filled the empty seats. Henry recognized some of his classmates, but not all of them. With three junior high schools that fed into the high school, there were plenty of new faces in the room.

One of the last students to enter the room right before the bell rang was another familiar face, one that Henry had not seen in about six weeks.

Molly Jacobs scanned the room looking for an empty seat. The front two rows were already taken by all the nerdy kids, and the back couple of rows were taken by all the troublemakers. That left the middle row. There were two seats available: one next to Henry and one in the back row right next to the old, noisy radiator. She chose the seat next to Henry. When she saw him looking at her, she waved and gave him that crooked little smile that Henry liked so much.

When Henry saw her smile, he quickly turned away and looked at Jackie all bug-eyed and panicky. At first Jackie smiled when he saw Molly enter the room. But after he saw Henry's panicked look, his smile changed to a look of genuine concern for his friend.

Molly squeezed past the rather large boy in the seat next to the one she was heading toward. "Hi Henry, long time no see," she said with a giggle. She tucked her hair behind her ear as she put her Trapper Keeper notebook on the desk. The notebook had a picture of a golden Labrador puppy on it. She waved at Jackie as well, who smiled politely, yet nervously at her.

As Molly sat down, Henry stood up. "I'll... I'll be right back," he said.

Henry darted for the door. Ever since the phone call debacle that one evening about six weeks ago, Henry had done everything he could to avoid running into Molly. He refused to go back to the community pool for fear that she might be there. He was even reluctant to go to the mall with his mom to do his back-to-school shopping because he knew that she liked to go there with her friends. Luckily, she was not there the day they went, but he was on high alert during the entire shopping trip, ready to run into a nearby store if he happened to see her approaching.

Henry had mentally rehearsed the moment he would see her again many times over the past six weeks. He worked through several different scenarios, but this was not one of them. He just had to get out of there.

And get out of there he did. Jackie was standing up, ready to follow him out the door, but the bell to start class stopped him in his tracks. He slowly sat back down and turned to face Mrs. Abbott at the front of the room, but kept the classroom door in his peripheral view.

When Mrs. Abbott called Henry's name from the roll sheet, Jackie tried to cover for his friend. "I think he had to go use the restroom or fill up his water bottle. He'll be right back."

Jackie knew it was a lame excuse and knew the teacher was not likely to buy it. But buy it she did. It seemed that Mrs. Abbott had been teaching long enough, and teaching freshmen long enough, to know that students sometimes have these bathroom emergencies on the first day of school. She just moved on in calling roll.

Molly looked at Henry's empty desk, then over at Jackie. She gave him a questioning look, like "What's up with Henry?" She could see the concern in Jackie's eyes. She wanted to ask him why Henry darted out of the room, but now was obviously not the time to do so. Molly did not want to make a bad first impression with the teacher.

As Mrs. Abbott began the class by introducing herself and telling the students about her four cats and her love for Shakespeare, Jackie kept looking over at the door, hoping to see Henry walk back into class. But after about five minutes, Henry hadn't come back yet.

At this point, Mrs. Abbott had the students turn to their neighbors and ask each other questions about their summer vacations. She had written specific questions on the board so that students didn't get off topic. During this time, Jackie got up from his seat, giving Molly a quick smile - she looked concerned about Henry as well - and went to talk to Mrs. Abbott in the front of the room.

"Hi, Mrs. Abbott," Jackie started. "I was wondering if I could go check on Henry. He said he had a stomachache before school, so can I go see if he's ok?"

Jackie hated himself for lying to the teacher on the first day of school.

Mrs. Abbott could see that Jackie was genuinely worried about his friend. After twenty years of teaching in a high school classroom, she had developed a pretty good "bullshit detector" and knew pretty well when a student was lying to her. She detected no BS from Jackie and told him to be sure to grab the hall pass - an 8.5 x 11 laminated picture of William Shakespeare - on his way out the door. Jackie gave the pass a funny look as he grabbed it from the hook on the wall next to the door.

Jackie stepped into the hallway and looked both ways to locate the nearest boys' restroom. He saw the sign to his left and headed in that direction.

"Where the hell is he?" Jackie muttered under his breath as he entered the boys' room. He then called out, "Yo, Hammer. You in here? Hammer?"

There was no response, but there was the sound of movement in the far stall. Jackie hesitated a moment before walking over there. He didn't want to risk the embarrassment of interrupting some stranger in the middle of doing his business.

"Hammer, is that you?"

Another sound came from inside the stall, the sound of the door unlatching. The hinges creaked as the door slowly opened. Henry peeked out at his friend.

"You ok, man?" Jackie asked. Henry just shrugged his shoulders, took a deep breath, and then spoke.

"Seeing Molly Jacobs walk in that door just... I don't know... sent me into panic mode. I... I mean, ever since that night I called her, I thought through a hundred different scenarios of how things would go when I saw her again... and having her walk into first period today was not one of those scenarios. I just froze up and all I could think was, 'I gotta get the hell outta here.'"

Henry stood there with his head hanging low. The sense of panic had subsided, but was soon replaced with a feeling of shame and embarrassment. How could he go back into that room? What would the class think? What would Mrs. Abbott think? Not exactly the best first impression. But most importantly, what would Molly Jacobs think? He had been utterly humiliated the last two times he had had any sort of contact with her. Henry was sure that whatever feelings she had for him that compelled her to kiss him outside the pool last summer had by now evaporated. He would never be able to ask her out let alone ever talk to her again. Maybe he could just transfer schools or talk his parents into moving out of state or something.

As Henry wallowed in embarrassment, Jackie had the perfect idea. "Come with me."

Henry followed closely behind Jackie down the hallway toward the main office. Jackie explained the plan to Henry; they would go to Mr. Alvarez - one of the assistant principals who also happened to be a good family friend of the Marcuses - and call Jackie's dad to come and pick them up.

Henry, still overwhelmed with embarrassment, agreed it was a good idea, assuming Mr. Alvarez would go for it. Henry had his doubts that an assistant principal would let a couple of kids play hooky on the first day of school just because one of them was embarrassed at the sight of his crush walking through the classroom door. But Henry could not think of any other plans; so hey, it was worth a shot.

Jackie went straight into Mr. Alvarez's office when the two friends got to the main office. Mr. Alvarez was in the middle of lecturing a flunky upperclassman about the importance of an education and how he – Mr. Alvarez – would be personally giving this student an application to go work at McDonald's if this student didn't get his act together this semester. Jackie was caught off guard; he didn't expect to find anyone in Mr. Alvarez's office, and he had never heard Mr. Alvarez raise his voice like that before. Jackie paused awkwardly in the doorway before taking a few steps backward into the office common area.

The secretary at the front desk didn't know what to make of this scrawny kid who so boldly walked right past her desk toward Mr. Alvarez's door. So instead, she looked to Henry to provide some answers.

"May I help you?" she asked indignantly.

Henry mumbled something about Jackie needing to talk with Mr. Alvarez.

"Speak up, hon," said the secretary.

"My friend Jackie needs to talk with Mr. Alvarez."

"About what? Do you have a hall pass? Does he have an appointment? You can't just waltz in here…"

Her voice tapered off as she turned to see that the flunky upperclassman was on his way back to class and that Jackie was sitting comfortably in Mr. Alvarez's office. The two were chatting it up like old friends. Jackie turned around in the chair and waved for Henry to join them in the conversation. Henry walked past the secretary without saying a word.

"Have a seat, Henry," Mr. Alvarez said. "Jackie was just telling me about what happened in homeroom."

Henry shot Jackie a look, wondering how much his friend had told the assistant principal. Henry could barely live with himself, he was so embarrassed, and he wanted as few people as possible knowing about it.

Mr. Alvarez continued, "He said that you felt really nervous or panicky all of a sudden."

"Yes, sir," Henry replied.

"You know, Henry, this sounds a lot like an anxiety attack. Has this sort of thing happened before?"

Henry thought for a moment, then recounted the incident at last summer's Royals game and a few other times he felt all nervous and panicky. Mr. Alvarez just nodded his head patiently as he listened to Henry's rambling story.

After Henry finished, the awkward silence was broken by Mr. Alvarez. "Look, here's what I'm going to do. It sounds like you had a pretty major panic attack back there in homeroom. It might be best for you to go home for the day to relax and try to get your body and brain back to normal because you really do need to be back in class tomorrow. I will call Reverend Marcus to come and get you guys."

Henry nodded his head at this. Mr. Alvarez continued, "I'll let him explain all this to your parents, and I will talk to your teachers. Your mom can expect a phone call from me with any assignments you missed today. Sound good?"

Henry and Jackie both nodded in agreement.

"And I'm not an expert," Mr. Alvarez said. "But I'd recommend going to see your doctor about this. This attack might be the sign of an anxiety disorder."

Henry got another look of panic on his face. Mr. Alvarez tried to calm him down by changing the subject. "I understand you're quite a baseball player..."

"Yes, sir," Henry said.

Mr. Alvarez stood up and reached out to shake Henry and Jackie's hands. "And I want you to know that my office door is always open, Henry. If you are feeling overwhelmed or feel a panic attack coming on, just ask your teacher to let you come to my office."

"Yes, sir," Henry answered as he shook the assistant principal's hand.

"Now, Jackie, why don't you go get your and Henry's backpacks from Mrs. Abbott's class. Henry, you sit there in the waiting area, and I will call Reverend Marcus."

"Yes, sir." This time both boys said it as they got up from their chairs and left Mr. Alvarez's office. There was already another flunky upperclassman waiting to see Mr. Alvarez. This dude reeked of a type of smoke that neither Henry nor Jackie had smelled before. They each coughed after walking by him.

Mr. Alvarez turned to the pothead and said, "I'll be with you in a minute." Then he closed the door to make his phone call to Reverend Marcus.

"Where are we going, Dad?" Jackie asked as they pulled into a seemingly random parking lot. They were about fifteen minutes away from school and in the industrial part of town, nothing but huge concrete buildings. But Henry knew exactly where they were. He had been here many times with his dad. Once they parked the car, the business's sign was visible:

"Monarch's Batting Cages."

Simple proof that Reverend Marcus was a pastor in touch with his community. Even though the Mitchells rarely attended services - they did show up most years for Christmas and Easter, and Henry was sure to be there for Jackie's Confirmation a few years ago - Reverend Marcus did take a vested interest in his son's best friend's family. He understood that the batting cages were one of the local parishes of Henry Mitchell's house of worship.

Jackie and Henry waited near the cages while Reverend Marcus went into the clubhouse to purchase their tokens and borrow some bats. He had been to enough of their Little League games and overheard enough of their conversations to know what size bats to select for the boys. He soon returned to the boys with bats tucked under his arms and helmets in hand and a smile on his face. The boys, seeing that he was having trouble with all the equipment, ran over to meet him halfway. They grabbed the helmets and put them on, then grabbed the bats and headed for their favorite cages: the one that pitched 75 miles per hour, the average speed of most high school pitchers.

The tokens that Reverend Marcus bought kept the boys busy for about an hour. When the fun ran out, they emerged from their respective cages panting and sweating and smiling. It was the first time Henry had smiled since he met Jackie just outside the entrance to the school several hours earlier. They got into the car and stopped at 7-Eleven for drinks on their way home.

That night at dinner, the television in the Mitchell house was turned off, which meant that there was something serious to be discussed. Typically, they kept the TV on in the adjoining family room so that they could keep an eye on the evening news or on *Wheel of Fortune*, depending on whether Jack was away on business or not. So, it was an obvious sign when Diane told Henry to turn off the TV before washing up for dinner.

Henry's throat tightened a bit and his heart rate quickened as he saw that his mom had made sloppy joes, one of his favorite meals. The first five minutes or so of dinner were pregnant with an awkward silence. He knew they had to talk about what happened at school that morning, and he knew that his parents were not upset or angry with him - they had had a long talk with Jackie's father when he dropped Henry off at home - but he felt nervous nonetheless. And in those silent moments, he wasn't sure if they were waiting for him to bring it up, or if they were waiting until he was mostly done with his dinner, or what.

Finally, his father drew in a deep breath and said, "I'm really glad that Jackie's family is such good friends with the assistant principal at your school. It's important to have an ally like that..."

Jack paused a moment to gather his thoughts, then continued, "Look, I just want you to know that you have a lot of people here to support you, and that you can come to me and your mom, or Reverend Marcus and Victoria, or Mr. Aguilar..."

"Mr. Alvarez," Henry corrected him.

"Right, Mr. Alvarez."

That evening, the Mitchell family not only missed *Wheel of Fortune*, but also *Jeopardy*, *The Wonder Years*, and *Growing Pains*, as they talked through helping Henry cope with his anxiety. They talked about the people he could go to when he is feeling anxious or panicky and about personal coping mechanisms. Diane agreed with Mr. Alvarez about taking Henry to the doctor, writing herself a note to call in the morning.

It was also during this conversation - which ended with a trip to Baskin Robbins to get ice cream - that Henry told his parents about his years-long crush on Molly Jacobs and about the attempted phone call about six weeks ago and about how seeing her again set off this morning's panic attack. Even though he was nervous and embarrassed, he felt good in the end. His mother was all smiles listening to her son talk about his boyhood crush, which only made Henry blush.

After enjoying his chocolate malt, Henry thought it would be a good idea to go to bed early. After all, he needed to give his first day of high school a second try.

Chapter 12

October 13, 1989
Mitchell Home
Gladstone, MO

Henry chained his bike to a nearby streetlamp, then entered the building and meandered through the maze of hallways to Dr. Ferguson's office for his weekly therapy session. After the panic attack in homeroom, his mother took him to the doctor who recommended he start seeing a therapist once a week. Reverend Marcus recommended Dr. Ferguson - a member of Good Shepherd - to the Mitchells, thinking that he and Henry would get along nicely.

Henry took his usual spot on the couch and Dr. Ferguson sat in the chair across from him. Even though Henry had seen them in his previous three sessions, he was fascinated by the baseball pennants and other memorabilia that Dr. Ferguson used to decorate his office. Mixed in with the pennants from current MLB teams were those from Negro League teams. On the bookshelves behind Dr. Ferguson's desk were several autographed baseballs in little glass cases. Henry thought one of them was signed by Satchel Paige, but he couldn't quite tell for sure and he was too nervous to ask.

Most of the previous three sessions had been spent getting to know each other. Henry talked about his family, his friendship with Jackie, and his love for baseball. Dr. Ferguson, like Henry, loved to talk about baseball. He even shared a few stories about his uncle who once played in the Negro Leagues back in the day.

But during this session, Dr. Ferguson decided to pry a little deeper into Henry's anxiety and some of the things that triggered anxious feelings and panic attacks for him. This led to a conversation about Molly Jacobs and what happened in homeroom on the first day of school.

"So, what happened the second day of school, the next time you saw Molly?" Dr. Ferguson asked.

Henry explained how Jackie met him at the gate to the school, like he had the previous morning, and they walked to homeroom together. They sat close to the door, "just in case," and this time Molly sat in the row in front of them instead of next to them. Henry felt his pulse start to quicken, but he stayed cool and stayed in his seat.

About halfway through class, while everyone was doing a worksheet at their desk, Molly turned around to ask Jackie what he wrote for number four, and before turning back around, put a small, folded piece of paper next to Henry's hand. She gave him that crooked little smile he liked so much and went back to her work.

"What did the note say?" Dr. Ferguson said with the same enthusiasm that Jackie had when he pestered Henry to open the note.

"It said, 'U O K?'" Henry answered.

"And were you?" Dr. Ferguson prodded.

"Yeah," Henry said with the slightest smile.

Dr. Ferguson let the silence hang to allow Henry to continue his story, but it seemed to be over.

"Here's what I think we should do," Dr. Ferguson said as he shifted in his chair. These words made Henry a little nervous; the therapist seemed a little too enthusiastic about this idea.

Dr. Ferguson reached over to his desk and grabbed a notepad and a pen. He placed them on the coffee table that sat between him and Henry.

"I'd like for you to write a letter to Molly," he said. He could see Henry's eyes grow to the size of baseballs.

"I will help you with what to say and how to say it," the doctor was trying to sound reassuring. "And you don't have to actually give it to her unless you want to."

Henry was hesitant, but that last sentence eased his fears a little. He grabbed the notepad with his right hand and the pen with his left, and said "To whom it may concern" as he wrote "Dear Molly" at the top of the page. He gave Dr. Ferguson an ornery grin, and for the remainder of the session they composed a letter that expressed Henry's feelings for Molly Jacobs, as well as his embarrassment when he called her that evening during the summer, and the panic he felt when he saw her enter homeroom on the first day of school. Man, it felt good to get that all out of his system.

At the end of the hour, Henry folded up the letter and stuck it in his back pocket. He shook Dr. Ferguson's hand and headed for the office door. Outside, he unchained his bike and rode off toward home.

The route that Henry rode to get home took him past Jackie's house. As he coasted to a stop, he saw Jackie shooting hoops with his dad in the driveway. Jackie tossed the ball to his dad, then ran over to meet Henry at the curb. He asked how the session went.

"Good," Henry said. "Ferguson made me write a letter to Molly."

Jackie's eyes got big.

"I don't have to give it to her, though..."

"But you do have to show it to your best friend," Jackie cut him off and held out his hand.

Henry quickly changed the subject. "You coming to movie night?"

Jackie could see that he was not getting his hands on that letter unless he physically wrestled it away from him. He responded, "Only if I get to read that letter."

Henry rolled his eyes and said, "We'll see."

Jackie walked through the front door of the Mitchells' home without knocking or ringing the doorbell on that Friday evening. He grabbed a few slices of pizza from the kitchen counter and a soda from the fridge on his way to the living room, where he found Henry and his father in a deep debate about what movie they would watch that evening. Jackie had a standing unspoken invitation to join the Mitchells' movie nights on Fridays, assuming he had completed all his after-school chores at home. On this particular evening, he took his usual Friday-evening spot at the end of the couch and popped open his can of Dr. Pepper. Henry and his dad barely even looked in Jackie's direction as they both had their heels dug in in this debate over which film they would watch that evening. Jackie and Henry's mom smiled at each other; at least someone acknowledged the newly arrived houseguest.

Jack's argument was that since it was Friday the 13th, they should watch a cheesy horror film, and what film better fit that description than the 1978 cult classic, *Attack of the Killer Tomatoes*. Henry, who usually would be up for a cheesy cult classic horror film, really wanted to watch one of his new favorite baseball movies, *Field of Dreams*, which had just recently been released on VHS tape. Diane, who was not usually one to remain quiet in these decisions, stayed far away from this one. Jackie had also grown quite comfortable throwing his two cents worth into these conversations, but he took his cue from Diane and steered clear.

Jackie was well into his second slice of pizza before the two squabblers had reached an agreement... or more precisely before Jack decided to give in and watch the baseball movie. Jack had seen it last summer in the theater while on one of his business trips, and wanted to watch it with him Henry, but how does one NOT watch a movie like *Attack of the Killer Tomatoes* on Friday the 13th. Henry got up to get more pizza - and, of course, Jackie asked Henry to bring him another slice - and Jack put the movie into the VCR and was already fast-forwarding through the previews and FBI warning to start the evening's entertainment.

They had reached one of Henry's favorite scenes in the film: the part where Kevin Costner's character and James Earl Jones's character are somewhere in Minnesota trying to track down "Moonlight" Graham, the ballplayer whose name had appeared on the scoreboard at Fenway Park. They had found Graham's hometown, but learned that *Dr.* Graham had passed away several years earlier. Kevin Costner went for a walk around the town that night, and through some weird time warp thing, met a middle-aged "Moonlight" Graham. They talked about Graham's Big-League career that really wasn't. Graham told Kevin Costner that the one thing he'd always wanted to do was to stand in the batter's box and stare down a Major League pitcher. Then just as the pitcher goes into his windup, Graham said he would give him a little wink, just to mess with the pitcher's head. But alas, "Moonlight" Graham would have no such opportunity since his Big-League career was limited to one half an inning in the outfield.

Just as this scene ended, Henry's dad grabbed the VCR remote from the coffee table and paused the movie. "I gotta pee," he said. He quickly headed down the hallway to the bathroom and closed the door behind him. Jackie and Henry went to refill their empty plates with pizza.

"So, do I get to read your letter or what?" Jackie asked Henry quietly. The boys thought that by talking softly in the kitchen that they were out of earshot from Henry's mom in the living room. They weren't; she could hear everything they said, but she didn't let them know.

"Yeah, after the movie," Henry replied. But there was one little snag; Jackie had to be home by 10:00. There might not be enough time for him to read the letter after the movie. Both Henry and Jackie realized this at the same time.

"Mom, can Jackie..." Henry was cut off before he could finish his request.

"Yes," his mom said. She knew that Henry's question ended with "spend the night?" Anytime Henry said the words, "Mom, can Jackie" after 7:00pm, they were followed by "spend the night?" By the same token, almost any question that began with "Mom, can I" ended with "spend the night at Jackie's?"

Henry and Jackie quickly did their "secret" handshake, then Jackie grabbed the kitchen phone and called his house. He got out about the same number of words as Henry did before his mom gave Jackie permission to stay the night. The answer to this question was always "yes."

Henry's dad returned from the bathroom, grabbing another piece of pizza on the way back to his recliner. Diane gave him a look that said, "Haven't you had enough pizza?" Henry's father had put on a few pounds since turning 40 a few years ago, and his wife would always nag him about his penchant for junk food.

Jack saw the look from his wife and raised his hands and said, "What?" His mouth was full of pizza. "I had to skip lunch today because my sales meeting went long this morning."

A lame excuse he had given a hundred times before. Diane just shrugged and turned her attention back to the television. Jack pushed play on the remote and the movie resumed.

A little later in the film, Kevin Costner and James Earl Jones picked up a young "Moonlight" Graham along the side of the road and took him back to the Field of Dreams on Kevin Costner's farm in Iowa. After arriving at the field, the youngster was welcomed into the game and got his turn at the plate. And there, on a baseball diamond in the middle of a cornfield in Iowa, Graham got the opportunity to live out his dream. He winked at the veteran pitcher who then flipped out and threw at the kid's head. The rest of the players on both teams teased the pitcher who couldn't handle being winked at by this punk kid who had just arrived.

Henry let out a big laugh and got a look in his eye, a look that said he was concocting a very mischievous plan. He swiped the remote from the coffee table and paused the movie to make his declaration:

"Dad, write this down for me," Henry said as he got up and stood in the middle of the room. He didn't mean for his dad to actually write down what he was going to say; it was an expression that his dad used when he had something important to say to Henry. "If I make it to the Big Leagues..."

"Don't you mean WHEN you make it to the Big Leagues?" Jackie chimed in.

"Right, Jackie. WHEN I get to the Big Leagues - and you all are in the stands - in my first at bat, I'm gonna do it. I don't care who I'm hitting against... unless it's Nolan Ryan, that dude's a badass..."

"Jar!" his parents said in unison, referring to the "Swear Jar" that Diane had placed on the kitchen counter to curb the profanity in the Mitchell home.

"Sorry, Mom. I'll pay up after the movie," Henry continued. "In my very first at bat, I'm going to stare that pitcher down, and I'm going to give him a little wink, just like 'Moonlight' Graham."

Henry was so proud. Everyone in the room just chuckled as he sat back down, restarting the movie as he did so.

After the movie was over, Henry's dad hit the rewind button on the remote and Jackie made the rounds, picking up everyone's paper plates and soda cans. Henry cleaned up the mostly empty pizza boxes and other messes in the kitchen. Diane was so proud of herself and her ability to train two teenage boys to clean up after dinner. After the dinner mess was cleaned up, the boys scooped themselves some chocolate ice cream and headed back to Henry's room.

"Letter," he said, extending his hand toward Henry after the door was shut.

"But…" Henry was looking for any excuse not to hand it over. "Ice cream. We need to finish our ice cream. You don't want your ice cream to melt, now do you?"

Henry shoved a big spoonful of ice cream into his mouth, swallowed it quickly and gave Jackie the biggest, cheesiest smile he could. But that smile quickly turned into a look of excruciating pain. Jackie just laughed, almost spitting out his mouthful of ice cream, as he saw the all-too-familiar look of Henry in the midst of a massive brain freeze. Jackie extended his empty hand again. Henry gave in; he set down his bowl of ice cream, rubbed his forehead to soothe the brain freeze headache, then fished the neatly folded letter out of his desk drawer and reluctantly handed it to Jackie.

Jackie sat in Henry's desk chair, smoothing the letter out on the desktop, and grabbed his bowl of ice cream. With a big smile and a mouthful of ice cream, he dove into the letter.

Chapter 13

November, 1989
Winnetonka High School
Gladstone, MO

One of Winnetonka High School's oldest traditions had been the November Backwards Dance, in which the girls were supposed to ask the boys to be their dates to the dance. It was not a formal dance like homecoming or the senior prom. It was much more casual, and oftentimes students would attend in co-ed groups with their friends. Only well-established couples would make this evening a real "date." But for Molly Jacobs, this was her opportunity to make her big move.

At lunchtime on the Monday two weeks before the dance, Henry and Jackie were eating lunch at their usual table in the student cafeteria, two tables over from the varsity baseball players. Even though they knew most of the varsity players from their days in Little League, Henry and Jackie knew the unwritten rule: freshmen ballplayers were not allowed to sit at the varsity table unless they made the varsity squad. And tryouts weren't until January, so two tables away was as close as they dared to venture. Once in a while, Henry and Jackie would get invited to join in a conversation at the varsity players' table, but they knew to just stand near the table. They were not allowed to actually sit down at the table.

Molly Jacobs entered the cafeteria carrying her New Kids on the Block lunchbox. She usually sat on the opposite end of the room from Jackie and Henry's table, but on this day, she walked past her normal spot and headed straight for the boys' table. Jackie was the first to see her and he cut off Henry's complaining about how his curveball wasn't breaking the way he'd like it to. He tapped Henry on the arm and motioned with his eyes that someone was approaching the table from behind him.

Molly tapped Henry's right shoulder, then went around and sat in the chair on Henry's left. Henry fell for it, looking to his right, but then looked to his left when he heard her giggle. Henry and Jackie and Molly had been grouped together for a recent classwork assignment in Mrs. Abbott's English class, so Henry figured that Molly had a question about the night's reading assignment. He was racking his brain trying to remember what pages they had been assigned.

"Hi, Henry," Molly said as she sat down and scooted her chair a little closer to Henry. "Hi, Jackie."

Molly's hands fidgeted with the latch and handle of her NKOTB lunchbox. She wasn't quite ready to ask Henry what she came over to ask him, so she attempted a bit of small talk. "So, what's with that Boo Radley guy?" she asked, referring to *To Kill a Mockingbird*, the book they just started reading in English class.

Henry and Jackie looked at each other, a little dumbfounded by where this conversation was headed. All they could get out were a few "Uhhs" and "Umms." Molly could see that the tactic was not working, so she decided to just come out and say it.

"Henry, you know the Backwards Dance coming up in a few weeks?"

Henry glanced at Jackie, who now had a big grin on his face. Henry answered hesitantly, "Yeah..."

"Well, if you're not doing anything... and if no one has already asked you... I... I was wondering if you would like to go... with me... to the dance," Molly stammered out. She avoided eye contact with both boys at the table, staring intently at her NKOTB lunchbox.

"Oh... uh... um..." Henry wanted to say yes, but could not make the right shapes with his mouth and tongue in order to form the sounds to say "yes."

Jackie jumped in to bail out his friend. "I think what Henry is trying to say, Molly, is that he would love to go to the dance with you."

Molly gave Jackie a grateful smile.

Henry looked over and met Molly's eye and smiled sheepishly. Molly smiled her crooked little smile, which caused Henry to smile even bigger. Neither knew what to say next. After a few long seconds, Jackie slid a piece of paper over to Molly Jacobs. "Here's Henry's number. Call him tomorrow after school to work out the details." Everyone at the table knew that Henry was still a little gun-shy about calling her after last summer's phone call debacle. What would these two lovebirds do if it weren't for Jackie?

Molly put the slip of paper into her pocket as she stood up from the table. Henry and Jackie instinctively stood up as well - they had both been raised to stand up whenever a young lady approaches or leaves the table. Before she walked away, Molly Jacobs reached down and gave Henry's hand a gentle squeeze. "I'll call you tomorrow." Henry stared after her with a big goofy grin on his face.

Henry heard the phone ringing from his bedroom. He was supposed to be doing his math homework, but all he could think about was the call he was expecting from Molly Jacobs. He tossed the baseball he'd been handling onto his bed and ran down the hall to grab the phone before his mother did. But no such luck; she was already in the kitchen putting away groceries when it rang.

"Hello?" Mrs. Mitchell said. Henry got there just in time to see the huge smile on her face. "Yes, he's right here."

Henry would have sworn that his mother was able to hear his heart trying to pound its way out of his chest. But it was a good thing that she was too busy smiling at him.

"It's a girl!" she whispered as she handed him the cordless phone. Henry snatched it and didn't run, but walked as quickly as possible to his room and closed the door behind him. Diane laughed to herself as she went back to putting produce in the fridge.

"Hello?" Henry said as he sat on his bed. He was out of breath, not from his fifteen-foot walk down the hall, but from the fact that he was actually talking to Molly Jacobs. On the phone. Without her father accusing him of being a child predator.

"Hi, Henry. It's Molly," she said. Henry was too caught up in his own nervousness to not notice that her voice had a slight quiver to it as well.

"Did you ask your parents about the dance?" she asked.

"Yeah... yeah, I asked them this morning," Henry replied. "I think they were more excited than I was... I mean, not that I'm not excited... of course I'm excited... I mean..."

Molly threw Henry a life ring. "I'm really excited, too. My dad said he would drive us."

Henry's pulse rate about doubled, and it was as if Molly could hear it through the phone.

"But don't worry. After you tried to call me last summer and... well, you know... I told him that you are one of my classmates... and a very nice and sweet one, too."

Both Molly's words and Henry's deep breathing - he held the bottom end of the phone receiver away from his mouth so as to not sound creepy - brought his pulse rate back down closer to normal.

"So..." Molly was searching for something to say. "Are you excited about reading *Romeo & Juliet* in English next month?"

"Um, yeah... I guess."

After putting away the groceries, Diane had crept down the hallway to try to eavesdrop on her son's conversation with *the* Molly Jacobs. She couldn't hear much - partly because Henry did more listening than talking - but she felt the same giddiness that she felt as a young college student when she had her first phone call with Henry's father.

What a difference six days and three telephone conversations - and a long conversation between Henry and Dr. Ferguson - had made. First, when Molly Jacobs walked into Mrs. Abbott's homeroom every morning, she was greeted with a big smile from Henry. Henry's palms would get a little sweaty, but in a good way. No longer did he get that I-need-to-get-the-hell-out-of-here-because-I-feel-like-I'm-going-to-die sort of feeling. He welcomed the butterflies he got in his stomach when he saw her each morning.

Second, Molly and her friend Tisha started eating lunch with Henry and Jackie. Tisha was not in their English class, but she was in Algebra with Henry and in French with Jackie. As a lunchtime foursome, they clicked pretty quickly. Their lunchtimes were filled with lots of laughter;

typically, at least one of them would end up making a snorting sound or would almost shoot milk out their nose from laughing so hard.

On the evening of November 13, Henry was on the phone for the third time in a week with Molly Jacobs. He had finished his homework that afternoon and eaten dinner and was now in his room on the cordless phone. Henry's father had a late meeting at work, so Henry and his mother had eaten dinner without him. Henry and Molly weren't talking about anything in particular when he heard his dad come in through the front door and head down the hallway to Henry's closed door. Normally, Henry's father stopped in the kitchen or living room to say hello to Henry's mother, then used the restroom, then checked to see what Henry was up to. But not this time. He knocked on Henry's bedroom door and called out to Henry.

"Hey, Hammer. Get out here to watch the news with me," Jack said through the door.

Henry felt a little nervous. What could have happened? He hadn't heard about any big new events earlier in the day. And the Major League Baseball Winter Meetings didn't start until after Thanksgiving, so it couldn't have been about some big trade or free agent signing.

"Hey, Molly," Henry interrupted Molly's story. "I gotta go. My dad just got home."

"Oh, ok," Molly responded. Finishing her story about her new bloodhound puppy, Mortimer, would have to wait for another time. "I'll see you in homeroom."

Henry could hear that crooked little smile through the phone line. "Yup. See you tomorrow."

There was an awkward silence for a few long seconds before Henry heard Molly hang up the phone. Ending their conversations - both in person and on the phone - was always *weird*. They hadn't started dating officially yet; they were friends, but more than friends, but not yet boyfriend and girlfriend. So, they never really knew how to say goodbye.

Henry opened his bedroom door just as his dad walked by on his way to the living room. "Come on," Henry's dad said. "The sports report is almost on. Big baseball news."

Henry followed his dad to the living room. Henry put the phone back on its base in the kitchen while his dad turned the television to the

Channel 6 news. The broadcast was going to commercial with the teaser for the sports report. The image on the screen was first a dark-haired man sitting in front of a microphone, then cut to a clip of presumably that same man on the pitcher's mound clutching his left shoulder after delivering a pitch to home plate.

"Oh, thank you," Jack said as Diane handed him a plate of food.

"Who is that, Dad?" Henry asked, referring to the teaser clip that had just been on the screen. The television now showed an obviously low-budget commercial for a local personal injury lawyer.

"His name is Dave... something or other," Jack said to his son after swallowing a mouthful of food. "He's a pitcher for the Giants, I think. He announced his retirement today."

Henry gave his dad a puzzled look. *So, what?* he thought. It's November. It's a perfectly normal time for players to announce their retirement. And if Henry had never heard of the guy, and Jack couldn't even remember his last name, why was it so important that they watch clips from the news conference announcing his retirement? Henry's dad interrupted a phone call with Molly Jacobs for this?

Jack continued, "He had cancer in his pitching arm, was out for a while going through surgeries and other treatments, then came back this season... Oh wait, here we go."

The news broadcast had resumed, with the sports reporter's head and shoulders filling the right side of the screen. Dave Something-Or-Other's retirement announcement was the lead story. The reporter narrated the brief summary of Dave Dravecky's career as a Major League pitcher. Dravecky had made his debut with the San Diego Padres, and was later traded to the San Francisco Giants. He had been named an All-Star in 1983. Then came the cancer diagnosis in the deltoid muscle of his pitching arm. He'd had a large portion of that muscle removed and was told he might never pitch again. But Dravecky defeated the odds and made his comeback, returning to the Giants' starting rotation. But in his second game back, while pitching against the Montreal Expos, the bone in his upper arm snapped as he delivered the pitch; the bone had been so severely weakened by the cancer treatments that it couldn't handle the strain of throwing a Major League-caliber fastball. The sound of the bone breaking could be heard throughout the stadium, followed by a collective gasp by the crowd. After collapsing in pain, he had to be helped from the field. His comeback was over. His pitching arm was broken again several weeks later during a postseason locker room celebration, and today he was announcing his retirement.

"Oh shit," Henry muttered under his breath.

"Jar!" his parents called out in unison. Henry fished a quarter out of his pocket and sulked his way into the kitchen to drop a quarter into the Jar, then he returned to the living room to watch the rest of the sports broadcast. The reporter had moved on to football, basketball, and hockey scores, things that the Mitchell boys were only mildly interested in.

When Henry sat back down on the living room couch, he said, quite sarcastically, "What I meant to say..."

Henry's mother shot him a look. This phrase had become a running joke in the family. It started with Diane correcting Henry or Jack anytime they swore with, "I think what you meant to say was..." Jack and Henry now used this phrase after they had to drop a quarter into the Jar.

"What I meant to say," Henry started again. "Is that that's really messed up. I mean, he's so young and it sounds like he was really good."

Henry's parents nodded in agreement.

"Well, I've got homework to do," Henry said to break the silence. He had done most of his homework already but was looking for an excuse to go in the other room. After closing his bedroom door, Henry sat on his bed for a moment. For some reason, hearing about Dravecky's cancer and broken arm and retirement struck a nerve with Henry. Here's a guy in the prime of his career, only to be permanently sidelined with cancer. Henry tried to imagine how he would take the news if he was in a similar situation.

Henry was roused from his musings by the ringing of the phone in the kitchen. His mom answered it and then called out, "Henry, it's Jackie."

Henry got up off his bed, but before he could open his door, it swung open and his dad tossed the phone at him. "Think fast," he said without even looking at where he threw the phone as he continued on down the hallway. Henry had no chance of catching it at such close range, but he did manage to duck out of the way to avoid getting hit with the phone. The phone receiver bounced off the bed and onto the floor before Henry picked it up.

"Hello?" Henry said.

"Yo, Hammer," Jackie said on the other end of the line. "You'll never guess what just happened."

"Yeah, I just saw it on the news," Henry replied. His one-track mind was still stuck on the baseball news.

"Wait, what?" Jackie was so confused. "What are you talking about?"

"That Giants pitcher, Dave Dravecky, announced he's retiring. It was just on the news."

"Dude... what the hell are you talking about?" Jackie didn't let him answer that. "I don't really care about baseball right now..."

"Whoa..." Henry could not believe those eight words just came out of his best friend's mouth.

"Oh, relax. I just mean that I have other important news to tell you."

Henry was still getting his shorts out of a twist as Jackie continued.

"I just got off the phone with Tisha," Jackie said. "She was at Molly's house, and they both called me, actually."

"Uh huh," Henry said.

"And Tisha asked if I wanted to go to the Backwards Dance with her. We can, like, go as a double date."

"That's great," Henry was actually very excited for his friend, but his tone of voice certainly didn't show it.

"Well, you could at least pretend to be excited for me," Jackie complained.

"No, no. I am excited for you. Your first real date."

"Yours too," Jackie reminded him.

The next two weeks before the Backwards Dance went by very quickly, and Henry had spent those two weeks agonizing over every little potential detail for the evening. *What if Molly actually wants to dance?* Henry may have been graceful on the baseball diamond, but that gracefulness did not extend past the foul lines. His little cousin had dragged him out onto the dance floor several years ago at their uncle's wedding, which made for the most uncomfortable four minutes of his young life. He held her waist at a very stiff arms' length, swayed back and forth and probably bruised his little cousin's toes by stepping on them with his big old clumsy feet.

Henry did not have the rhythm for a fast song, and the thought of a slow dance made his heart go pitter pat... but not in a good way. How close

126

should he stand to her? Should he hold one of her hands out to the side, or put both hands on her waist? What if his hands got too sweaty? What if holding her that close to himself made him, you know... *excited*?

And what would they talk about? The dance was three hours long, after all. What if he ran out of things to say? Or worse, what if they ran out of things to talk about, and she suggested they go out and dance?

Henry had certainly lost sleep during these past two weeks worrying about these things, but what had him most scared was having to meet her father. Molly had assured him that she had talked with her dad and cleared up the misunderstanding, and that everything was going to be fine. But those assurances did not stop Henry from living on the verge of an anxiety attack for the three days leading up to the dance.

On the big night, Jackie was over at Henry's house so they could get ready together, and then Molly's dad was going to come pick them all up to take them to the dance. Henry's father talked them through ironing their shirts, something he said every young man should learn how to do. Both boys had buzz cuts, but that didn't keep them from obsessing over their hair in the bathroom for fifteen minutes. And despite careful instructions from Henry's father on its proper use, the boys put on way too much Old Spice cologne. After they realized this, they tried to wash it off, but it had already soaked into their skin and clothes. Henry's father said they would probably blend right in with all of the other freshmen who also got a hold of their fathers' cologne or aftershave.

At 6:45pm, there was a knock at the door. The girls were here! As he walked to the front door to let them in, Henry whispered to himself over and over, "Be cool. Be cool."

He opened the door and there stood Molly Jacobs and Tisha Roberts. They both looked amazing in their matching (in color, not in style) blue dresses. Henry, with Jackie standing right behind him, said hi and welcomed them into the entryway. Henry wasn't sure how to greet Molly; was it too weird to give her a hug? A handshake would have just been weird; they never shook hands or high fived. But a hug? In front of his parents? She and Tisha just stepped past them, giving him and Jackie big, uncomfortable smiles.

Henry's mom knew he would forget to get the corsages out of the fridge, so she went to the kitchen to retrieve them while the four adolescents stared awkwardly at each other. She caught Henry's eye when

127

she returned, and he went to her to get them. He gave one to Jackie, and then the boys gave them to their dates. They were wrist corsages, so they were spared having to try to pin them to the girls' dresses. They were about to leave when Henry's mom stopped them and insisted on taking "just a few" pictures before they left. When she was finally finished, they were walking out to Molly Jacobs' dad's car. Henry's heart was pounding and his palms were sweating. Welcoming Molly Jacobs into the house was one thing; meeting her father face-to-face was a whole other ballgame.

Molly's dad was not much taller than Henry or Jackie were, but he was an intimidating presence. He was a solid mass of humanity, the type of guy you want on your side in a barroom brawl. He stepped out of the car and greeted the boys, extending his hand to shake theirs. "You must be Jackie," he said, sizing up the young man. Molly's dad was one of those old-fashioned men who believed you could learn everything you need to know about another man by the firmness of his handshake. Fortunately, Jackie had learned from his dad – also a rather old-fashioned man – the proper way to shake another man's hand. Molly's father gave him a smile as he released his hand.

"Daddy, this is Henry Mitchell," Molly Jacobs said as she gave her nervous date a little nudge toward her dad. Henry tried to be sly about wiping the sweat from his hand before shaking Mr. Jacobs' hand, but Molly's father definitely noticed. He liked that the young man taking his daughter to the school dance was a little intimidated.

"Nice to meet you, sir," Henry said, offering a firm handshake. Despite every natural inclination, he forced himself to make eye contact and smile as he said this.

"And a pleasure to meet you, young man," Mr. Jacobs said, giving Henry's hand an extra little squeeze, as if to say, "You're alright, kid," before releasing his hand.

Molly had prepped her father by telling him that Henry was a big baseball fan and that it might help him to not feel so nervous if he brought up baseball in the car. Mr. Jacobs, who was himself a baseball fan, was happy to oblige. All it took was asking what Henry thought about the earthquake in San Francisco that interrupted that year's World Series to get Henry going. During the ten-minute drive to school, no one else could get a word in edgewise. Molly was happy to see her dad engaged in conversation with her... *friend*. She still wasn't sure how to define her relationship with Henry.

Mr. Jacobs parked in the lot nearest to the school's gymnasium to let the foursome out of the car. Molly gave her dad a quick side hug before starting to walk toward the gym. Music was already pouring out of the open doors and could be heard in the parking lot. Henry was about to follow Molly, but Mr. Jacobs stepped in front of him to block his way. He had something to say before Henry took Molly into the gym, "I like you, kid. But Molly is my little girl, and I love her very much. So, take good care of her."

"Yes, sir," Henry said. Then Molly's dad stepped aside to let Henry pass.

As he joined the group, he turned around to see if Mr. Jacobs was still standing there, but he had already gotten into the car. He stared at the car for a moment before Molly touched his arm to get his attention.

"What did my dad say?" she asked.

"N... nothing," Henry replied. "He said to have a good time."

"Well, I'm not one to disobey my father. So, let's go!" Molly took Henry's hand and walked quickly toward the open doors of the gym.

Tisha and Jackie headed straight to the middle of the dance floor, but it took about an hour before Molly finally managed to get Henry to go out and join them. Tisha was on the girls' cross-country team, and a number of her teammates and their dates were out there too. Henry was very slow to warm up to the idea of dancing, but he soon realized that most of the girls' dates could not dance either. Everyone was just jumping around and waving their arms around; every once in a while, they did so to the rhythm of the music. Henry could do that. In fact, after a couple of songs, he was actually enjoying himself.

By the time the DJ changed things up and put on a slower song, the group of ten to twelve freshmen were in a sweaty cloud of body odor, cheap perfume, and their dad's Old Spice. This seemed like a good time to visit the punch bowl and maybe step outside for a breath of fresh air. Even though his shirt was drenched in sweat and his tongue was parched, Henry fought the urge to guzzle his cup of punch. He did refill his and Molly's cups several times, then looked out onto the dance floor. All the couples were standing very close to each other and swaying gently to the slow song. Henry liked the idea of slow dancing with Molly Jacobs, but was not ready to be that close to her.

"Wanna go outside for a minute?" he asked.

"Sure, I could use some fresh air," she answered. They put their cups in the nearby trash can. Molly grabbed Henry's hand, interlocking her fingers with his. She gave him that crooked little smile, and he smiled back. They walked toward the exit, Jackie and Tisha following close behind. They, too, were holding hands. And had big smiles on their faces. Jackie and Tisha were, in the words of Friend Owl from Disney's *Bambi*, "twitterpated." Or maybe it was just the overactive hormones.

The four friends sat at a nearby picnic table, far enough away from the gym doors to be able to have a conversation over the sound of the music, but not too far away to arouse the suspicion of the chaperons who were making regular rounds to make sure students stayed out of trouble. They talked and laughed - mostly at Henry's earlier attempts at dancing - for about fifteen minutes. It was a typically chilly November evening, and Molly wanted to go back inside. Henry agreed that it was a good idea.

"You two coming in?" he asked as he and Molly stood up from the table.

Jackie and Tisha smiled at each other, then Jackie said, "Nah, you guys go ahead. We're going to stay here for a few more minutes."

Tisha gave Molly an impish look that the boys were oblivious to, to which Molly gave a disapproving glare. If those two wanted to risk getting in trouble for the sake of a quick make-out session, then that's on them. She grabbed Henry's hand and the two went back into the gym.

The last hour of the dance went by quickly. Henry and Molly had a wonderful time on and off the dance floor. The final song was "I'll Be Loving You (Forever)" by the New Kids on the Block, one of Molly Jacobs' favorites. She dragged a reluctant Henry out onto the dance floor for their first slow dance together. He wrapped his hands around her waist, and she rested her head on his shoulder with her arms around his neck. They swayed back and forth - completely off rhythm - but neither seemed to mind. Those three minutes and fifty-two seconds were a little slice of eternity for these two. Everything else around them - sans the music - faded away and it was just the two of them on that dance floor. As the song came to an end, they just kept on swaying back and forth, wanting the moment to last forever.

When they did stop dancing, Henry's hands slipped from her waist as he began to pull away from Molly, but she held on tight, not letting him get away. He looked down at her; she looked up at him. Then as if being cued by a stage director, they both closed their eyes and leaned in for a kiss. This time neither was caught off guard and neither was in a hurry for it to end. Whether it was ten seconds or ten minutes, it didn't matter.

The house lights came on and the other students jostled past Henry and Molly, interrupting the bliss of that kiss. Their lips parted and their eyes opened, and they looked long into each other's eyes, not wanting the moment to end. But like all good things, it had to end. They had to find Jackie and Tisha - whom they had not seen for about an hour - and get out to the parking lot where Molly's dad was sure to be waiting for them. And they had to fight through the crowd of smelly, sweaty teenagers to do so, something Henry was not going to enjoy.

Molly took hold of Henry's hand and guided them through the throngs of students toward the door. They had no choice but to join the bottleneck as far too many students tried to exit through the only two open gym doors at the same time.

Once out in the fresh night air and away from the crowds, Henry and Molly began looking around for Jackie and Tisha. Molly could see her dad's car pull into the driveway at the far end of the parking lot, and their search for their friends got a little more frantic. *Where the hell could they be*, they both thought.

Fortunately, Jackie and Tisha emerged from around the side of the gym just as Molly Jacobs' father pulled up to the curb where Molly and Henry were standing. By the look on Jackie's face and the wrinkles in his shirt and Tisha's dress, it was easy for Molly and Henry to guess what they had been up to for the last hour. Jackie gave Henry a big guilty grin as they got into the back seat of the car. Henry just rolled his eyes at his friend. As Molly's dad drove them all home, Henry thought he caught a glimpse in the light of a streetlamp that looked like a hickey on Jackie's neck. It was hard to tell against the dark complexion of Jackie's skin if it was actually a hickey or just a shadow from Jackie's loosened collar. Jackie sure had gotten over his shyness around girls. Honestly, this was so unlike Jackie and so unexpected that Henry really didn't know what to think of it. On his very first date – not just with Tisha, but with any girl – Jackie had gotten to first base, maybe even second, something Henry never would have expected.

Henry remained lost in thought for pretty much the entire ride home. It had been a perfect first date with Molly. They held hands. They laughed. They danced. And they shared an amazing kiss on the dance floor.

And based on the big, goofy grin on Jackie's face, he had a pretty damn good time as well.

Chapter 14

March, 1990
Mitchell Home
Gladstone, MO

Ever since the Backwards Dance, Henry and Molly were spending a lot of time together. And Jackie and Tisha were spending a lot of time together. Which meant that Henry and Jackie were not spending a lot of time together. This was not at all intentional, just the result of young love... or in the case of Jackie and Tisha, young hormones.

Molly started showing up on Friday evenings for the Mitchell family's movie night. She was not much of a movie fan, but she was willing to put up with it for a chance to spend time with Henry and his parents. After they had finished their pizza – Henry's parents were quite surprised by how much pizza that girl could scarf down – Molly would tend to snuggle up close to Henry, or hold his hand, or rest her head on his shoulder. Henry was a little embarrassed at first by her displays of affection, but when he saw that his parents didn't care, he just went with it.

Adding Molly to the mix on Friday evenings also had an effect on the movie selections. Wanting to be sensitive to the new guest, Jack didn't bring home the typical action films or psychological thrillers that he used to. Instead he brought home from the video store films like *Some Like It Hot* and *An Affair to Remember*, films that were great in their own right, but not what Henry had grown accustomed to. Diane, on the other hand, welcomed the change.

Across town, Jackie and Tisha spent a lot of time at Tisha's house. Her parents were divorced, and she lived with her mom. But her mom worked the late shift as a waitress at a fancy restaurant in Kansas City, so Tisha's older sister was left to look after her. Tisha's older sister was even more boy crazy than Tisha was, so on Friday evenings, she would pick up Jackie and Tisha from school, grab dinner for them from a nearby drive-thru, and then drop them off at her house before going to her boyfriend's house a few blocks away. Of course, Tisha's mom thought that Tisha's sister was there to supervise the young lovers, and Jackie's parents assumed Tisha's mom was home, but no; Jackie and Tisha were left home alone for several hours almost every Friday evening. Henry and Molly knew about this arrangement, but they weren't going to tattle on their friends. But they also did not want to know what was going on at Tisha's house. They had a "don't ask, don't tell" rule when it came to those lovebirds.

On this particular Friday evening in early March, Henry Aaron Mitchell came bursting through the door, dropping his school bag and athletic bag in the entryway... in the exact spot his mother always yelled at him for dropping his stuff.

"Mom! Hey, Mom. Where are you?" Henry shouted as he raced first into the kitchen, only to find it empty. So was the living room. He continued shouting for her as he headed down the hallway toward his parents' bedroom. He was quiet long enough to hear the toilet flush in the master bathroom, followed by the sound of the sink running, then the sound of the door opening.

"Not a moment of peace around here, I tell ya," Diane complained as she dried her hands and turned off the bathroom light. Henry stood in the middle of her bedroom, almost out of breath. He was wearing his baseball practice uniform: old baseball pants cut just below the knee with a big dirt stain on the butt from sliding on the infield dirt, knee-high socks, a three-quarter sleeve cut t-shirt with a big Winnetonka Griffins logo on the front, and – of course – his Kansas City Monarchs cap.

Diane could see that Henry had important news to share with her. She thought for a brief moment about teasing him and bringing up some completely irrelevant topic to prevent him from sharing his news, but the last time she did that it did not go over well. Henry just ended up pissed off.

"Mom! Guess what... I made varsity!" Henry was nearly jumping up and down with excitement. Henry was, in fact, the first freshman to make the varsity squad at Winnetonka in over fifteen years.

"That's great!" Diane said. She was so happy and proud of her son. She knew it meant a lot of time in the car for her as she would have to drive him to and from practices and games, and it would mean time spent sitting in the car in the parking lot while Henry spent time at the batting cages. But this was nothing new; she had long since gotten used to the life of a baseball mom.

Diane extended her arms to give her son a hug. She could feel the sweat that was still clinging to his t-shirt and could smell the funk from a long, hard tryout that afternoon. She wanted to hold her son for a moment, but was overcome by the cloud of stench she had stepped into.

"I'm very proud of you, Henry," she said as she released him from her embrace. "Why don't you go shower and get ready for dinner."

Henry turned around and stepped toward the door, but his mom stopped him. "Is Jackie coming over for movie night?" she asked.

"No, I think he's going over to Tisha's house tonight," Henry replied.

"He's been spending a lot of time with her, hasn't he?" Diane asked.

"Umm... yeah," was all Henry said. He still had lunch with Jackie, and they did have a couple of classes together, but they did not spend much time together outside of school. Sure, it was partly Henry's fault because he and Molly were spending a lot of time together, but Jackie was spending *a lot* of time with Tisha.

"What about Molly?" Diane asked.

"Umm... I think she is coming. I can call her after I take my shower."

Henry headed to the shower as his mom went to the kitchen to call in the pizza order.

Even though Satchel Paige High School was named for the Negro League star and Major League Hall of Famer, they had not fielded a decent baseball team in over a decade. They did dominate the league in other,

135

less popular sports like boys' golf and girls' tennis, but the other baseball coaches in the league knew that a game against Paige was a good opportunity to give the second-string players a chance for some extended playing time.

This was the first time this season that Winnetonka High School would be playing Satchel Paige High School. It was a home game for Winnetonka, and the coach gave Henry Aaron Mitchell the game ball as the starting pitcher. As a freshman, Henry was a strong second-string utility player, playing mostly first base and in the outfield. He had also pitched in relief in a few games in the young season, but the coach wanted to see what he could do in an extended start. The coach saw Henry's potential, and wanted to give him opportunities to learn and grow, even as a freshman.

And what a game Henry was having against the Satchel Paige Panthers. On the mound, he was throwing a game for the record books. The coach had planned on allowing Henry to throw about 75 pitches, which he figured would get him into the fourth or fifth inning (high school baseball games only go seven innings instead of the nine innings of a college or professional game). He wasn't going to be quick to go to the bullpen; he wanted to see if Henry could pitch his way out of any tough situations he got himself into.

But the coach never got the chance to see Henry pitch his way out of a tough situation. The toughest situation he found himself in was when Henry walked a batter in the third who then reached second base on a passed ball. But Henry got the next three batters in order; the first struck out, the second grounded out to the shortstop who was able to keep the runner from advancing, and the third batter flied out to shallow center field.

Even though Henry was having a great game, the coach knew that it wasn't just Henry's greatness on display. The defense behind him was also having a great game. They were fielding the ball cleanly and making good throws to the appropriate bases or to the cutoff men. The passed ball that allowed that one runner to advance to second in the third inning was the only thing that could really be considered an error. All those ground balls and pop flies that the coach had the team field in practice were already paying off, and it was only the third week of the season. If they kept this up, it was going to be a very good season for Winnetonka baseball.

Not only was Henry having a good day on the mound, but he was also having a good day at the plate. Henry batting leadoff, so when the team batted through their entire line-up in the first inning, he had a double and a two-run home run before he went back out to pitch in the second inning.

After the second inning, the Winnetonka Griffins were winning by a score of 12-0. If they held onto at least a seven-run lead for the next three innings, the "mercy rule" would go into effect at the end of the fifth inning, and the Griffins would win the game. The rule states that if any team has a lead of at least seven runs at the end of the fifth inning, then the game would end... so as to not embarrass the losing team.

Going into the bottom of the third inning, when the Griffins were due to bat, the coach had a quick meeting with the team. He was going to start substituting second string players into the game, and he set down two rules for the offense: that no matter how hard or far they hit the ball they were to stop at first base, and no stealing bases. With a 12-0 lead, he felt bad for the other team, and he didn't want to be accused of running up the score. The Winnetonka boys had no problem abiding by these rules, and even with these rules, they still scored a few more runs to make it 15-0 going into the bottom of the fourth inning.

The bottom of the fourth was going to be the Griffins' last opportunity to bat in this game; since they were winning by enough of a margin to put the mercy rule into effect and since they were the home team, they would not bat in the bottom of the fifth.

In the previous inning, Henry Aaron Mitchell hit a single, a short fly ball into right field that was beyond the reach of the infielders and hit the ground in front of the outfielder. When Henry stepped into the batter's box in the fourth inning with one out and one man on base, he couldn't help but think of what one of his teammates said as he left the dugout.

"All you need is a triple and you'll have hit for the cycle."

Hitting for the cycle means that a player hits a single, double, triple, and a home run all in one game, but not necessarily in that order. It has always been one of the most elusive feats in the game of baseball, right up there with pitching a no-hitter. To accomplish this feat, it takes equal parts skill, luck, and good timing. In the history of the Major Leagues, it has been done just over 300 times. Most players, even the great ones like Babe Ruth and Hank Aaron, are never able to do it. And only a very rare few have done it more than once, such as Kansas City hometown hero George Brett.

Henry pin-wheeled the bat a few times as the pitcher took his place on the mound. The pitcher looked at the runner on first, who had a very non-threatening lead off the bag. The first baseman was not even positioned to take a throw from the pitcher.

Henry stood there, loose and relaxed, waiting for the pitch. When the pitcher released his fastball, it looked like a huge beach ball headed right down the middle of the plate. Henry's eyes grew big as saucers when he saw it coming: 70 miles per hour tops with no funny spin or curve. Just a straight fastball. Henry waited a split second, and then stepped in toward the pitch, swung the bat, and PING! the ball shot out toward the gap in left center field. The outfielders were playing Henry to pull the ball to right field – his last three hits were all to right – so there was no one anywhere near the ball when it hit the ground in shallow left center. The ball bounced a few times, then went into a hard roll toward the outfield fence. The outfielders knew they didn't stand a chance of cutting it off, so they ran into position to play the carom off the fence. But as soon as the ball reached the chain link fence, it hit one of the links and went off in a different direction from where the outfielders thought it would. They scrambled after the ball as the shortstop jogged deeper into left field to catch the relay throw.

After Henry hit the ball, he started running at about half speed down the first base line, remembering his coach's instructions. But when he saw how deep the ball went and how there was no one there to field it and how it took a bad bounce off the outfield fence, he impulsively decided, *to hell with it, I'm running!* And run he did. Within about three steps, he was at a full sprint and was taking a wide angle so that he could round the base without losing speed.

The coach in the dugout was watching the ball roll around in the outfield, so he didn't see what Henry was up to at first. It wasn't until he heard the first base coach – one of the seniors on the team who had been taken out of the game earlier – start cheering loudly that the coach realized that Henry was not stopping at first.

"What the hell is he doing?" the coach said under his breath as he watched Henry take a wide turn around first to go for extra bases.

The problem was that Henry's split-second caused his footwork down the base path to be out of step. He had run down the first base line so many times that he had committed every step to muscle memory. But changing his mind from running through the bag to rounding it to take extra bases totally screwed up his pacing. So, when he approached first base, his outside foot was going to land on the bag instead of his inside foot, like it was supposed to. He made a stutter step to try to correct this, but it was too late and his outside foot – his right foot – ended up stepping on the corner of first base, causing his foot to slip ever so slightly and his ankle to twist underneath him. The injury to his ankle would end up being worse than it felt in the moment. It hurt when it happened, but Henry was too amped up on adrenaline to let it slow him down. But his gait did take on a noticeable limp.

The runner ahead of Henry coasted into second base, but then realized when he heard all the shouting from the bench that he needed to keep running or else Henry might pass him on the base path. He took off toward third with Henry only about fifteen steps behind him. He could see that Henry was not slowing down at second, so he rounded third and headed for home.

The further around the base paths that Henry got, the louder the bench got. Half the bench was cheering him on as he tried to make it to third base. The other half – the half that wanted to stay on the coach's good side – was yelling at him to stop. No one could believe that as Henry rounded second base that he was a mere ninety feet away from achieving something that had never been done in school history.

Even though the coach was furious at Henry for deliberately disobeying his earlier instructions, and for showboating in his team's final at-bats when they already had a 15-0 lead, there was a small part of him that wanted to see Henry slide safely into third base. Under any other circumstances, he would be cheering on Henry louder than any of his players. But good sportsmanship was an essential part of his coaching strategy. It wasn't just his knowledge of the game and his winning record that had earned him two Coach of the Year awards in his tenure as head coach at Winnetonka. He had gained a lot of respect among the other coaches in the league through his fair play and classiness.

Henry's limp became more pronounced and his speed greatly diminished as he ran from second to third base. By this time, the left fielder grabbed the ball and nailed the throw to the cutoff man – the shortstop – in shallow left field. The shortstop spun around, pulled the ball from his glove, and threw a bullet to the third baseman.

The third base coach – also a senior on the team – was down on one knee motioning to Henry to slide into the base to try to beat the tag. Henry slid into third, his right foot extended. If he had thought about it, he would have slid with his left foot extended to protect his injury, but his only thought was to beat that throw from the shortstop. Out of the corner of his eye, Henry could see the throw from the shortstop heading for the third baseman's glove. The infield umpire was hustling toward third to get a good view of the play. It was going to be a close call.

When the dust of the play settled, the umpire paused for a second before issuing his call.

"Safe!" The umpire said as he emphatically spread his arms to signal the call. When he saw that Henry lay there on the red dirt of the infield, his twisted right foot touching the edge of the base and the rest of his body spread in every other direction to avoid the tag, the umpire called time out to give him a chance to stand up and dust himself off. Hesitant cheers erupted from the Griffins' bench. All of his teammates knew Henry had done something worth celebrating; he had become the first player in school history to hit for the cycle. But he did it by directly defying his coach's explicit instructions.

Untwisting his body proved to be difficult, and standing up even more so. When Henry tried to put weight on his right foot, he felt a searing pain shooting up from his ankle as its strength gave way. He nearly collapsed again to the ground. He doubled over, reaching for the injured ankle while trying to balance on one foot.

The third base coach was the first to notice and began yelling to his coach in the dugout on the opposite side of the infield. The infield umpire saw this and joined the third base coach in calling for the coach. When the defensive players saw what was happening, they all took a knee, a sign of respect for the injured player.

Winnetonka's head coach and athletic trainer jogged out onto the field and over to third base where Henry was standing on one foot, using his teammate – the third base coach – to support his weight. Henry was helped off the field by the trainer and the base coach, followed closely by the head coach who now had some important line-up decisions to make, not just about the rest of this game but potentially for several games to come. Once in the dugout, Henry sat on the bench and elevated his right foot by placing it on top of a big Gatorade cooler that had been dragged over to him. The ankle had already begun to swell. The trainer removed Henry's cleat before it would have to be cut off of his foot, and applied ice to the injury.

When the coach saw that the situation had calmed and all the players had gone back to standing at their spots along the dugout fence, he went and sat down next to Henry. Henry saw the angered look on his coach's face and decided to look straight ahead at the baseball diamond in front of them.

"You know, kid, you're kinda lucky you messed up your ankle on that play," the coach started in a nearly whispered tone. If he was yelling at you, it meant that you made a silly mistake, but if he sat down and started talking softly, then you knew you were in real trouble. He continued, "Because if you took that slide cleanly and were standing out there on third base, I would have pulled your ass out of this game so fast..."

Henry was afraid to make any sort of eye contact. He knew that he deserved every bit of this tongue lashing he was receiving.

"Did I not tell you we are stopping all base hits at first?" Henry gave the slightest nod of affirmation.

"Did I not tell you that we are not going to rub it in against Paige?" Another nod from Henry.

"I don't know who taught you to play, but this is not how we play ball here..." The coach caught himself mid-thought. "No wait, actually, I do know who taught you to play ball. I know your Little League coach, and that is not the kind of baseball his team plays. So, shame on you for not only disgracing me and this team, but disgracing your previous coaches."

Henry was no longer looking at the field, but down at the big bag of ice that rested on his ankle. He convinced himself it was because sweat had dripped into his eye, and not his coach's scathing words, that was causing his eyes to well up.

The coach paused for a moment.

"I can see you're in a lot of pain with that ankle," the coach continued. Henry nodded his head. "But this conversation is not over, young man. I'm very disappointed by your decisions out there."

The coach got up from his seat on the bench and addressed the other boys on the team. A Griffin batter grounded out to the second baseman to end the bottom of the fourth inning, and the Panthers were trotting off the field knowing there was no way in hell they could come back from a fifteen-run deficit.

"Tommy," the coach said to the group of boys grabbing their caps and gloves, "You're pitching. The rest of you, let's finish this game."

Tommy Snyder, a junior with limited pitching experience, gave up two runs on four hits before retiring the side. After the game, all the players except Henry went out to shake hands with their opponents.

The coach was conflicted in how to respond to his team's overwhelming victory against the Satchel Paige High School Panthers. They played a clearly inferior team, but they didn't allow that to make them sloppy. Defensively, they played an outstanding game. Henry had pitched four strong innings. The coach was very pleased by what he saw. Henry had great control over the placement and velocity of his pitches and the weak hitters he faced didn't stand a chance against him. And offensively... well, it was like they went to the slow-pitch batting cages. Even the younger and weaker hitters were making good contact and driving the ball.

But that ridiculous showboating by Henry in the bottom of the fourth left a really sour taste in the coach's mouth. He tried to see it from Henry's side. He had the chance to make school history. He had the chance to do something that not even his namesake, Hank Aaron, had done. And he was only a freshman. Henry was young and immature and somewhat impulsive. But still, he disobeyed direct instructions. There was no need to go for extra bases. And more importantly, that was not the sportsmanlike game that he wanted his team to play. There was no place for that kind of theatrics on this Winnetonka team. And the coach knew the right thing to do was to call the Paige coach the next day to apologize for his player's cockiness.

"Let's get this place cleaned up, and be out here for practice tomorrow," the coach said. "We'll talk about this game tomorrow."

The coach's lack of words quieted the rest of the team as they cleaned up their gear. They all knew that the coach was upset at Henry, and they didn't want to do anything to redirect his wrath toward them. A few of them gave Henry a high five and complimented his hitting and/or pitching, but their congratulatory remarks were nothing compared to the game he had had. The rest of them glared at him as they exited the dugout.

142

Most of the players had cleared out of the dugout when Henry's father and Jackie stepped in to help Henry gather his things and walk to the car. Jack had a look of concern on his face when he saw how swollen Henry's ankle was already. Jackie had an impish smirk as he tried to hold in so many things he was feeling at the moment.

It wasn't just the many red lights and the rush hour traffic that made it a long drive home, it was the deafening silence between Henry and his father. Even though he'd had the game of a lifetime, Henry was not in the mood for talking. He was in a lot of pain with his swollen ankle, and he was still upset about the talking-to he received from his coach. The coach spoke briefly to Jack, mostly to tell him to get Henry to the doctor to look at that ankle. It wasn't an emergency; just keep icing it and keep it elevated, and take him to the doctor in the morning.

On that long drive home, Jack tried to break the tension by telling Henry a story.

"You know, when I was stationed in the Philippines..." Jack started his story. Jack had turned 18 just a few months before the end of the Vietnam conflict. And rather than risk being drafted, he enlisted in the Navy. He hoped that between the weeks of Boot Camp and – hopefully – months of specialized training, he would avoid being deployed to an actual warzone. And his plan worked out quite well for himself. He trained to be an electrician and spent his entire tour of duty at the Naval Base Subic Bay in the Philippines. He worked on the electrical systems of the ships that stopped there in order to restock supplies and undergo routine maintenance checks. He hated almost every minute of his tour, but it kept him out of the combat zones.

Even though Jack considered himself extremely lucky not to have had any really traumatic experiences during his time in the service, he didn't talk about it much. But he knew this story would put a smile on Henry's downcast face.

"... We had every Sunday off for what they called 'liberty;' it was time off, but we weren't allowed to leave the base. So, it was up to us to entertain ourselves. There were quite a few guys in my unit who, like myself, were big baseball fans. None of us were very good at baseball, but that didn't stop us from attempting to play on those hot and humid Sunday afternoons."

Henry was listening. With the busyness of his own schedule and his dad's frequent travels, they didn't get many moments like this anymore. And deep down, Henry kind of missed hearing his dad's stories.

"Well, young guys who are really bored and not very athletic can find some pretty creative ways to make a pick-up game of baseball a little more ... uh... *interesting*..."

Henry's interest was piqued.

"Of course, if you add alcohol to anything, even baseball, it's bound to be more fun. Over time, we developed a game that came to be called 'Beer Baseball.'"

"What is 'Beer Baseball'?" The moment Henry asked the question, he realized that it was a dumb question.

"Well, it's kinda self-explanatory. We'd play a game of baseball and every player had to have an open can of beer in his hand at all times."

"But how would you bat?" Henry asked, intrigued by the idea of this game. Not that he had had more than a sip of his dad's beer a few times, and not that he had any desire to try this game anytime soon, but he began to smile a little at the thought of a bunch of half-drunk sailors running around the baseball diamond with beer sloshing all over themselves.

"Well, some guys got really creative, but most of them would hold the beer in their weaker hand, and the bat in their stronger hand. And they would kinda have this really open stance where they are kinda almost facing toward the pitcher." Jack did his best to mimic these actions while still keeping at least one hand on the steering wheel.

"So, everyone's got a beer in their hand, and it's hot and humid, so everyone is also drinking their cans of beer. Anytime someone finished off a beer, play would stop so that he could go grab another one from the stack of cases of beer. We didn't have any way of keeping the beer cold, so it just sat out there in the sun on those hot afternoons. By the end of the game, most everyone was pretty sloshed."

By now Henry had a big smile on his face imagining how funny one of these games would be to watch. He smiled even bigger thinking that his own father was involved in such a thing.

"So... so... one time, this guy... what was his name? Well, I don't remember his name, but he was a big dude. Like 6'4" and 250 pounds. We called him 'Tiny.'"

Henry rolled his eyes at the clichéd nickname.

"So Tiny gets up to bat. It's late in the game and it was a really hot Sunday afternoon. And Tiny had had *a lot* to drink, like at least five or six beers. He swings at the first pitch and barely makes contact. The ball just dribbles toward third base. Tiny starts running toward first, but you know that game where you spin around a bat ten times then try to run across a field? Well, he looked kind of like that. He staggered down the baseline and pretty much collapsed onto the first base bag... well, it was one of the guy's shirts or something. But you know what? I don't think he spilled a single drop of beer, even after falling flat on his face."

Henry let out a chuckle.

"He skinned his knees and I think he sprained his wrist when he fell, but not one drop of beer spilled from that can."

Just about the time that Jack finished his story, they pulled into the driveway at their house. After turning off the engine, Jack went around to the passenger side to help Henry limp up to the front door.

In the living room, Diane had set up a spot for Henry to recline on the couch with an extra pillow for his ankle. It took a few minutes, but Henry was able to get comfortable there before Diane brought him another ice pack. Not long after that, she brought him his dinner. Henry remained pretty quiet the rest of the evening.

Chapter 15

Summer 1990
Gladstone, MO

Henry Mitchell was typically a pretty fast healer – he got over colds quickly and bumps and bruises typically cleared up in a few days – but that was not the case for his badly sprained ankle. X-rays showed that nothing was broken, and an MRI showed no tears to tendons, ligaments, or other sensitive tissue. But he had jacked it up pretty bad. The intense pain went away after a few days, but the injury was bad enough to end his baseball season.

If Henry had not gotten injured, and if he was able to maintain the kind of performance he'd had in the first few weeks of the season, he would have likely been voted First Team All-League and maybe even earned a spot in the All-State All-Star Game, something that was unheard of for a freshman. Instead, he sat on the bench for the rest of the season keeping track of his teammates' statistics while his teammates would go on to win the league championship that year. It absolutely killed him not to be on the field.

The severity of Henry's injury did not, however, prevent the coach from ripping Henry a new one for his arrogant and foolish behavior. At the next practice that Henry attended – he stayed home for two days because he could barely walk, even with crutches – the coach laid into him about how his decision was one of the most selfish things he had ever witnessed on the baseball diamond. Henry was not only showboating against a really weak team, but he was making the rest of his team and his coaches look bad. The coach and school's athletic director had a PR nightmare on their hands the next day. Not only did the head coach have to apologize to the Panthers' coach for Henry's actions, but the local newspaper caught wind of the fact that Henry did, indeed, hit for the cycle that day and wanted to get a quote from the coach about this record feat. Not an easy tightrope act. How do you tell a local reporter that you are very proud of a kid's accomplishment when, deep down, you are really pissed at him for disobeying your explicit instructions?

Henry took it all like a respectful young man. He didn't try to make excuses or try to claim ignorance; he apologized sincerely. He even, of his own free will, wrote an apology note to Paige's baseball coach and team. And as a further part of his penance, Henry still went to every practice and game. Even though he was not out on the field, he learned more about the game of baseball that season than in his entire Little League career.

As summer was approaching, Dr. Ferguson felt that they could meet a lot less frequently than they had during the school year. He wanted to let Henry enjoy his summer and let him try to cope with his anxiety on his own. It was time to push the baby bird out of the nest, so to speak.

Henry walked into Dr. Ferguson's office on that early summer afternoon and noticed there was an additional person in the room. Henry gave his therapist a puzzled look.

"Henry," Dr. Ferguson said. "This is my uncle, Oliver Ferguson. He's the one I told you about, who played pro ball in the Negro Leagues."

Henry's face lit up. He wished he had brought a baseball with him to have Uncle Oliver sign. As if he read Henry's mind, Uncle Oliver pulled a baseball out of his pocket. Dr. Ferguson handed him a pen, and he signed the ball and gave it to Henry.

"Boy, I can't even remember the last time I signed a baseball. These days, I usually only sign mortgage checks," Uncle Oliver joked as he signed the ball. Henry admired the signature in dark blue ink. He gently set the ball on the coffee table, then sat down in his usual spot on the couch. Dr. Ferguson sat behind his large mahogany desk a few feet away. Today's conversation would be all about baseball, and Dr. Ferguson didn't want to get in the way.

Henry had a million questions swirling round his head, but had no idea where to begin. Sensing this moment of awkward hesitation, Uncle Oliver graciously got the conversation going. He told Henry about when he first started playing ball before he signed with the Negro League team, playing pick-up games in the fields near his house and playing at his segregated high school in Alabama. His high school team mostly played other all-black schools, but they did also play predominantly white schools too. And nine times out of ten, they kicked those white boys' butts. Henry laughed, mostly at how proud Uncle Oliver was to tell him that last bit of information.

And then he told him about playing in the Negro Leagues. About how they sometimes played two games in one day with a long bus ride in between. About how they came up with rather peculiar names for their pitches, like "Midnight Creeper" and "Wobbly Ball." And about how they faced all kinds of racism and animosity in so many cities. People enjoyed watching them play at the ballpark, but didn't want to see them in the local restaurants or bars or hotels after the game.

Then Uncle Oliver launched into stories about some of the all-time greats to play the game. And not just great by Negro League standards, but great by all of baseball standards. Unfortunately, they didn't always keep very accurate statistics in the Negro Leagues, so it can be difficult to objectively compare these players to the great players of the Major Leagues. Nevertheless, the greatness of these Black players had become the stuff of legend. For example, Uncle Oliver said, many referred to Josh Gibson – the second Black baseball player to be inducted into the Baseball Hall of Fame despite never playing in the Major Leagues – as the "Black Babe Ruth," when a more accurate assessment would be to call Babe Ruth the "white Josh Gibson."

Of course, Uncle Oliver's favorite stories to tell – and Henry's favorite stories to listen to – were the ones about Satchel Paige. Satchel Paige pitched for almost a dozen Negro League teams before playing in the Major Leagues. He was not only one of the greatest pitchers to ever play the game, but also one of the biggest showboats to ever play the game. He was as much an entertainer and performer as he was an athlete, always seizing the opportunity to dazzle the crowd.

Satchel Paige was famous for his impeccable control when pitching. He had laser-like precision on the mound, even into the later years of his career. Rumor has it that when throwing warm-up pitches he had the catcher put a chewing gum wrapper on home plate; not only could he hit the corners of home plate with pinpoint accuracy, but he could hit the corners of the gum wrapper with that same accuracy.

He was also notorious for his trash talking. There were a number of stories about how Paige would taunt a batter by having the outfielders come into the infield, implying that there was no way the batter would even hit the ball past the infielders. Not only that, but he would sometimes tell his infielders to just sit down on the grass because he knew he was going to strike the batter out. And he had the goods to back up his audacious words. Not once did he fail to strike out those batters he was taunting.

The greatest legendary feat of Satchel Paige came during the 1942 Negro World Series. In game two of that series, Paige put on the ultimate spectacle by intentionally loading the bases with two outs before *the* Josh Gibson came to the plate. It was a showdown between the League's greatest – and, in reality, probably the nation's greatest – pitcher and hitter. Paige intentionally put himself in the pressure cooker and turned up the heat... and then struck out Gibson on three straight pitches.

By the end of the hour in Dr. Ferguson's office, Henry was all smiles. This felt like the fastest of his hour-long sessions and the time seemed to just fly by. And Uncle Oliver would have gone on for another hour – and Henry would have gladly sat there and listened – had it not been for Dr. Ferguson clearing his throat to break up the conversation; after all, he did have an appointment with another client in a few minutes and Uncle Oliver had another engagement. Oliver was the first to stand, and Henry quickly followed. Henry shook Uncle Oliver's hand and thanked him for both the autograph and the stories. Henry then shook Dr. Ferguson's hand and thanked him for this amazing opportunity. Dr. Ferguson wished Henry a fun-filled and non-anxiety-filled summer vacation.

It was another hot, muggy early summer day in Gladstone, Missouri. The type of day that kept the kids whose houses had air conditioning inside and drove the less-fortunate youth of Gladstone to the local community pools. And to make an early-afternoon swim even more appealing, Henry's doctor said that swimming was a good way to regain strength and mobility in his injured ankle. He was ready to do anything he could do to get back into top shape for the next baseball season.

Molly Jacobs would join Henry at the pool a lot, too. And she looked even better in her bikini than she did last summer. When she and Henry were at the pool together, they spent a lot of time playfully and flirtatiously rough housing in the water. They would get into splash fights or games of tag or other things that twitterpated teenagers do in the pool. And not wanting to disobey his doctor's orders, Henry also spent some time swimming laps, dodging other kids in splash fights and moms on floating lounge chairs. Sometimes Molly swam laps with him, but she was a much slower swimmer than he was. But Henry didn't mind slowing down his pace for her because he sure enjoyed watching her glide effortlessly through the water.

On this particular day, Jackie was also at the pool, along with his siblings. He said his mom had "had enough of you kids constantly being underfoot," so she sent them to the pool to give herself a few hours of peace and quiet.

Unlike the previous summer, Henry hadn't seen much of Jackie in these first couple weeks of summer. That's what happens when young teenage boys hit puberty and discover the opposite sex. Henry was spending more and more time hanging out with Molly Jacobs, and Jackie was spending more and more time making out with Tisha. And in the midst of it all, neither of them seemed to really notice the absence of their best friend.

But earlier that day, Tisha had told Jackie that she was going to her cousins' house in Kansas City, so he joined his siblings for an afternoon at the pool. He quickly met up with Henry and Molly and joined in their fun and games. They played Marco Polo and challenged each other to races across the pool.

Exhausted from the ten or so laps they'd swum at a sprinter's pace, Henry and Jackie decided to join Molly Jacobs who was sunning herself in a lounge chair on the pool deck. They were there at the pool during one of the rare times of day when it actually wasn't all that crowded. The time between about 11:30am and 1:00pm tended to be a lot less crowded because most of the morning swimmers went home or to nearby fast food restaurants to have lunch and the after-lunch crowd had not yet arrived. Of course, this was Henry's favorite time to be at the pool because he hated large crowds.

Henry couldn't help but admire Molly Jacobs' curves and smooth skin as he approached the lounge chair next to hers. *Damn, she's hot*, he thought as she grabbed his towel and threw it at him. He caught it and started rubbing the freshly buzzed top of his head. Jackie just stood there, mouth agape as if to say, "what, no towel service for me?" Molly saw his expression and said apologetically, "I couldn't reach your towel all the way over there."

She stretched out her arm to show him that she couldn't reach the towel and gave him a big crooked smile. He smiled in return and grabbed his towel and began to dry himself. He and Henry both laid out their towels on the chairs, then sat down to sun themselves dry and catch their breath from swimming laps in the pool.

The three friends lounged there and started talking about television shows they had watched that week. Henry, of course, always found a way of turning the conversation to baseball; this time, talking about how the future Hall of Famer, Nolan Ryan, had pitched the sixth no-hitter of his career just a week or two ago. Jackie was at least somewhat interested in what Henry had to say, but Molly only feigned interest. She tried really, really hard to like baseball. After all, her dad was a big baseball fan, so she often heard him talking about it. Her dad even dragged her to a couple of Royals games over the years. And now her boyfriend was an even bigger baseball fan than her dad was, so there was no escaping it. But try as she might, she just couldn't find it in herself to enjoy the game the way her dad and Henry did. The pace of the game was too slow, and the players were always adjusting themselves and spitting.

Right in the middle of Henry singing the praises of the great Nolan Ryan, something – or, rather, some*one* – near the main entrance of the pool caught Molly's eye. She sat upright and lifted her sunglasses from her eyes to get a better view of what – or whom – she thought she saw. She squinted and shaded her eyes from the sun to confirm her suspicions. She then looked over at the boys, who – thankfully – did not see who it was.

"Uhh…" Molly Jacobs interrupted Henry. "Are you guys hungry? I'm hungry. Jackie, are you hungry?"

Henry and Jackie gave each other dumbfounded looks. Yes, Molly could be somewhat random and spontaneous, but not like this. She knew not to interrupt Henry in the middle of a good baseball story. She had made that mistake once, and it only took that once to learn her lesson. Henry hadn't been rude or angry when she interrupted his story, but she could tell that he wasn't happy.

But, the boys were both feeling kind of hungry. It was lunch time, after all. And Henry did have a hard time saying no to Molly Jacobs, even if she did interrupt his story about Nolan Ryan's sixth no-hitter.

"Um, yeah, I guess I could eat," Henry said. Jackie nodded his head in agreement. Molly Jacobs was already gathering her things and putting on an oversized t-shirt over her swimsuit. She stood there all fidgety as the boys took their time folding and rolling their towels, and putting on their t-shirts and sandals.

"Come on, guys," she said. "I've got a *real* hankering for a corn dog. You guys feel like corn dogs?"

There was a Hot Dog on a Stick in the strip mall a few blocks away, and Molly really liked their corn dogs and lemonade. But that was not the real reason she wanted to leave in such a hurry. The real reason for her sudden hankering for a corn dog – and for wanting to get the hell out of there with Henry and Jackie – was that she saw Tisha walk through the main gate arm-in-arm with some guy who was not Jackie.

Honestly, she did not know how Jackie would respond. He was a rather emotional young man, wearing his heart on his sleeve. But she also knew that he knew the proper times and places for displaying his emotions. Yes, Jackie had broken into tears on the baseball diamond on more than one occasion. And yes, he had literally jumped out of his seat with joy when he aced his math final just a few weeks ago. But she had no idea how he would respond to this, and she hoped that she could get the boys to leave so that she wouldn't have to find out.

Molly could see that Tisha did not see her or Henry or Jackie; Tisha was too busy fawning all over this other guy to notice much of anything. But, unfortunately, they were headed right toward Molly and Henry and Jackie. It seemed as though this guy, whoever he was, saw that Molly and the boys were leaving and was going to grab their lounge chairs when they left. There were plenty of empty chairs, but he was set on theirs.

"Come on, guys, I'm *really* hungry," she urged.

"What's the rush?" asked Henry. "I mean, it's not like they're going to run out of corn dogs."

Molly had a panicked look, her eyes darting back and forth from Henry to something just over Henry's shoulder. Henry finally caught on that this wasn't just about corn dogs and lemonade. He turned his head to see what Molly had been looking at; Molly's eyes grew wide, knowing that the shit was, indeed, about to hit the fan. Henry gave her a little nod.

Henry quickly grabbed his towel while slipping his sandals onto his feet. He joined in trying to get Jackie to hurry up. "Come on, man. Corn dogs. Let's go."

"Oh, now you're in a hurry, too?" Jackie asked, annoyed with his friends. "What is it with you guys and those damn corn dogs?"

Jackie made a big show of slowing down in folding his towel and putting on his shoes. Molly had a frantic look on her face and Henry grew more and more worried, looking several times over his shoulder. Jackie finally noticed that Henry and Molly kept looking at something behind them, something he couldn't see because they were blocking his view. He stood up and put his hand on Henry's arm to move him out of the way.

And that's when the shit hit the fan.

"Da fuck?" Jackie muttered under his breath as he squinted to get a better look at the very affectionate couple approaching their lounge chairs. He gave a rather confused look to both Henry and Molly. Henry just shrugged his shoulders as his head whipped back and forth between looking at his friend and looking at Tisha and the very hunky guy whose arm she was hanging on. Molly just tried to shrink into the background behind her man, Henry.

Tisha's friend – who was completely oblivious to any of what was going on – asked Henry if they were leaving so that he and Tisha could have their chairs.

"Uh... yeah... yeah..." Henry stammered. Jackie just stood there scowling, waiting for Tisha to see him.

But it was obvious that Tisha was not very aware of her surroundings; all she was focused on was this guy that she was hanging all over.

Tisha's friend began to pick up on the fact that something was going on; after all, the people whose lounge chairs he wanted to take were not moving. An awkward silence hung in the hot summer air until Jackie finally broke it.

"What the hell, Tisha?" Jackie's eyes were reddening and beginning to water. He would later say that it was because of the chlorine in the pool water.

Tisha finally stopped staring at her hunky fella and looked in the direction of the familiar voice. Her smile quickly faded as she purposely tried to avoid Jackie's gaze.

"What the hell?" was all Jackie could say. He grabbed his things and pushed his way past the others. Henry gave an awkward smile as he followed his friend. Molly was the last to leave, giving her now former best friend an angry glare as she followed after the boys.

The next several weeks were filled with high drama for Jackie as he went through a nasty break up with Tisha. Lots of yelling. Lots of tears, mostly on Jackie's part. Apparently, Tisha only thought of him as her boy-toy, but Jackie was downright smitten. Tisha was Jackie's first girlfriend, and he was head over heels. So, Jackie was not very pleasant to be around for a good portion of the summer.

And this nasty break up put Molly Jacobs into an awkward position. She had been friends with Tisha since 5th grade, but not really close friends with her. Molly did her best to avoid Tisha, but Molly was one of Tisha's only real friends, so Tisha was calling her quite a bit, not really able to take the hint.

There was lots of drama that summer. But Jackie and Henry had their own way of coping with it all: baseball. Henry's ankle was healthy enough at this point for running and batting and the like. So, on many a day when they weren't at the local community pool, these two best friends could be found at the local elementary school playing catch or pepper for hours on end. There is something cathartic and therapeutic about tossing a baseball back and forth.

While Henry was trying to help Jackie get over the feeling of being discarded like last week's funnies section, Molly was eyeing her calendar and the fact that the one-year anniversary of her first kiss with Henry - the one outside the pool, not the one at the Backwards Dance - was fast approaching. Yes, they had agreed that the kiss on the dance floor was their "official" first kiss, but now, a year later, Molly thought that the anniversary of the "unofficial" kiss was still worth celebrating.

And, almost exactly one year ago, everything went exactly according to plan... well, almost exactly. There was just one variable that Molly had not anticipated: her dad answering the phone when Henry called. Even though things didn't go as planned, Molly treasured that moment outside the pool locker room, and she thought it was worth celebrating with Henry. So, for a couple of weeks leading up to the anniversary, Molly tried dropping subtle hints to Henry to try to get him to think about doing something.

She said things like:

"Hey, whatcha got planned for next Wednesday? Maybe we could hang out or something."

"Have you seen that new burger place on Main Street? I've heard they have really good milkshakes."

But Henry was both slow at taking the bait.

Molly was not too thrilled by Henry's lack of response. Why couldn't he just suck it up and enjoy a nice evening with his girlfriend celebrating the anniversary of their unofficial first kiss? Was splitting a chocolate malt and a plate of French fries too much to ask?

She thought about asking Jackie for some help in convincing Henry to do something, but Jackie was still moping around from his break up with Tisha and was in no mood to talk about romance.

The big day had arrived, and Molly Jacobs had heard nothing from Henry about any sort of plans for that day. Around midmorning, she had had enough and decided to give him a call.

"Hi, Mrs. Mitchell, is Henry home?" she asked.

"No, Molly," Mrs. Mitchell responded. "He and Jackie went to the schoolyard to play ball. Do you want me to tell him you called when he gets home?"

"No, no... that's ok."

Mrs. Mitchell could hear the sadness in Molly's voice. She paused a moment before hanging up the phone. She really wanted to know why Molly sounded upset, but she had promised herself the day that Henry announced to his parents that he and Molly were dating that she would not be "that" parent. She would not meddle in her son's love life. She liked

Molly and thought that she and Henry made such a great couple, but she was going to let them work out their own issues.

Jackie and Henry were in their usual spot at the schoolyard – the same spot where Henry got his ass kicked the summer before – playing catch. The ball flew back and forth and back and forth, making a THWAP! sound every time it smacked the leather of their baseball gloves. Their conversation, of course, centered on baseball, particularly the struggles that their local Kansas City Royals were having that year. George Brett was on his way to another batting title and Bo Jackson was taking the league by storm, but their pitching staff wasn't pulling their weight and was dragging the team down.

The boys were well into their second hour of throwing the ball when Jackie saw someone approaching them from across the field. The sun was in his eyes, so all he could see was this person's silhouette.

But this distraction did cause Jackie to take his eyes off the baseball, which would have hit him square in the face had Henry not shouted at him to get his attention. Jackie ducked just in time, but the ball flew past him and rolled about fifty feet behind him. Jackie threw his hands in the air as he turned around and started running to get the ball.

"What the hell, man?" Henry yelled after him.

Jackie turned around mid-stride, intending to give his friend the finger for throwing the ball when he was obviously not paying attention, but then he caught a glimpse of who it was that was walking toward Henry.

Oh shit, Jackie thought. He used his glove hand to point past Henry to get him to turn around and see her approaching. Without missing a step, he turned back around to retrieve the ball.

Henry turned around to see what Jackie was pointing at.

It was Molly Jacobs.

Jackie hustled to get the ball, scooping it into his glove midstride, then ran back toward Henry and Molly.

To say Henry was surprised to see Molly walking toward him, especially with such determination in her step, would be an understatement.

"Hey, Molly. What's up?" Henry asked.

Molly said nothing, but just kept walking toward Henry, her eyes fixed on his. Henry had never seen her like this before. Was she angry? Was she upset about something? Did she have some bad news for him? She wasn't about to break up with him, was she? All of Henry's worst fears regarding their relationship came screaming to the forefront of his mind. But she did not say anything and just kept walking toward him.

Jackie slowed from a run to a jog to a walk, not wanting to interrupt whatever was about to go down between Henry and Molly. He didn't know if this was a friendly visit from Molly, or if it was a "we-need-to-talk" visit. Either way, he was going to keep his distance… but not too far away that he couldn't hear anything. He wanted to know what was about to happen, he just didn't want to get sucked into any drama.

"What's going on?" Henry asked. Molly's silence was growing more and more unsettling. His heart rate began to climb and his hands grew sweaty.

Molly Jacobs walked right up to Henry, cupped his face in her hands – a bit more tightly than normal to prevent him from escaping – and planted a big ol' kiss right on his lips, then said, "Happy anniversary, Henry Aaron Mitchell." Then she turned right around and walked back the way she came.

Once she was out of earshot, Jackie took a few steps closer to Henry and tossed him the ball.

"Dude, you just got middle-named by your girl. What the hell did you do?" Jackie said.

Henry just shrugged his shoulders as he tossed the ball back to Jackie. If only he knew.

Chapter 16

October 31, 1990
Good Shepherd United Methodist Church
Gladstone, MO

Molly Jacobs could not stay angry with Henry for very long. And it helped that Diane had a talk with him after he got home from the schoolyard. Jackie couldn't resist telling her about how Henry got "middle-named" by Molly. Diane explained to the boys that girls think about these things differently than boys, and when it comes to these petty conflicts, it is better to be happy than it is to be right. So, that evening, Henry called to apologize and then asked Molly to meet him at Al's Diner. They met that evening and shared a chocolate malt.

In the first several weeks of the new school year, the student events planning committee of Winnetonka High School decided that the Backwards Dance was, well... backwards and antiquated. They decided, instead, to hold a Halloween Costume Dance. Flyers were put up all over school, and this new event generated quite a buzz around campus.

The community around the school was also appreciative of this new event. There was not a lot to do in the little suburban community of Gladstone, Missouri. There was a mall, and the community pool, and a small second-run movie theater, but not much of a teenage nightlife. If teens wanted to have fun, they typically had to go into Kansas City for that. So, on Halloween night, most high schoolers – at least those who couldn't drive – went trick-or-treating in the neighborhoods. And being bored teenagers, many of them would cause problems, like smashing jack-o-lanterns on people's porches or stealing candy from younger kids. Nothing worthy of actual police intervention, but enough to annoy the community. So, the high school providing an event on Halloween night that kept the older kids off the streets earned a great deal of support from the community.

Henry bought tickets for him and Molly during the first week that they were for sale. That day at lunch, all Molly wanted to talk about was ideas for matching costumes for the dance. She threw out a few ideas: Thing 1 and Thing 2 from *The Cat in the Hat*, or Doc Brown and Marty McFly from *Back to the Future*.

"Sure, sure," Henry said, then took a bite of his sandwich.

"I have an idea," Molly said, her eyes lighting up the way they would when she got excited about something. "What are you doing on Saturday?"

Henry looked over at Jackie, who was obviously not interested in this conversation.

"Nothing, I guess," Henry said.

"Great. Meet me at the mall after lunch," Molly said. "We can go shopping for our costumes and then go to Al's for fries and malts. What d'ya say?"

"Um... sure."

The bell ending lunch rang. Henry, Jackie, and Molly cleaned up their spots at the table. Molly gave Henry a peck on the cheek as she went off in one direction while he and Jackie went in another.

That Saturday morning, a week before the dance, Henry and Jackie were working on geometry homework at Jackie's house. The assignment should have taken about an hour tops to complete, but they kept getting sidetracked with conversations about potential trades and free agent signings that the Royals should make this offseason.

160

It was around noon when Jackie's mom knocked on the open bedroom door and asked if the boys were ready for lunch. She had bought Subway sandwiches for them.

"Thanks, mom."

"Yeah, thanks. Mrs. Marcus."

"You boys are welcome," Victoria replied. "There are chips and drinks in the kitchen."

The boys went into the kitchen and joined Jackie's siblings and dad for lunch.

Soon, Henry and Jackie had scarfed down their sandwiches, a family-sized bag of Ruffles potato chips, and a can of soda each. Their belches quickly drove Jackie's brothers and sisters from the kitchen. Henry cleaned up their trash, then found a brand-new package of Double Stuf Oreos in the pantry. He held them up to show Jackie and made a face as if to ask if they could have some. Jackie shrugged to say, "sure why not." When the phone rang an hour later, they had finished off half the package of cookies and each had another can of soda. Jackie let it ring a couple of times, hoping someone else in the house would answer it, before he picked up the receiver from the wall-mount.

"Hello... yeah, he's right here, Mrs. Mitchell."

Jackie handed the phone to Henry. Henry gave his friend a puzzled look. Why would his mom be calling?

"Hi, Mom," Henry said. "What's up?"

Henry winced as his mom spoke on the other end.

"Ah, shit!" he muttered.

"Jar," Jackie said instinctively.

"Ok... ok..." Henry said. "I'll call her."

Henry hung up the phone and looked at Jackie. It didn't take long for Jackie to realize why Henry's mom had called.

Meet me at the mall after lunch. Molly's words echoed in both their brains. It was almost two o'clock; still technically after lunch, but Henry was supposed to meet Molly over an hour ago.

Henry dialed Molly's number and sat back down at the kitchen table. Jackie grabbed another Oreo cookie and took his ringside seat.

The phone only rang once before a familiar voice said, "Hello?"

"Hi, Molly. It's me," Henry said. "Look, I am so sorry. I've been here at Jackie's house..."

161

"I know," was all Molly said. She didn't sound angry, which meant that she was very angry.

"I've got my bike here. I can meet you at the mall in twenty minutes."

Jackie stuffed another cookie into his mouth and smiled. There was no way Henry could make it to the mall in twenty minutes on his bike.

"No, no. That's ok," Molly said. "There's no need. Besides, we are leaving to go to my aunt's house for dinner in about an hour, so we wouldn't have time to go shopping anyway."

"But, I... I... I'm sorry," was all Henry could say.

After a long silence, Molly said, "I know you are."

There was another long pause, and Henry knew not to fill it with another apology.

"Henry Aaron Mitchell," Molly finally said. "If you'd rather spend the day with Jackie, then maybe you'd rather spend next Saturday with him, too. And not with me at the dance!"

Henry pulled the phone away from his ear; the sound of Molly slamming down her phone was loud enough that Jackie cringed when he heard it. Henry just crumpled into his chair as Jackie took the receiver from him and hung it up.

As the day of the Halloween Dance approached, Henry and Jackie were both without dates to the dance and without plans for Halloween evening. They were too old to go trick-or-treating, all of their other friends were going to the dance, and the 1990 baseball season had officially ended eleven days ago with the Cincinnati Reds winning the World Series.

Reverend Marcus could see the plight that the boys had gotten themselves into, and decided to offer them a job of sorts for Halloween evening. Since the boys were both almost sixteen years old, he figured that they were old enough to work as night watchmen at his church on Halloween night.

Good Shepherd United Methodist Church held services in a very old church building in the old part of town that the congregation had bought back in the 1950s. It was one of those old brick buildings with a white steeple topped with a cross. The Sunday school classrooms were in the basement, and there was an old churchyard cemetery behind the church building. Very seldom was anyone buried in the churchyard any more since it was nearly full of graves and headstones. In fact, the Missouri State

Historical Society was considering making the church and its cemetery a historical landmark.

The job that Reverend Marcus had in mind was to stay the night at the church and call the police if any Halloween vandals targeted the church and/or cemetery. Good Shepherd had become a popular target for teenage hooligans looking for trouble. It had become something of a tradition over the past four or five years for these hooligans to throw eggs at the windows or toilet paper the trees, but Reverend Marcus hoped to break this tradition. He was thankful that the vandalism was not destructive or vindictive – just harmless pranks – but he never looked forward to the cleanup he would have the next day.

But not this year. Reverend Marcus hatched a plan to thwart the hooligans, and to give Jackie and Henry something to do to take their minds off their girl troubles. He wanted to hire the boys to spend the night at the church, hoping that any potential vandals would see that someone was at the church, and think twice about their pranks. Or if it didn't stop them, Henry and Jackie could call the police, who were only a few blocks away.

Henry's dad had a great idea: the day before their night watch gig, he went to the local video rental store and rented approximately nine hours' worth of Alfred Hitchcock films. Henry and Jackie had seen a couple Hitchcock films during Friday movie nights, but Henry and Jackie were about to receive an overdose of Hitchcock. Films like *Rear Window*, *Vertigo*, *Strangers on a Train*, and of course, *Psycho*.

The big night arrived. The elementary- and junior high-aged kids took to the streets in their costumes to ask their neighbors for candy. The high schoolers made their way to the school's gymnasium for a couple hours of bumping and grinding to the latest tunes. And Reverend Marcus drove Jackie, Henry, the stack of VHS tapes, and a couple grocery bags full of snacks to Good Shepherd United Methodist Church.

The Reverend gave them some last-minute instructions and showed them where the list of important phone numbers was by the phone in the office. Then he showed them to the multipurpose room where he had set up the thirty-inch television set and VCR. His parting words were, "Don't hesitate to call me, but if it's after midnight, please make sure it is an *actual* emergency."

"Yessir," the boys said, almost in unison as Reverend Marcus closed the door behind himself as he left the room. A short moment later, they could hear the engine of his car start up, then see the headlights flash through the window as he turned the car around to head home.

Henry and Jackie scoped out their room for the evening. It was a large multipurpose room, approximately twenty feet by thirty feet in size. At the end opposite the door was a small stage about eighteen inches high. An old upright piano sat on the stage. On one side of the room were large windows that faced the parking lot; if anyone was going to come onto the church property, they would see them. The other side of the room was covered with old paintings depicting scenes from the life of Christ. One end of the row of paintings started with Christ's birth and the Nativity scene, the other end showed the risen Christ emerging from the tomb, and the rest filled in the gap.

Reverend Marcus had wisely placed the television in front of the wall of windows. He knew the boys would get distracted watching the movies, so with the TV in front of the windows, they would have to be dead asleep to not see a car or pedestrian approaching the church buildings. Across from the TV, he had placed a large sofa that had been moved from the youth room. The couch was old and lumpy and smelled kinda funny, exactly what you would expect from a youth room couch.

Next to the stage in the front of the multipurpose room was a door that led into the church's kitchen. Many a church potluck had been served out of that kitchen, but all the boys cared about was finding room in the fridge to keep their sodas cold and room on the counter for their snacks. Jackie put the food and drinks in the kitchen while Henry set up their first movie of the evening: *Rear Window.*

After getting the VHS tape ready to play, Henry joined Jackie in the kitchen to select his first round of snacks and drinks. One must select these things carefully when readying for an all-night movie marathon. You don't want to eat too much sweet stuff early on because it can spoil your appetite for the rest of the evening. He opted for a big bag of Ruffles potato chips and a couple cans of A&W Root Beer. Jackie, following Henry's lead, grabbed some Cheetos and 7-Up.

The boys were absolutely riveted by Jimmy Stewart's performance in *Rear Window.* But right at the scene when he is using the flashbulb in his camera to blind the intruder in his apartment, a set of headlights shown in through the window from the church parking lot. Both boys jumped ever so slightly, then looked at each other to see if the other had also jumped. Jackie started to rise from his seat as Henry grabbed the remote control and paused the movie. They both walked over to the window to see who might be disturbing their suspense-filled evening. They stood still, one on each side of the window, peering out of the shadows.

The car came to a stop in the middle of the lot and turned off its headlights. As the boys saw the driver and passengers opening the car door, Jackie had an idea. They had kept the lights off in the multipurpose room, mostly to avoid a glare off the television screen. But from the outside, it appeared that no one was in the room. Jackie ran over to the wall with the door to the kitchen and flipped on the light switch. He thought that, perhaps, if the interlopers saw that someone was in the church, they might be dissuaded from their plans of vandalism or other shenanigans.

And he was right. As soon as those in the car saw the lights turn on and saw the silhouettes of Henry and Jackie in the room, they got back into their car and sped out of the parking lot. Jackie turned the lights off again, and both boys stood there for a moment, allowing their eyes to adjust to the darkness once again. Then they walked back over to the couch, Henry gave Jackie a high five for his brilliant idea, and they sat back down to resume the movie.

The final scene – Jimmy Stewart asleep in his wheelchair while Grace Kelly reads her fashion magazine – filled the television screen and Henry let out a huge belch that he had been holding in.

"Dude, that was gross," Jackie said as he slugged Henry in the shoulder.

"At least I didn't do it during the movie," Henry said to defend himself. He got up from the couch and headed toward the kitchen to reload his snack stash before they started the next movie. Jackie followed him. They rummaged through the fridge and the grocery bags they had brought to get enough snacks to last them the two-plus-hour running time of their next film.

"Hey, what kind of chips are in the bag, Hammer?" Jackie asked as he grabbed several cans of Mountain Dew.

"Uhh... let's see... Cheetos, Doritos, and... Sour Cream and Onion Lays," Henry replied.

"Grab me some Doritos, will ya?"

"Sure thing," Henry answered, grabbing the bag of Doritos for Jackie and the bag of Cheetos for himself.

"You know, speaking of Doritos," Jackie said, "What's going on with you and Molly?"

Henry almost walked into the door frame. "Wha... What are you talkin' about, man?"

Jackie gave Henry his signature "Whatcha talkin' 'bout Willis?" look.

"I don't know what you mean," Henry said.

The look again, followed by another look that said, "are you kidding me?"

"Dude, it's... I don't know," was all Henry could muster.

"Seriously?" Jackie said.

Henry just turned around and walked through the door and into the multipurpose room. Jackie followed him. They sat in silence for several minutes, then Henry got up to put the new video cassette into the VCR. But Jackie grabbed the remote and told Henry to sit his ass back down.

"Seriously, what is going on between you two?"

"I don't know, man," Henry said. "I apologized like a hundred times last week."

This was a slight exaggeration, but wasn't that far off. Last Saturday, after realizing he had stood her up, Henry called Molly again after dinner to apologize. He tried several times throughout the week to apologize, but she had perfected the art of ignoring him.

Henry knew it was time to simply own his mistake.

"Dude..." he said. "I fucked up. Plain and simple... I want her back... I want to... to make things right... But..."

Jackie just sat in silence. A long silence. Not knowing what to say – and letting too much time slip awkwardly by – he grabbed the remote control and started the next movie.

After the movie finished and Jackie hit the rewind button on the remote, the boys just sat there staring at the blank television screen. They had no idea what they had just watched; partly because it was a Hitchcock film and was lost on these two teenagers, but mostly because they were distracted by their previous conversation. Henry was obsessing about getting Molly back, and Jackie was racking his brain to come up with a brilliant plan to help him.

Jackie broke the silence. "I gotta take a piss."

He walked out of the multipurpose room and down the hall toward the restrooms. Henry followed him. After all, he'd had about three cans of soda in the last couple of hours and also had to pee.

Jackie didn't see that Henry was following him, something that Henry decided to use to his advantage as he plotted a little Halloween prank of his own.

In the hallway outside the multipurpose room, the men's room and women's room were right next to each other; the door to the women's room coming first. Henry tiptoed down the hall several steps behind Jackie and then ducked into the women's room instead, making sure to open and close the door as quietly as possible.

Henry took care of his business as quickly as possible, turned off the light, then stood silently in the doorway. He waited and waited. *Man, that's a lot of pee,* he thought. Jackie finally emerged, turning off the bathroom light and stepping into the darkened hallway (Henry had turned off the hallway light after Jackie had walked into the men's room). Jackie wasn't expecting the hallway to be dark, and his eyes were slow to adjust to the darkness. He took a few cautious steps in the direction of the multipurpose room. After his third step, Jackie felt a tap on his shoulder and if he had not just voided his bladder, he would have pissed himself right then and there.

"Boo," Henry whispered, causing Jackie to jump and shriek like a little girl.

"What the hell, man?!" Jackie gave Henry a shove. Henry could not stop laughing. Jackie just turned around and walked to the multipurpose room, leaving Henry in the hallway wiping his eyes from laughter. As Henry started walking back to the multipurpose room, he could barely make out that Jackie was flipping him off as he walked through the doorway.

During the break between the next two films, the boys took another trip to the kitchen. This time, Henry went to the fridge to get drinks and Jackie rummaged through the shopping bags for snacks. They agreed that after all the chips they had eaten earlier, something sweet sounded good. The big bag of M&M's buried at the bottom of the grocery bag would really hit the spot.

As they took their spots on the couch, Jackie said, "So you gonna call Molly tomorrow, or what?"

Jackie knew how to get straight to the point.

"Yeah, I guess," Henry said, followed by shoving a handful of M&M's into his mouth. This allowed him to dodge any more questions from Jackie. After all, it is rude to talk with your mouth full.

"Good, 'cause I've got a plan to get her back."

Chapter 17

March 25, 1991
Satchel Paige High School
North Kansas City, MO

Even though this was not a home game for the Winnetonka Griffins, a pretty significant group of fans traveled to see their baseball team play their crosstown rivals from Satchel Paige High School. There were almost seventy parents and students sitting in the bleachers behind the Griffins' dugout, almost as many as were there to cheer for the home team.

SPHS had improved significantly since last season – when WHS had mercy-ruled them – thanks to a very talented freshman class. When the two teams played each other earlier that month, Winnetonka won by a score of 7-4, but it was not an easy win. If not for a late-inning rally, led by Henry Aaron Mitchell, Paige might have come away with a victory.

This game, now in the top of the sixth inning, was tied three all. The Griffins had two on with two out. The right fielder had drawn a leadoff walk and took second on a single by Jackie Marcus. The next two batters struck out, but Jackie and the right fielder advanced to second and third on a passed ball by the SPHS catcher. This brought up the Griffins' clean-up hitter, Henry Aaron Mitchell.

Henry was having another league MVP-worthy season. He could have been a contender for the award last season if he hadn't blown out his ankle in that now infamous game against Paige. But with a good doctor and physical therapist, no one could tell that Henry had injured himself so badly, not even the scouts who were watching Henry very closely this season. A couple of coaches from local colleges and universities had contacted his coach, and scouts from the Oakland Athletics and Atlanta Braves had contacted his parents. If Henry continued on his current trajectory, he would be signing a contract with an NCAA Division 1 school or a professional team in about two years' time.

As Henry dug into the batter's box, the Winnetonka fans began chanting, "Ham-mer! Ham-mer! Ham-mer!" and the loudest voice in the crowd belonged to Molly Jacobs.

Jackie had come up with the perfect plan for Henry to win back Molly. He told Henry to go over to her house, stand on her front lawn, and play her favorite song on his boombox, just like John Cusack's character in Say Anything. Molly couldn't resist the gesture. She came out and gave Henry a big forgiving hug. They walked to the nearby park. They made up. They made out. And Henry reached second base.

The visiting crowd from Winnetonka was in a frenzy, yelling and screaming and stomping their feet on the metal bleachers. Henry took his place in the batter's box and looked down the third base line to get the signs.

Swing away.

Henry nodded and caught Jackie's eye as he turned his head to face the pitcher. Jackie gave him a quick thumbs up as he took his lead from second base.

The Paige pitcher wound up and threw a curve ball outside, trying to get Henry to chase the bad pitch. But Henry knew better and let it go. He adjusted his grip on his bright orange aluminum bat, pinwheeled it around three times, then glared at the opposing pitcher.

The next pitch was a fastball on the inside half of the plate. Henry sized it up and lined it into right field. The Griffins' baserunner scored easily from third, and it was obvious that Jackie was not stopping at third. Henry watched the play as he coasted around first base, stopping a few steps from the bag.

The Paige outfielder read the ball perfectly, fielded it perfectly, and then threw the perfect throw toward home plate. It was going to be a close play; the ball arrived on a short hop to the catcher just as Jackie started his slide into home plate. Jackie could see the catcher was in position to block the plate, so he knew he was going to have to slide hard if he hoped to touch home plate and try to knock the ball loose. The catcher braced himself for the impact.

Jackie, already going in for a head-first slide, decided not to slide and lowered his shoulder to plow through the catcher.

The collision was not pretty. Jackie's shoulder ran straight into the catcher's chest, knocking him over as Jackie tumbled over on top of him. The catcher dropped the ball as he lowered his arms to brace his fall. Jackie landed on the other side of the plate and had to scramble back to tag home. He then sprang to his feet and pumped his fist as adrenaline pulsed through his body. The catcher outweighed Jackie by a good thirty pounds, but the pure momentum that Jackie had created by sprinting toward home plate was enough to send him flying backwards.

The nearby umpire was all set to call Jackie out until he saw the ball drop out of the catcher's mitt. He waived his hands wildly as he called Jackie safe instead. Jackie started skipping off toward his team's dugout, but the catcher – still stumbling and trying to regain his balance – stepped in to block Jackie's way.

Henry stood on first base, removing his batting gloves and watching the scene unfold at home plate. The catcher glared at Jackie and had a few words for him. Jackie stared back at him for a quick moment, then shook his head and walked to the dugout to be greeted by high fives from his teammates.

Later in the dugout, while trading his batting helmet for his cap and glove, Henry asked Jackie what the catcher said to him after Jackie plowed into him. And he couldn't believe the slur Jackie had been called. Henry knew that people used that kind of language, but he had never actually witnessed that word being used, much less directed at his best friend.

As Henry exited the dugout to resume his position in the outfield, his coach pulled him aside. "I want you to close out the game. You got us the lead, now hold onto it for us."

He gave Henry a pat on the shoulder, then followed him onto the field. Henry jogged out to the mound and his coach walked over to the home plate umpire to tell him of the defensive changes. Henry took his warm-up pitches, thrilled at the chance to pick up the save and the game-winning RBI.

Henry got the first batter to ground out to the shortstop. Then the next batter - Paige's catcher - stepped into the batter's box. Henry's heart rate increased significantly, so he stepped off the mound for a moment to take a few deep breaths. He looked over at Jackie, who was playing first base. Jackie gave him a look, as if he knew exactly what Henry was thinking. Jackie shook his head. *Don't bean him, Henry*, he thought.

After another deep breath, Henry dug his left foot into the mound, the outside of his foot pressed against the pitching rubber. He held the ball behind his back in his left hand as he leaned in to get the sign from his own catcher. The batter snarled as he glared at Henry and took a few practice swings.

The catcher called for a fastball, high and tight. Henry reluctantly shook it off and waited for the next sign. Fastball, high and tight. Henry rolled his eyes and nodded. He placed the ball in his glove and adjusted his grip with his pitching hand. Henry went into his windup and threw the pitch. It was high and a little tight, nothing that could be construed as a brushback pitch. The batter didn't budge and just glared at Henry. Henry glared back.

The catcher called for another high and tight fastball. Henry nodded and went into his windup. This time the ball was a little higher and a little tighter and a little faster, forcing the batter to duck out of the way. This time he did more than glare at Henry. He threw his bat down and stepped toward the mound. The umpire, seeing what was about to go down, grabbed him by the arm.

"You're not going anywhere, son," he said. He let go and gave the batter a look to show him he meant business. The umpire then took a few steps towards the mound to give Henry a formal warning: another pitch like that and he'd get himself ejected from the game. He then turned to the Griffins' dugout and issued the same warning to Henry's coach.

Henry walked a lap around the mound to calm himself down again. The batter went back to the on-deck to get a little more pine tar for his bat. They both took their respective places to finish this duel.

Henry had gotten behind the batter, 2-0. From atop the pitcher's mound, he leaned in for the sign. The catcher called for a curveball down the middle. Henry nodded, then threw his pitch to the exact spot the catcher wanted it.

The batter got a perfect read on the ball, but overswung on the breaking pitch, causing it to dribble slowly toward the second baseman. The Griffins' second baseman charged the ball, fielding it with his bare hand. He saw that the batter was not exactly a world-class sprinter, so he planted his feet to make a strong throw to Jackie at first base. The throw beat the runner by at least three steps, but that didn't slow him down. The baserunner veered to the inside of the baseline toward Jackie, who was a bit slower than normal in taking his foot away from the bag. The batter missed the base completely and stepped down hard onto Jackie's ankle, his spikes ripping through Jackie's stirrup, sock, and flesh. Jackie crumpled to the ground in pain. Blood quickly soaked his torn sock. He screamed in pain.

The batter stood over Jackie, gloating in his revenge. "Take that, you little bitch," he said.

Henry was there, in the batter's face, in what seemed like about two steps. "What the hell, man?!" he yelled as he shoved the batter hard in the chest.

The field umpire, who was just a few paces up the first base line, ran to break up Henry and the opposing player before any punches were thrown. But Henry's fists were faster than the overweight, middle-aged umpire. He got in a right jab to the guy's ribs and a left punch to his face before the umpire grabbed Henry by the back of his jersey and flung him away, toward the middle of the infield. The umpire may have been slow on his feet, but he was surprisingly strong.

Meanwhile, both benches cleared to join in the scuffle near first base. Luckily for Jackie, who was still crumpled in a heap on the infield dirt, the Griffins' coach headed straight for him to get him away from it all. The coach had seen enough of these bench-clearing brawls to know that lying on the ground was not a good place to be. He handed Jackie off to the trainer, who rushed him to the dugout.

The home plate umpire grabbed hold of Henry's shoulder and started walking him out toward right field, away from the melee. The field umpire grabbed the Paige catcher and started walking him out toward left field.

The umpires wanted to get the instigators away from the gathering crowd of players in hopes of diffusing the situation. It seemed to be working; the two coaches, who before Henry's showboating against Paige last season had been very collegial toward each other, did not want to see an all-out brawl, so they did the best they could to keep the players from resorting to fisticuffs. There were no punches thrown, not even any shoves, but there was a lot of name calling and swearing at each other. After everyone said what they felt they needed to say to the other team, the coaches were able to herd their respective players back into their dugouts.

Meanwhile, the stands on both sides erupted with shouting and yelling and stomping on the metal bleachers. Several of the school's security guards stepped out onto the field to make sure that all the fans stayed put. Some fans threw soda cans and water bottles and candy wrappers onto the field to express their anger, but that was about all.

Both Henry and the opposing catcher made their ways to their dugouts to rejoin their teams. The umpires met briefly on the mound before delivering their judgment to each team: this game would be suspended until the league officials could weigh in on what happened. Both teams were told to pack up and go home.

Jackie was not at school the day after the game against Paige High School, so Henry and Molly Jacobs went to visit him at his home after school. The coach cancelled practice that day because he had to go meet with league officials to try to convince them not to give Henry too long of a suspension.

Molly's dad dropped her off at Henry's house. She had baked a batch of Jackie's - and Henry's - favorite chocolate-oatmeal cookies, but she knew to leave a few at the house for Henry's dad. He loved those cookies almost as much as Henry did. Molly and Henry walked the couple of blocks to Jackie's house. They found him reclining on the living room couch with his foot elevated on an ottoman and an ice pack on his ankle. He was watching afterschool cartoons, but turned off the TV when they walked in.

"Dude, how's the foot?" Henry asked.

"Hurts like a mofo," Jackie replied.

"Here, these are guaranteed to make it feel better," Molly Jacobs said as she handed him the plate of cookies. She had removed the plastic wrap in the kitchen on the way to the living room; she knew Jackie always had a hard time with that stuff.

Jackie took two cookies, shoving the first one whole into his mouth. He chewed and swallowed it quickly, then smiled. It was the first time he'd smiled in about twenty-four hours.

Molly returned from the kitchen with a glass of milk for each of them. She handed one to Henry and one to Jackie. She sat at the other end of the couch from Jackie, and Henry sat in a nearby chair. Jackie reluctantly offered each of them a cookie. Henry was about to grab three or four, but Molly shot him a look, so he settled for two.

After a few minutes, Molly shyly asked Jackie if she could see the wound on his foot and ankle. She had taken a recent interest in medicine after talking with her older cousin who had recently become a nurse.

"What the heck?" Henry protested. "Not while we're eating!"

It wasn't just the fact that Henry didn't want to see the wound while they were eating; any sight of blood made him squeamish.

Molly rolled her eyes at him. "Well, you can go in the other room if you're too much of a baby to handle it."

"Who are you calling a baby?" Henry shot back. He wasn't actually offended, but was a little embarrassed that his girl was calling him out in front of his best friend.

Jackie was a bit hesitant as well. After all, there was a lot of blood yesterday. "I guess. If you really want to see it. I need to change the bandage anyway."

"Oh, I can help," Molly said.

"I'm just going to take these glasses into the kitchen," Henry said as he stood.

Molly and Jackie looked at each other, smiling at their friend's cowardice. Jackie pointed to the fresh gauze and tape on the end table next to Molly. She grabbed it while he removed the ice and started unwrapping the wound. There was not much blood now; only the layer of bandaging closest to the skin had a little on it. When the bandage was completely removed, Molly could see the extent of the damage done by the Paige catcher. His spikes had easily cut into his skin, but also created long slices in his ankle and heel as his cleat slid down the side of Jackie's ankle and foot. The cuts were deep, requiring stitches. Fortunately, the spikes did not injure his Achilles tendon or any muscle tissue. But these lacerations were going to keep him off his feet and off the ballfield for several weeks.

Henry purposely took his time rinsing the glasses and putting them in the dishwasher because he was not interested in seeing Jackie's injuries. Not just because the sight of the stitches and bruising would make him nauseous, but because he was still very angry at the guy who did this to his best friend. He really wished the ump hadn't broken them up so quickly; he wanted to give that catcher a season-ending injury as well.

When he rejoined the others, Jackie was telling Molly about his exchange of words with the catcher after his hard slide into home plate. When the catcher regained his balance and stood back up, he got in Jackie's face and called him a racial slur that Jackie didn't feel comfortable using in front of Molly Jacobs. Hearing Jackie telling the story again made Henry's blood boil.

"Yeah, and I would've beat the shit out of him if the ump hadn't stepped in," Henry said as he sat back down in his chair.

"Language!" came a shout from Jackie's mom in the other room.

"Sorry, Mrs. Marcus," Henry apologized.

Molly once again rolled her eyes at her boyfriend.

"Thanks for having my back, Hammer," Jackie said. He reached out to shake Henry's hand. They did an abbreviated version of their secret handshake. He knew, and was thankful, that Henry was always ready to stick his neck out for him. Henry was very sensitive to how people – especially white people – treated his friend, sometimes even overly sensitive. It was this oversensitivity that led to Henry getting his ass kicked a few years ago by a schoolyard bully. But in this instance, when Jackie couldn't step up and defend himself, he was grateful for a friend like Henry.

Chapter 18

July 23, 1991
Wrigley Field
Cincinnati Reds vs. Chicago Cubs

The details of their trip to Chicago could not have come together more perfectly.

The firm that Jack Mitchell worked for had recently been bought out by a large multinational corporation based in Chicago. The merger took over a year to complete, and there was a lot of nervous speculation about whether this large multinational corporation would keep the Kansas City firm as a regional office or whether those working at the Kansas City firm would be out of a job come summer of 1991. All the nervousness and anticipation ended when it was announced that the sales staff in Kansas City would be retained, but the management team would be let go and replaced by mid-level managers from the larger corporation. Apparently, they wanted to be sure that the Kansas City office would run the way they wanted it run.

This was really good news for Jack Mitchell who was the top salesman at the firm. He had been considered for a promotion to assistant manager, but his boss decided to delay that decision until this whole merger thing had blown over. So instead of looking for a new job that summer like the managers and assistant managers, Jack was preparing for a trip to the corporate office in Chicago to meet his new bosses. And, to make things even better - the large multinational corporation was trying to entice its new employees not to jump ship - he was allowed to bring his family along on this trip for an all-expenses-paid vacation to the Windy City.

At the same time that the Mitchells were planning their trip to Chicago, Reverend Marcus had been invited to be a guest speaker at a regional conference in Chicago for the United Methodist Church. As a black man pastoring a predominantly white church, he was asked to speak on topics of race relations in the Midwestern church. And to sweeten the invitation, he was allowed to bring his family along with him. Jackie and Victoria were the only ones to join him; Jackie's other siblings were all spending their summer working at a Methodist youth camp a few hours outside of Kansas City.

So, due to some very fortuitous circumstances, both the Mitchells and the Marcuses would be in Chicago during the week of July 21, 1991. It also worked out quite nicely that the Cubs were playing at home that week, so Jack, Reverend George, and the boys enjoyed a game at Wrigley Field while Diane and Victoria enjoyed a day of shopping.

It was the bottom of the 7th inning and the Cub had a comfortable 5-2 lead. Henry had left his seat in the middle of the inning to get a refill of Dr. Pepper. The concession stands were running a special on soft drinks: for only four dollars, you could buy a commemorative plastic 24-ounce cup that entitled you to free refills throughout the game. You just had to stand in the glacially slow concession lines to get that free refill. And it quickly became apparent that Henry was not going to make it back to his seat before play resumed. Fortunately, there was a TV mounted on the wall near the concession stand, but the glare from the sun and the rather tall man in front of him in line made it very difficult for him to see.

The Cubs sent the middle of their lineup to the plate to face Reds pitcher, Norm Charlton. The first batter, future Hall of Famer Ryne Sandberg, hit a pop fly to the shortstop for an easy first out. Next up was future Hall of Famer Andre Dawson. As Dawson stood in the batter's box waiting for the first pitch from Charlton, Henry finally reached the front of the line and handed his commemorative plastic 24-ounce cup to the cashier, asking for a refill of Dr. Pepper.

"Do you want more ice?" the young woman behind the cash register asked.

"Um, sure," Henry answered, trying his best to see the game on the monitor above his head.

The cashier handed the cup back to Henry, who tried to snap the lid back on as he walked toward the gate and back to his seat. He was having trouble with it, which was made even worse by the rising tumult around him. Something exciting was happening on the field, and the fans in the stands and on the concourse were getting rowdy.

What happened was Andre Dawson had been called out on strikes on a questionable pitch on the outside corner of the plate. The home plate umpire called strike three in rather dramatic fashion, and the Cubs' slugger took umbrage with the call. Dawson got right up in the umpire's face, expressing his dissatisfaction for the call with what can only be assumed to be very colorful language. The umpire just stood there and let Dawson speak his mind. But as Dawson stepped back a second to catch his breath, the umpire waved his arm to eject him from the ballgame. Dawson was ushered to the dugout by some of his teammates, but the Cubs manager came out to say a few things of his own to the umpire. He, too, was quickly ejected.

At this point, the entire stadium was in an uproar. Those in the stands were yelling and booing and cursing the series of bad calls made by the umpire, and those on the concourse were rushing back to their seats to get in on the action.

Even though he had already been ejected from the game and was now in the dugout, Andre Dawson was not going quietly to the clubhouse. He continued to yell at the umpires and, perhaps egged on by the crowds, grabbed an armful of bats and hurled them onto the field. And apparently one armful of bats wasn't enough for Dawson, so he grabbed another six or seven bats and threw those onto the field as well.

Many of the 34,000 fans in attendance decided to follow Dawson's lead and began throwing all kinds of things onto the field: half-full cups of beer, open bags of peanuts, partially eaten hot dogs. They made quite a mess of things.

Meanwhile, Henry just wanted to return to his seat and the relative safety of the company of his dad and best friend. But there were a lot of people and noise in his way. People were rushing past him to see for themselves what was happening on the field and to join in the melee. Henry was bumped into from the left, then some big dude ran right into him from behind, causing Henry to spill Dr. Pepper all over himself as well as several people near him. This caused even more jostling and bumping and yelling, which caused Henry's heart rate to begin accelerating. Thump thump. Thump thump. Thump thump. All the noises began to blur together. It was happening again.

All the commotion around him sent Henry spiraling into a panic attack, the first he'd had in a very long time. Fight or flight. Fight or flight. Henry had to get out of there. He dropped the now nearly empty commemorative soda cup and pushed and fought his way out of the crowd into the nearest open space. He reached a safe place near a trash can and far away from the crowds. The stench of stale beer and mustard and nacho cheese invaded his safe space, but Henry didn't move other than to drop into a crouching position. He reached up and took off his cap and began running his hand back and forth over his buzz cut hair.

His heart continued racing. Thump thump. Thump thump. He tried to slow his heart and mind with deep breathing. Thump thump. Thump… thump. Thump… thump. The blurred noises around him slowly became more distinct as the cacophony on the field and in the stands died down.

Soon enough, order was restored on the field and fans returned to their seats, except for Jack Mitchell. He stood on the concourse near the concession stand where Henry had gotten his refill. He looked back and forth and finally spotted Henry near the trash can. Seeing Henry there, he knew instantly what had happened.

Jack jogged over to Henry and helped him to his feet and wrapped his arms around his son. Henry resisted at first, but once he realized it was his father, he allowed himself to be shielded from the turmoil around him and within him. Jack just stood there with his son for a few more minutes.

Jack slowly released his hold on Henry. Henry took a deep breath and looked up at his dad. His heart rate had slowed back to normal and the trembling in his hands was hardly noticeable.

"Let's get out of here," Jack said.

Henry nodded. Jack kept his arm around his son's shoulder as they made their way back toward the gate. They had to tell Jackie and his father that they were going back to the hotel.

Later that summer on a hot August afternoon, Henry and Molly and Molly's friend, Kara, were hanging out at Jackie's house trying to decide what movie to go see. If they could hurry up and decide what to watch in the next fifteen minutes, they could save themselves about two dollars per ticket because they'd be paying "early bird" prices instead of full price for an evening showing. Henry and Molly really wanted to see *Bill & Ted's Bogus Journey*. But Jackie hadn't seen the first film, so he didn't want to watch the sequel to a movie he hadn't seen. Jackie wanted to see *Hot Shots!*

Round and round they went, spending way more than those fifteen minutes arguing about which movie to see. When they realized that they were at a stalemate and that, even if they did decide on what to watch, they would have to pay an extra two bucks a ticket, they decided not to go to the cineplex after all. Now what would they do?

Victoria Marcus couldn't help but overhear all twenty minutes of the teens' bickering over what movie to go see, and it took every ounce of strength she possessed not to tear her hair out over the ridiculousness of it all. And now that their plans were completely up in the air again, she just couldn't take it.

"Look, Jackie, call Tony's Pizza and order a couple of pizzas for you and your friends. Henry, run to your house and pick out a movie that everyone will enjoy."

Jackie and Henry knew better than to hesitate when Jackie's mom prefaced her instructions with the word "look," so they jumped right into action. The girls just sat in stunned silence. Seeing that her work was finished, Victoria turned around and went back into the den.

After the movie and the pizza and the root beer floats that Rev. Marcus made for the teens, Kara did that glance-at-your-watch thing to signal to Molly that it was getting close to her curfew; Molly was her ride home. Jackie and Henry were oblivious to the nonverbal exchange between the girls. They were still laughing at some dumb joke from the movie they watched. Molly interrupted them, "Well, I need to get Kara home. It's almost 9:00."

"Yeah, my parents are really strict like that," Kara chimed in.

"9:00? During the summer?" Mrs. Marcus hollered from the den. The four teenagers chuckled.

"Yeah, I know, right? We're driving to see my Grandma near St. Louis, and my mom wants to be sure we all get a good night's sleep because we're leaving early," Kara said, the tone of her voice becoming more mocking of her mother as she got closer to the end of her sentence. The others just shook their heads in pity.

"Well, it's still early," Henry said. "Molly, do you want to meet me and Jackie at Denny's after you drop off Kara... if it's ok with you, Mrs. Marcus."

Jackie nodded his head approvingly. He knew that Henry knew better than to make plans without consulting Queen Victoria first. That's a mistake you only make once. Victoria gave a wave of permission from her chair in the den.

"Umm... sure. Let me call my mom real quick," Molly said. Kara's head fell and she just stared at the floor. She wanted to go hang out at Denny's, too.

After Molly called her mother, the plan was set. She would take Kara home and then meet the boys at Denny's. Since both Jackie and Henry had gotten their driver's licenses at the beginning of summer, they were arguing over which of them got to drive. Henry was able to convince Jackie that since he still needed to ask his parents' permission, it would be best if he drove. They could walk to his house, and if his mom said no, then they could call Kara's house and leave a message for Molly to just go on home herself.

With a quick kiss between Henry and Molly, they were all on their way.

Jackie and Henry were on their second round of sodas, swallowed up by the enormous booth they were sitting in, when Henry asked Jackie if he could borrow a quarter for the payphone. They had been there for almost half an hour and Molly had not yet arrived. Henry and Molly always split a chocolate malt and he didn't want to order until she got there.

Jackie fished three dimes out of his pocket and gave them to Henry, who walked to the payphone down the hallway near the restrooms. He dialed Molly Jacobs' number and saw the waitress roll her eyes at Jackie as he sent her away. The phone rang twice before the line was disconnected. Luckily, since the call was not actually answered, the three dimes dropped into the coin receptacle. Henry tried again, and the same thing happened. Two rings. Disconnected line. Henry tried once more. This time, someone picked up but it wasn't Molly.

The girl's voice said, "Hi, Henry. Molly can't come to Denny's because she's getting her nails done."

The voice giggled and hung up the phone. Henry slowly hung up the phone and returned to the booth.

When Henry sat down, Jackie shrugged his shoulders as if to say, "so, what'd she say?"

Henry took a sip of his nearly empty soda and said, "She's not coming."

Jackie took a long drink of the last of his soda. "That's weird. Everything ok between you two?"

"Yeah, everything's good. Kara answered the phone and said that Molly's not coming because she's getting her nails done," Henry replied with a shrug of his shoulders.

"What a bitch," Jackie said.

"Watch it," Henry snapped. Jackie gave him an apologetic nod. He sipped the last of his soda from the glass. He was about to say something else, but the waitress came by again, this time looking really annoyed.

"You two gonna order or what?" she barked at them while smacking her gum. "'Cause I'm not giving up a booth for an hour for two sodas and a lousy tip."

The boys quickly grabbed their menus and frantically scanned them.

"I'll have the bacon cheeseburger, no onion, and a chocolate malt," said Henry.

"Do you want regular fires or seasoned fries?" the waitress asked. She wasn't writing any of this down. She was one of those veteran waitresses who could memorize the order of any group, no matter how big or how complicated the order.

"Seasoned fries. And a side of barbeque sauce, please," Henry answered.

Jackie began ordering before the waitress even turned her gaze to him. "I'll have the same thing, but with grilled onions, no pickle, and regular fries."

"You want the malt, too?" the waitress asked.

"Yes, please."

"Alright, I'll have that right out for you."

"Dude, I can't believe she stood us up," Jackie said as the waitress walked to the kitchen to put in their order.

"Yeah, what I can't figure out is why Kara answered the phone. I thought she had to be home early, and she's hanging out at Molly's house... What the hell, man?"

Henry's voice got louder than he intended at the end, causing the few other patrons of the restaurant to turn their heads. The boys sat in silence, staring at the melting ice in their soda glasses, until the waitress brought their food. She also placed the bill on the edge of the table.

"I hope your daddies taught you about tipping pretty waitresses," she said with a sarcastic smile.

The boys paid little attention to her and dove straight into their food, burning their tongues on their freshly cooked fries. Even though they had had pizza, root beer floats, and other snacks just a few hours earlier, they scarfed down their burgers, fries, and malts like they were starving.

When they were each about three bites away from finishing, Jackie asked, "So what do you want to do next?"

Henry just shrugged his shoulders.

"I mean, I figured that if Molly had actually showed up, you two would have just ditched me after we ate to go make out somewhere," Jackie said with a big smile. "Since I ain't gonna go make out with you, whatcha wanna do?"

Henry shrugged his shoulders again.

Jackie's eyes and his smile got even bigger. Henry could tell that whatever Jackie was about to say was probably going to be a really bad idea.

"Dude," Jackie said, his eyes lighting up, "Let's go toilet paper Molly's house!"

Henry took a long slurp to get the last bit of chocolate malt from the bottom of the glass.

"Man, I don't know," Henry said.

"Ah, come on. It's just a little harmless prank to get her back for standing us up."

Henry took another long slurp of his milkshake, even though nothing came up his straw. It certainly wasn't the worst idea Jackie had ever had. But it was still kind of early, not even 10:00 yet. They wouldn't be able to strike just yet. But Molly did kind of deserve it, hanging out with Kara instead of meeting them for late night burgers.

Henry grabbed the check from the middle of the table and studied it, trying to calculate how much of a tip to leave. Jackie just stared at him, awaiting a response from his friend.

"If we did TP Molly's house," Henry finally said as he fished his wallet out of his back pocket. "We'd probably have to wait a couple of hours..."

Jackie listened eagerly. He knew if he just sat there quietly, Henry would talk himself into the plan.

"But we could go to the store to buy toilet paper now before the store closes..."

Jackie continued his silence. He could practically see the gears in Henry's head turning as he listened to his friend.

"We could go back to my house," Henry continued. "We could watch the first part of Letterman, then go out about midnight..."

Jackie nodded in approval.

"My dad is away on business, and my mom is a pretty sound sleeper..."

Checkmate. Jackie knew it was only a matter of time before Henry would give in.

"Alright, let's pay this bill and get out of here." Henry had grown tired of trying to figure out what the tip would be on his half of the bill. He put ten dollars on the table and Jackie did the same. They got up from the table and waved a "thank you" goodbye to their waitress who was bussing a nearby table.

Henry and Jackie each lay on one of the two couches in the Mitchells' living room. Henry's room was on the west side of the house and just baked in the afternoon sun, so summer nights were too hot to sleep in there. With the ceiling fan on and only covered in a thin bedsheet, the two boys lay there on the verge of sleep.

Their plan of revenge had gone off without a hitch. After leaving Denny's they drove a few blocks to Kmart, where they bought several packages of cheap toilet paper, the kind that is so thin and rough that the only thing it is good for is decorating someone's front yard. The middle-aged woman working the register gave them a sideways look as she took their money.

185

Trying to make light of the situation, Jackie said, "My friend here has to go *really* bad."

The checker gave Henry the change and wished them a good night.

After waiting for Henry's mom to go to bed, the boys drove over to Molly Jacobs' house, but parked half a block away. The house appeared dark as if everyone had gone to bed, but they didn't want to risk being seen. They unwrapped the rolls of toilet paper, closed the squeaky car doors as quietly as they could, and made their stealthy approach up to the Jacobs's house. They paused at the mailbox by the curb to listen for their dog. Molly's bloodhound, Mortimer, had very sensitive ears and always started barking whenever Henry came over. Mortimer loved Henry and could hear him as soon as Henry started up the driveway.

But so far, no barking.

Henry and Jackie began by decorating the bushes that lined the Jacobs's driveway, then moved on to the forty-foot-tall oak tree in the middle of their front yard. And then while Jackie wrapped rolls of toilet paper around their mailbox, Henry decided to giftwrap Molly's 1978 Datsun B210. She had been given the car by her grandparents shortly after she got her license. The car, which had been quite "slick" when Molly's grandfather drove it, was definitely showing its age. But Molly didn't care; it was a car and it was free.

After about fifteen minutes and thirty-something rolls of toilet paper, Henry and Jackie paused to admire their work. If only they had a camera. But as they walked past the driveway, they could hear Mortimer's faint bark coming from Molly's bedroom at the back of the house. Henry and Jackie ran to their car, jumped in and sped off toward Henry's house.

Just as they were on the verge of sleep, Henry's mom walked into the living room and turned on the nearby kitchen light. The boys both pulled their bedsheets up over their faces to block out the blinding light.

"I think some of your friends are outside," Mrs. Mitchell mumbled, herself squinting from the light.

Henry rubbed his eyes as he stumbled toward the front window to see why his mom was waking him and Jackie up at 2:00am. It was hard to see but it looked almost like Molly Jacobs and her friend Kara were in the front yard, dumping all of the toilet paper they had cleaned up from Molly's house onto the Mitchells' front lawn. Jackie soon joined Henry at the window.

"Da fuck?" Jackie muttered. Even though she was on her way to her bedroom, Mrs. Mitchell still heard Jackie.

"You owe me a quarter in the morning, Jackie," she yawned. "Now you two go clean up that mess out there."

The boys noticed that Molly and Kara could see them through the window. The girls waved, and then Molly blew a kiss at them before they ran back to Molly's car.

"Shit, man," Henry said, turning to look at Jackie. "I guess we'd better go clean that up."

They grabbed a couple of trash bags from under the kitchen sink and went out onto the front lawn, not even putting shoes on their feet. As they bent down to start scooping up the toilet paper, they heard a hissing noise coming from the grass. It started softly, almost unnoticeable, but quickly got louder. The boys paused and looked around near their feet to locate the source of the hissing sound. But before they could find it, it found them.

The sprinkler heads popped up and started spraying them with water, which caused the cheap toilet paper to begin turning into a wet, sticky substance that no longer resembled paper of any kind. Jackie sprinted the six steps to the dryness of the driveway and was headed back to the comfort of his couch in the living room. But he stopped in his tracks when Henry yelled at him.

"Dude, my mom will kill me - and you - if we don't get this shit cleaned up," Henry said.

Jackie was about to say something in protest, but he knew it was no use. He stomped back out into the wet lawn, opened his trash bag that he had dropped on the grass when the sprinklers turned on, and began scooping the soaked toilet paper up off the wet lawn and into the bag. Henry was already doing the same. It quickly became nearly impossible to actually pick the stuff up, it practically melted in their hands. But they knew a worse fate awaited them if they did not have it all cleaned up. So, they carried on, water dripping down their faces and soaking their clothes.

The next few minutes were filled with all kinds of "shits" and "dammits" every other profanity as they cleaned up the mess. If Henry's mother had been listening, she would have demanded they both put the rest of their summer's allowance in the Jar in the kitchen.

Chapter 19

Fall 1991
Gladstone, MO

As Henry's junior year of high school began, it was not unusual for his father to miss family dinners because of his new work schedule. He was on the road less, but he often had to work later hours in the office. Since Jack's firm had been bought up by a large multinational corporation, they now had customers all over the country. And with the growing use of computers and other technologies in the office, the salesmen could conduct their business over the phone and fax machines instead of in person. Jack soon became the sales supervisor for many of the firm's West Coast clients. And because of the two-hour time difference between Kansas City and the West Coast, Jack often stayed much later than he used to.

"Hi, Dad," Henry said as he saw his dad putting his sport coat in the closet by the front door. Henry and Jackie were headed toward the front door after rinsing their ice cream bowls and putting them in the dishwasher.

"Where're you two going... at 7:46... on a school night?" Jack asked.

"Library," Henry answered. "Mr. Simpson assigned us a big research project in US history last week, and we need to turn in our topic tomorrow."

All underclassmen at Winnetonka High School spent their first two years living in fear of the 11th grade US History research project. Some saw it as a rite of passage; others saw it as the guarantee of an early demise. It was rumored that, over the past four decades, six students had been admitted to Southside Mental Hospital because of this project.

The project was to write a twenty-page research paper about what was - in the opinion of the student - the most significant moment of the past hundred years of American history. This paper needed a title page and endnotes and a bibliography, and exactly one-inch margins and a 12-point font size. The really mean teachers would go to the library to investigate suspicious-sounding sources or use a ruler to measure the exactness of the margins. The slightest infraction - rumor had it - could result in a failing grade.

But Henry and Jackie had found one saving grace in all the hysteria over this research paper. Over the last several years, the 11th grade history teachers had relaxed things ever so slightly. The honors classes still had to complete the dreaded research paper as it had always been done, but that the regular classes could complete it with a partner. This was the sole reason why Henry and Jackie did not join Molly Jacobs in taking Honors US History.

Jack was glad to see the boys taking the initiative of going to the library to work on the assignment, but also a bit disappointed that they had waited to start the night before the first step was due. *At least they didn't say the entire research paper is due tomorrow*, Jack thought.

"Whatcha guys gonna write about, Hammer?" Jack asked.

"I don't know," Henry answered, glancing at Jackie who only gave a shrug. "That's why we're going to the library."

"Well, maybe I can help you guys," Jack said as he walked into the kitchen. Henry and Jackie paused in the entry way for a moment. Things did not always go well when Henry's dad tried to help him with homework. Jack Mitchell was a walking example that formal education is not always necessary for personal or professional success. He got decent grades in high school and attended community college for a couple of years, but soon realized that school just wasn't his thing. So, he quit going to school and got a job as a salesman, and the rest, as they say, is history.

Higher education had not been Jack's ticket to success, but he didn't want his son to limit his own opportunities through a lack of education. And besides, if Henry Aaron Mitchell was going to play baseball beyond high school, he needed his grades to match his baseball stats. Gone were the days of "dumb jocks" getting full-ride athletic scholarships.

Even though Jack pushed his son to do well in school, his own lack of formal education meant that he was not much help to Henry when it came to homework. Jack's helpfulness ended somewhere around 8th grade. But, Jack was a bit of a history buff, especially if that history was in any way related to baseball.

Jack grabbed a beer and his dinner from the fridge and sat down at the kitchen table. He gestured toward the other chairs and motioned for Henry and Jackie to join him. Henry grabbed cans of soda for himself and Jackie and they both reluctantly sat down. He tossed the assignment handout onto the table in front of his father. Jack grabbed his glasses from his shirt breast pocket so he could read it.

"What is the most important event in American history in the last one hundred years? Choose an event from the past century and write a 20-page essay in which you argue the importance of that event. You must cite at least five sources in your paper," the directions said.

"Easy..." said Jack as he tossed the paper back onto the table. "Jackie Robinson breaking the color barrier in baseball."

Henry and Jackie gave each other a puzzled look. Sure, it was probably the most important event in baseball history, but American history? Henry was a bit skeptical, although Jackie was quickly coming around to the idea. Henry was thinking maybe the stock market crash that led to the Great Depression. Or Pearl Harbor. Or the assassination of JFK. Or Martin Luther King, Jr.'s "I Have a Dream" speech. But no, his dad suggested they write about Jackie Robinson? But after only a few seconds, Jackie was really liking the idea of researching and writing about his namesake.

Henry took a long sip from his soda can. Maybe they could make it work. At least they would enjoy finding and reading all those sources. Henry always loved an excuse to learn more about the National Pastime. He gave Jackie a long, hard look. A smile was starting to creep across

Jackie's face. Henry took another sip of soda and tried to hide a burp. He gave another shrug.

Jackie knew what the shrug meant.

It meant that he and Henry would get to watch the rest of that night's playoff game because they no longer needed to go to the library because they had themselves a research paper topic.

But would Mr. Simpson go for it?

Mr. Simpson did go for it. In fact, he was kind of looking forward to reading something that wasn't about the Market Crash of '29 or about Martin Luther King, Jr.'s "Dream." He didn't necessarily agree with Henry and Jackie's assertion, but deep down he hoped the boys could pull it off.

That Saturday, after a trip to the library, Henry and Jackie spent the afternoon with books about Jackie Robinson and baseball and the Civil Rights Movement all over the living room at Jackie's house. They read and talked and wrote information on note cards. If only their parents could see them being all studious and scholarly.

"Ooh, write this down," Jackie said. Jackie was the reader, while Henry was the scribe who wrote the information on 3x5 cards. "It says here that Jackie Robinson had his own 'Rosa Parks' moment years before Rosa Parks did."

"What do you mean?" Henry asked.

"So, check this out. He was in the army during World War II, stationed at Fort Hood..."

"That's in Texas, right?"

"Yeah, yeah. I think so," Jackie answered, then continued with the story. "So, he was in the army, right. And he got on a bus and sat down next to this light-skinned woman who was the wife of some other guy stationed there. So, the bus driver tells him to go sit in the back of the bus..."

"Yeah... ok..."

"And Jackie Robinson refuses to get up and move. He just keeps on sitting there, and the MPs are called to escort him off the bus. So, they bring up all these lame-ass charges against him..."

"Like what?" Henry asked.

"They charged him - get this - with insubordination, drunkenness, conduct unbecoming of an officer, insulting a civilian woman, and disobeying the lawful orders of a superior officer..."

"Damn, dude. All because homeboy didn't move to a different seat on the bus?"

Jackie sat silent for an awkward moment.

"First of all," Jackie finally said. "You do not have enough melanin to pull a 'homeboy.'"

"Second of all, yes, all that because *homeboy* didn't move to a different seat," Jackie continued. "This was the Jim Crow South, so yes, it wasn't all that unusual for a black dude to face those kinds of charges."

Henry realized he wasn't writing anymore. He flipped over the note card to continue writing the story on the other side.

"So, the NAACP and the Negro press caught wind of what was going on and protested the charges against Robinson."

"So, what happened? At his trial?" Henry asked.

"Homeboy was acquitted of all charges," Jackie said. "And a few months later, he received an honorable discharge."

"That is so badass," Henry said as he wrote down the last of the details.

"Oh, oh... copy this down. This is a good quote," Jackie said. "'It was a small victory, for I learned that I was fighting in two wars; one against the foreign enemy, and one against the prejudice at home.'"

"Prejudice... at home," Henry repeated as he wrote down the quote.

Jackie closed the book and set it on the coffee table and said, "Snack break?"

Jackie stood up and Henry followed him into the kitchen. Jackie grabbed a couple cans of soda while Henry rummaged through the pantry looking for chips and cookies. He found some sour cream and onion potato chips and Oreos, and followed Jackie back into the living room. He set the food down on the coffee table next to their stack of library books; Jackie handed him one of the cans of soda. They popped the cans open in unison and plopped back into their respective seats to get back to work.

For Jackie and Henry, this felt nothing like homework. The fact that they were reading about one of the all-time great baseball players and one of their personal heroes made this the most fun they'd ever had doing schoolwork.

They read about why Jackie Robinson was selected by Branch Rickey, the general manager of the Brooklyn Dodgers, to be the first Negro League player to be signed by a Major League team; not because he was the best player in the League, but because he was one of the most even-tempered. Everyone involved knew that, even though integrating the sport was good for the game and good for the nation, there was a lot riding on this. If the first Black player proved to be hot-tempered and not able to handle the ridicule and prejudice and scorn, then it might set back the cause of desegregation.

Robinson, who was a very vocal advocate for equal rights, agreed to keep his mouth shut for his rookie season; after that he gained a reputation of not being one to walk away from a conflict. He argued with umpires and fought with opposing players, when the need arose. But it was what he did with his bat and glove that spoke louder than any of his words. He won the Rookie of the Year award in 1947 and Most Valuable Player in 1949. He helped lead the Brooklyn Dodgers to six pennants and was elected to the Baseball Hall of Fame in 1962.

After his baseball career, Robinson became an important part of the Civil Rights Movement in the 1960s. As a businessman, he invested in Black-owned businesses and in Black communities. He worked with the NAACP and other civil rights organizations. But after a while, he grew frustrated with how slow the progress toward equality was going. He later resigned from the NAACP because he felt they needed younger and more progressive leaders. He also spoke out about baseball's slowness in hiring African Americans as managers, coaches, and members of the front office.

In so many ways, Jackie Robinson donning a Brooklyn Dodgers uniform and breaking the color barrier paved the way for the Civil Rights Movement that would take the stage less than twenty years after Robinson's debut.

"Dude, write this one down," Jackie said. "Martin Luther King, Jr. once said to Dodgers pitcher, Don Newcombe, 'You'll never know what you and Jackie and Roy [Campanella] did to make it possible to do my job.'"

"To do my job," Henry repeated as he wrote it down.

The boys sat back and surveyed the damage they had done to the Marcus's living room while working on this research paper. They had each left a couple empty soda cans on various flat surfaces. There were several piles of books around the room, some looking like they were about to topple over. And then there were half-empty bags of chips and cookies here and there. Jackie took a quick glance out the front window and saw his mom's car driving up the street.

"Dude, mom alert!" Jackie said as he and Henry jumped into action. This was not the first time they had trashed the living room and had to quickly clean up after themselves. There wasn't even any of that "deer in the headlights" panic; they each knew exactly what to do to get the room back to its pristine condition. And just as they both walked back into the living room after throwing away the last of the trash, they could hear Jackie's mom's car pull into the driveway. They high-fived each other and flopped onto the couch. It had been a very productive afternoon.

About six weeks later, Henry and Jackie were putting the final touches on their research project. Mr. Simpson decided to pull a fast one and make his students present their research papers to the class. None of the other history teachers were making their classes do this, but Mr. Simpson felt his students were up for the challenge.

The dreaded day arrived. Henry and Jackie had US History during fifth period, after lunch and before sixth period baseball practice. Which meant that Henry had almost the entire school day to worry about giving the presentation. He spent most of his morning - when he should have been focused on geometry and English - doing his deep breathing exercises. But even with the deep breathing, his heart rate was not slowing down.

Lunch was a welcomed distraction. Molly Jacobs had given her big presentation in her honors History class earlier that day, so she was full of stories of how it went. Molly's enthusiasm for her project and its subject - the fight for women's suffrage - was contagious. For a few brief moments during lunch, Henry's mind was not focused on his own presentation. But his heart rate only slowed slightly, and then shot back up as he heard the bell ring to end lunch.

The bell rang to start fifth period, and Henry and Jackie were in their seats in the third row. Mr. Simpson took roll, then asked for volunteers to go first in presenting their projects. There was an awkward moment of silence as everyone looked at their shoes or out the window, anything to avoid eye contact with the teacher. Then, catching Henry completely off guard, Jackie shot his hand up in the air.

"What the hell?" Henry said a little too loudly. There were chuckles and snickers from all over the classroom.

"Mr. Marcus," Mr. Simpson said. "I appreciate your enthusiasm and I look forward to hearing your and Mr. Mitchell's presentation."

Jackie stood up and gestured for Henry to get out of his seat. Henry rolled his eyes and reluctantly stood up and followed Jackie to the front of the room. There were a few slow claps coming from various parts of the room. Henry took a few deep breaths as Jackie pinned their poster to the bulletin board behind the teacher's podium.

One of the things Henry had worked on with his therapist over the past couple of years was Henry's fear of public speaking. And since freshman year, Henry had made significant progress. That year, Henry had gone from being "sick" the day he had to recite a poem in English class to pulling a solid C+ on the oral presentation part of his science project. And honestly, it was not just stage fright that was getting the best of Henry. No, this seemed different. His heart rate was up, causing his hands to tremble slightly. He kept his hands in his pockets to hide this. His mind was racing; he just couldn't slow down his thoughts. He felt himself spiraling, but this was more than one of his panic attacks. *What the hell is wrong with me?* he thought.

Henry stood there, practically frozen, and hadn't realized that Jackie had already begun the presentation. The two friends had rehearsed a number of times, and it was a good thing because Jackie was almost finished with the first segment, which meant that Henry would soon have to begin speaking. He heard Jackie say, "And now Henry is going to tell you about Jackie Robinson's own 'Rosa Parks' moment."

Jackie took a step back and looked at Henry to continue the presentation. The seamless transition they had rehearsed did not go so seamlessly. Henry looked at Jackie, then looked at the class and at Mr. Simpson standing in the back of the room with his clipboard in hand, then back at Jackie. Jackie's eyes got really big, as if to say, "If you don't start talking, I swear to God..."

Henry swallowed hard and turned to face his audience, taking his trembling hands out of his pocket. He began to speak, "Y... yes, thank you... uh, thank you Jackie."

Another hard swallow and the hands went back into his pockets.

He continued, "J... J... Jackie Robinson was a... uh... lieutenant in... in the army, and s... stationed at Fort... uh, Fort Hood..."

Jackie gave his friend a puzzled look, then looked back at their teacher in the back of the room. Mr. Simpson - who could certainly be a hardass, but was also very sympathetic toward his students - gave them both an encouraging look, but it was pretty apparent that he thought Henry's nerves were just getting the best of him.

Henry took a deep breath, looked frightenedly at Jackie, then tried to go on.

"One d... day, Jackie Robinson got... got onto... uh... a bus and sat down next... uh, next to a... uh... light-skinned woman. She... she was the... uh... um... the wife of a... um... fellow officer..."

Jackie had seen this before, but this was worse than one of Henry's anxiety attacks. Was something truly wrong with him? What should he do? How could he help his friend? Should he take over and continue the presentation? What the hell was going on?

Jackie made the split-second decision to take over the presentation, and he absolutely nailed the rest of it. Mr. Simpson had been skeptical of their thesis, but the boys' presentation was rather convincing. The class applauded as Jackie returned to his seat; Henry kept walking past his desk to Mr. Simpson in the back of the room.

"Can I use the restroom?" Henry whispered.

Mr. Simpson just nodded, and Henry exited the room. Jackie watched as his friend left.

The next pair of students got up to deliver their presentation. When they had finished some seven minutes later, Henry had not returned. Jackie was not very good at pretending to pay attention; he kept looking over his shoulder at the classroom door to see if Henry was coming back. Mr. Simpson noticed that Henry had not yet returned and that Jackie kept staring at the classroom door, so when the current group finished and were returning to their seats, he walked over to Jackie and suggested he go check on his friend.

Jackie exited the classroom and walked down the hallway toward the boys' bathroom. He stepped into the restroom and called out, "Yo, Hammer. You in there?"

No response.

Jackie listened for a second, but didn't hear any sounds coming from the inside of the restroom. It was obviously empty; Henry was not in there.

Jackie looked back and forth in the empty hallway. Henry was nowhere to be seen. Jackie jogged past the restroom to the main door of the building and looked outside. Henry was over to the left of the entrance, pacing back and forth. He held his baseball cap in one hand, and the other hand was rubbing the top of his head. Jackie recognized this behavior and approached Henry cautiously.

"Yo, Hammer. What's up?" Jackie asked.

Henry looked startled at the sound of his friend's voice. He instinctively smoothed back his buzz cut hair and put his cap back on and looked over at Jackie. Henry's eyes appeared wetter than normal. He would say it was because of allergies - which was often true - but Jackie knew it wasn't.

Jackie sat on the bench near where Henry had been pacing. Henry reluctantly sat down next to him, took off his cap, and went back to rubbing his scalp. He wouldn't make eye contact with Jackie.

There was an awkwardly long silence between them. Jackie knew not to wait for Henry to speak, because that wasn't going to happen. But he didn't know what to say either. On the one hand, he'd been through this with Henry before. All the way back to Henry's first real panic attack on the first day of ninth grade, Jackie had seen Henry at his worst. But on the other hand, they had spent so much damn time on that damn project. He truly felt bad for his best friend, but he was also a little angry with him.

But, surprisingly, Henry was the one to break the silence.

"Dude, I... I'm sorry," Henry said. He paused, then opened his mouth to speak again, but said nothing.

Jackie looked over and began to talk, not knowing what he was going to say or where he was headed, but if Henry wasn't going to fill the silence then he was going to.

"Look," Jackie said in a tone similar to his mother's. "Dude, we spent so much time on that damn project..."

"I know," Henry said, again avoiding eye contact.

"And we rehearsed the presentation so many times..."

"I..."

"What the hell happened in there?" Jackie's tone grew sharper. "I mean... what the hell?"

Jackie found himself much angrier than he thought he was.

"I thought you had this under control, man. I ain't seen you like this in... in like... I don't know how long."

Henry was not only avoiding eye contact at this point, but was looking off in the totally opposite direction. Jackie was only building steam.

"I mean, what's all that therapy and deep breathing and all that shit for anyway?"

Jackie knew he should stop. He knew he was hitting very sensitive spots. But he just couldn't stop.

"I mean, we had that bitch down pat. We had that shit memorized. And... you blew it. You goddamn blew it."

Jackie knew he shouldn't have said those things. The second he heard those words coming out of his mouth, he wished he could take them back. He wished he could just pop the dialogue bubble before Henry heard any of them.

Henry didn't say a word. He just stood up and started walking away. Jackie wasn't sure if he should follow or not. But Henry took only a few steps before he turned around and faced his friend. He took something out of his pocket and tossed it at Jackie. Jackie caught the object and looked at it. It was a small plastic cylinder, the kind that a woman might use to keep some aspirin in her purse. The labeling had been rubbed off, so there was no way to know what was inside the tube. Jackie gave Henry a puzzled look, and Henry returned the look with a little head nod, motioning for Jackie to open the tube. There were three white capsules inside.

"What the hell are these?" Jackie asked as Henry sat back down on the bench.

"Diet pills," Henry said with a deep exhale.

"Why the hell you takin' diet pills?" Jackie asked. "Molly thinks you're fat?"

Henry let out the faintest hint of a smile and shook his head. "No, Eric... Eric Lanford gave them to me at practice a few weeks ago. He said they... they would give me an edge on the field. And I mean, you've seen how I've been hitting and throwing the past couple weeks..."

Jackie closed his fist around the pills, as if he was trying to smash the pills with his anger. He had been willing to accept the circumstances if what happened back there in Mr. Simpson's classroom was a genuine panic attack and he was ready to apologize for the things he had said a moment ago. But now he was really pissed. He just shook his head as his fist clenched tighter and tighter.

"Look," Jackie said the word just like his mom did. "You've done some stupid stuff in the past…"

Henry nodded in agreement.

"But this has got to be the stupidest thing you've ever done," Jackie paused a moment as if he were trying to think of something stupider than this.

"I just can't believe it, man," Jackie continued. "So freakin' stupid, man."

Jackie unclenched his fist and tossed the pills on the ground and stomped on them several times. Henry watched in shameful silence.

"I hope you're happy," Jackie said as the bell rang to end the period. "I have to go get my stuff."

Jackie walked back into the building before the flood of students came out the main entrance doors. Henry followed at a distance and had to fight his way against the stream of students to get back into the building to Mr. Simpson's classroom.

When he reached Mr. Simpson's classroom, he could see that Jackie was already halfway down the hallway in the other direction. Henry saw his belongings still at his desk and the room was empty of students. He approached Mr. Simpson, before getting his things.

"Mr. Simpson," Henry said, causing Mr. Simpson to turn around. "I… I'm really sorry about what happened earlier, you know…"

Mr. Simpson nodded in acknowledgement.

Henry continued, "Please don't take points off of Jackie's grade. That was all my fault. I guess my nerves got the best of me."

Mr. Simpson nodded again, not saying anything.

"If we lost any points because I couldn't get through the presentation, please take them off my grade… not his."

Mr. Simpson finally spoke.

"Well, this is a group project, and the instructions do say that part of your grade is working together to produce a quality project and presentation."

Henry looked down, nodding his head dejectedly.

"But," Mr. Simpson continued. "I'll think about it."

Henry looked up at him. Mr. Simpson gave him a half smile.

"Now get to class," Mr. Simpson said as he turned back around to the board. Henry turned around, grabbed his things from his desk in the third row, and left the classroom.

Chapter 20

Spring 1992
Gladstone, MO

Mr. Simpson did only take points off of Henry's grade for messing up the presentation, which meant that Jackie still got an A, while Henry got a B-. This was the first of several small steps toward Henry making amends with Jackie for his decision to take diet pills to enhance his performance on the baseball field. By the holidays, they were pretty much ok, or at least had agreed not to talk about it anymore. And this meant with anyone; Henry was very embarrassed and, despite Jackie's encouragement to do so, did not tell his parents or Molly about it. He was just hoping to chalk it up as a foolish mistake not to be repeated or discussed again.

With the tossing out of the old calendar and the putting up of a new one came the excitement for a new baseball season. As he had done for several years now, Henry had written two countdowns on the calendar that hung near the kitchen wall-mounted phone: one looking forward to the start of his own baseball season, and the other to the start of the Major League Baseball season.

One day in early March, Henry and Jackie walked into Henry's house after baseball practice to the smell of Diane's lasagna. They had a math test the next day, so Jackie was going to have dinner with the Mitchells, then the boys would spend the rest of their evening studying for the test. Molly Jacobs would have joined them as a tutor - she was a level ahead of them in math - but she had her own test to study for. But she was only a phone call away if they needed her.

This was also one of the few evenings in recent memory that Jack was actually home to eat dinner with his family. When he heard that Diane was making lasagna, he was sure to wrap up his conference calls early to make it home just as she was taking it out of the oven. Jack hung up his sport coat by the door and put his briefcase under the table in the entryway and greeted his lovely wife with a big kiss on the cheek. Deep down, Henry hoped to be able to one day greet Molly Jacobs the same way after he got home from a day at work.

Henry and Jackie were in their usual spots at the dining room table, and Jack sat down with them.

"Are you guys ready for me to blow your minds?" Jack asked the boys. They responded with a shrug. This was not the first time that he had said those words as he sat down at the table, ready to repeat some news story he'd heard on the radio while driving home. A story that usually was not to be described as "mind-blowing."

"I was listening to the news on my way home from work," Jack Mitchell was not going to let an eye roll stop him from telling his story. "And they get to the sports report. News out of Chicago, the Cubs signed their second baseman..."

"Ryne Sandberg," Henry and Jackie said in unison.

"Right, Ryne Sandberg," Jack continued. "They signed him to a four-year, 28.4 million-dollar contract extension!"

Both Henry and Jackie perked up at this news.

"That's $7.1 million per year," Jackie chimed in. He was a bit quicker in the math department than Henry was, and continued doing the mental math. "And say he plays 150 games each season, because homeboy's got to rest every now and then, that comes to... $47,000 and change per game!"

Henry just sat there dumbfounded, and Jackie continued to work the crowd with his skills. "And say he hits... Hammer, how many homers did he hit last year?"

Henry bit his lower lip as he gazed at the ceiling fan above the table, trying to remember. "Uhh... he hit, if I remember right, like 25 or 26 home runs last year."

"So, if he hits 25 home runs again this year, that comes to... $284,000 per home run!"

As much as Diane didn't want to interrupt this mathematical fun the boys were having, dinner was ready to be served. She put the plates of food on the table, along with a basket of garlic bread in the middle for everyone to share. The plates had barely touched the surface of the table before everyone was scarfing it down. In the mind of a teenage boy, the faster you eat, the sooner you get seconds.

There was about ten minutes of virtual silence, interrupted only by yummy noises as everyone ate. During this silence, Henry's brain was swimming in numbers. Big numbers. After all, Henry did have a real chance of playing professional baseball someday. He was trying to imagine himself signing a contract like the one Sandberg just signed. By the time he was onto his second plate of lasagna and his fourth piece of garlic bread, he had picked out his dream house, vacation home, and dream car.

After dinner, the boys cleared their dishes, then went back to Henry's bedroom to study for their math test.

The 1992 Northern District League baseball championship came down to the final game of the regular season between Winnetonka High School and Satchel Paige High School. Winnetonka was 11-0 in league play and Paige was 10-1; Paige's only loss was an extra-innings nail biter to Winnetonka. If Winnetonka won the game, they would be the outright champs. If Paige won the game, it would create a tie for first place, and league rules said that a tie in the standings would be decided by each team's runs scored versus runs allowed differential. If it came to that, it would be incredibly close. And the last thing the Winnetonka Griffins wanted was for their quest for a league champion to come down to a tiebreaker.

The score was tied 3-3 in what was shaping up to be quite a pitchers' duel. Both teams' offenses had to work hard for the few runs they each had on the scoreboard, relying on a few timely hits and defensive mistakes by the opposing team. Here, in the bottom of the seventh, the Griffins couldn't have asked for better luck because the heart of the lineup was due up: Jackie Marcus, Henry Mitchell, and Eric Lanford.

Jackie drew a leadoff walk from the tiring pitcher. On the first pitch to Henry, Jackie stole second easily and then took third base when the throw from the catcher went past the shortstop and into shallow centerfield. The stage was set for Henry to once again be the big hero.

With the count 1-0, no outs, and one of the league's fastest baserunners on third, the Paige head coach called a timeout to talk with his pitcher. The Griffins' third base coach called Henry over to chat with him and Jackie about what to expect from the pitcher and what to do in this situation. The umpire called an end to the timeout; the pitcher returned to the mound and Henry returned to the batter's box.

The pitcher was working from the stretch. He peered in to get the sign from his catcher and then started into his pitching motion. Focusing on the catcher's glove that was on the inside corner of the plate, the pitcher didn't see the suicide lead that Jackie was taking off third base. As the pitcher wound up to throw the ball, Henry squared up to bunt and Jackie broke for home plate.

At the last second, Henry stepped out of the batter's box, not wanting to be involved in the collision that was about to happen right in front of him. Jackie, charging down the third base line, let out a yell to distract the catcher as he went into his foot-first slide into home plate. The yell did its job; the catcher looked away for a millisecond, and the ball - a perfectly placed pitch - tipped off the catcher's glove and rolled toward the backstop. Jackie was called safe at the plate and jumped up into Henry's arms. Their fellow Griffins rushed out onto the field to congratulate the hero of the game. Jackie's suicide steal won them the game and crowned them the uncontested league champions.

That Memorial Day weekend, the Marcuses hosted a barbeque for friends and neighbors. When Henry and Molly arrived at about 2:00, Reverend Marcus was at the grill in the backyard, Mrs. Marcus was in the kitchen, and Jackie was in the den playing *The Legend of Zelda* on his Super

Nintendo. Henry tapped lightly on the open door as he and Molly entered the den.

"How come you're not out there with your folks?" Henry asked as he sat down on the couch next to Jackie. Molly sat on the arm of the couch so as not to walk in front of Jackie while playing his game.

"My mom said if I finished helping set up the dining room that I could play video games until guests arrive," Jackie answered without even looking up.

"Well, I think we are the first ones here," Henry replied.

Jackie didn't seem himself this afternoon. Normally, he would at least pause the game to greet his friends when they came over, but not today.

"There's sodas in the fridge," Jackie said. "Help yourself."

"I'm good for now," Henry replied. "You want anything, Molly?"

"No, I'm fine," she said.

Several minutes went by and the only sounds in the room were the annoyingly repetitive music and sound effects from Jackie's game. The monotony was finally broken by Jackie's mother hollering from the kitchen for him to help his father bring in the burgers. And besides, guests were starting to arrive, so it would be rude of them to stay isolated in the den. Jackie turned off the game, stood up, and left without saying anything to Henry or Molly. They got up and followed Jackie to the kitchen. Henry grabbed sodas for himself and Molly, and then snatched a deviled egg from the spread on the table before going into the living room. Molly followed him in there, where they both sat on the couch.

"Is Jackie acting weird," Molly asked. "Or is it just me?"

Henry swallowed his mouthful of soda then answered, "Yeah, that was kinda weird earlier. I mean he does like *Zelda*, but he didn't even look at us."

Their conversation was interrupted when Henry's parents walked through the front door and Jackie and his dad walked in the back door with two large trays of hamburger patties and hot dogs. Henry's mom gave Molly a hug, and the four of them walked into the kitchen to join the Marcuses and their other guests.

Reverend Marcus said grace and then invited everyone to dive into the spread set out in the kitchen. There were burgers and hot dogs and all the trimmings. There was macaroni salad and potato salad and deviled eggs. There was everything you could want from a Memorial Day backyard barbeque. As people loaded up their plates, they took their food to the backyard to enjoy.

Once everyone was outside, Reverend Marcus stood in the middle of the group and said, "Excuse me, everyone, I have an announcement to make. I will be telling my congregation this tomorrow, but I wanted you all to hear it from me rather than through the grapevine."

There were a lot of awkward glances among the guests, most of whom were not members of his church.

He continued, "I've been in a number of meetings with the district superintendent during these past couple weeks, and she has decided that my skills in ministry would be of benefit to St. Luke's United Methodist Church in Columbia, about two hours east of here."

The awkward looks turned to surprised ones at the news that the Marcuses would be moving away.

"We will be moving at the end of June so that Jackie can finish the school year."

All eyes turned to Jackie, who obviously knew this announcement was coming but was still visibly upset by it. After his father began talking again, he went back into the house. Henry and Molly gave each other a look that said, "Oh, that explains it," and then followed Jackie into the house.

Chapter 21

Summer 1992
Jackie Marcus's House
Gladstone, MO

Henry spent much of the first couple weeks of his summer vacation at Jackie's house, helping him pack up his things for his family's move to Columbia, Missouri. If they really got down to business, they could have had Jackie's room completely packed in just a few hours. But most of the time they spent together was taken up with talk of baseball.

They spent one afternoon hunting down loose baseball cards that were scattered around Jackie's room. Jackie had a ton of baseball cards, and the boxes and binders he used were not enough to contain them all. He was sure to keep the truly valuable ones in protective sleeves in designated boxes or in protective pages in the binders, but inevitably, there were a few hidden gems to be found in sock drawers or being used as bookmarks on Jackie's bookshelf. These cards were most often rookie cards of players who had a breakout second or third season, but were used as bookmarks when the players were still relatively unknown.

Henry was thumbing through books on Jackie's shelf, searching for any loose cards as he put the books into cardboard moving boxes. In Jackie's copy of *The Adventures of Huckleberry Finn* - a book they were assigned to read this past school year - Henry found a Ken Griffey, Jr. Upper Deck rookie card. This was *the* Ken Griffey, Jr. rookie card that had been at the center of one of the biggest fights between Henry and Jackie.

"Hey, look what I found," Henry said. "*My* Ken Griffey, Jr. rookie card."

Jackie finished taping a box shut and slowly turned around.

"What do you mean, *your* Ken Griffey, Jr. rookie card?" Jackie scowled. He couldn't believe what he was hearing.

"Hey, we shook on that deal and you know it," Henry said.

Jackie just shook his head in disbelief as the memory of that summer evening came screaming back to him. They were hanging out there at Jackie's house last summer; one of their typical evenings of pizza, movies, and trading baseball cards. Even though most of their friends and teammates had kind of outgrown the whole baseball card thing, Henry and Jackie could spend hours and hours trading cards.

Henry and Jackie had pooled their money from mowing neighbors' lawns that summer and bought several boxes of baseball cards. One Topps, one Donruss, one Upper Deck, and one Fleer. Each box contained thirty-six packs of cards. They decided before opening any of the boxes that they would divide them evenly, sight unseen. But as they were opening the individual packs of cards, it became apparent that Jackie had received a much luckier draw; he was opening packs with all-star players and breakout rookies. Henry, not so much. When Jackie ended up with two Ken Griffey, Jr. rookie cards - a card that, by itself, was worth more than the entire box of cards it came in - Henry begged and pleaded for Jackie to give him one. He even offered to buy Jackie lunch the next day. Jackie reluctantly agreed and handed over the card.

But Henry was unable to take Jackie out to lunch the next day. Nor was he able to the day after that. Or the day after that. Finally, after about a week, Jackie demanded the card back. The deal was off. Henry refused. Jackie insisted. Henry refused and offered to drop everything he was doing and take Jackie out to lunch, even though it was 3:00 in the afternoon and Jackie's mom had made them grilled cheese sandwiches and tomato soup not more than two hours before. Jackie said it was too late for that and, once again, insisted he get his card back. This back and forth went on for about half an hour until Henry finally conceded (even though he insisted he was right) and gave back the baseball card. All this had been forgotten and forgiven until Henry had to go and make that comment.

Jackie walked over and snatched the card from Henry's hand.

"Thank you for finding *my* Ken Griffey, Jr. rookie card," Jackie said, standing uncomfortably close to Henry. He tossed the card onto his bed to keep it away from Henry. "I forgot that I put it there."

Henry did not like how close Jackie was standing to him and gave him a little nudge to get him to back up.

"Why you gotta get up in my face about it? I was only joking," Henry said. He gave Jackie another, playful shove to try to defuse the situation.

"Yeah, you didn't sound like you were joking," Jackie replied and shoved him back.

"Well, you did say I could have the card," Henry said as he got into Jackie's face.

"And you said you would take me out to lunch, which - by the way - you never did."

"That was not my fault," Henry contested.

"Not my problem," Jackie said. "We made a deal. You didn't do your part, so no card for you."

Jackie shoved Henry again, a little harder this time. Henry wasn't having it, so he shoved him back. The shoving went back and forth, harder and harder, until Henry lost his balance and fell backwards, knocking a glass of water to the floor. Not only did the water spill on a pile of Jackie's books, but the glass cracked on the hardwood floor. Jackie's father appeared as if by magic in the doorway within a second of the glass hitting the floor.

"What in the Sam Hill is going on in here?" Reverend Marcus shouted. The boys didn't say anything, but rather just knelt down to clean up the mess.

"Are you two fighting over that same damn baseball card?" Reverend Marcus asked, not really expecting an answer. "Give me the card."

Jackie put the pieces of broken glass gently into Henry's outstretched hands, wiped his hands on his shorts, and picked up the baseball card to hand to his father. Reverend Marcus pulled the card from its protective sleeve and tore the card in two and handed one half to each of the boys. "There. Now you don't have to fight over it anymore."

Jackie's dad left the room and the boys stood there in silence. They finished cleaning up the broken glass and mopping up the spilled water.

Henry stood there awkwardly as if he wanted to leave but didn't know how to excuse himself from Jackie's house. Jackie felt equally awkward, so he grabbed half of the baseball card and handed it to Henry. Not sure what to do with it, Henry took out his wallet and put the card in it.

"What time do you leave tomorrow?" Henry asked as he backed toward the doorway.

"Umm, like 10:00, I think," Jackie answered.

"Oh, ok," Henry said. "Well, if I don't see you tomorrow, have a safe drive."

And with that, Henry was out the door and on his way home.

"You have to go over there," Molly said.

Henry just took a bite of his donut and shrugged his shoulders.

"You'll regret it," Molly said. She took a bite of her bagel and looked at her watch. It was 8:47am. Henry and Molly decided to go get breakfast at the local donut shop. Molly had heard about Henry's fight with Jackie the day before, so she was going to be sure that Henry patched things up with his best friend before Jackie moved away. She finished her bite of bagel and silently stared at Henry.

He began to squirm in his chair, doing his best to avoid eye contact. He grabbed his mini carton of chocolate milk to take a drink, but realized it was empty. He put the opening to his mouth anyway to get the last few drops; anything to avoid Molly's stare.

"Alright, fine. I'll go," Henry said as he stuffed the last bite of donut into his mouth. Molly smiled and clapped her hands. She ate the last bite of her bagel and drank the last sip of her orange juice. Her mission was accomplished.

Henry and Molly parked a few houses away from Jackie's house. They walked past the large U-Haul truck that was taking up the curb in front of the house. Jackie and his dad were wrestling a mattress up the gangplank and into the back of the truck. As they set it down, Reverend Marcus saw Henry and Molly approaching and motioned for Jackie to turn around. Molly ran up and hugged Jackie's neck. He hugged her back, but scowled at Henry. Molly released Jackie from her hug and turned to look at Henry as if to say, "your turn." But Henry didn't move and neither did Jackie.

"Dammit you two!" Molly said. Both boys' jaws dropped. This was the first time they'd ever heard Molly use such saucy language. They quickly walked toward each other, not wanting to upset Molly further. Henry awkwardly reached out his hand to shake Jackie's. Jackie took his hand and the two did a pathetic excuse for their secret handshake. Before letting go, Jackie pulled Henry toward him to give him a hug. They couldn't stay mad at each other. They both felt pretty stupid about their fight yesterday over the baseball card. But internally, they each saw their half as a sort of "best friends" charm; you know, the kind that each form half a circle or heart or something. They both knew that their half of the card was both worthless and priceless.

Henry did not have much time, however, to wallow in the sadness of his best friend moving away. He had his own summer traveling to get ready for. After his high school baseball season was over, he tried out for a traveling scout team; a team of high school players from the Kansas City area who had a good shot at playing ball at the next level, but weren't likely to get much attention from scouts on their own. These teams would play exhibition games against similar teams, and these games would attract local college and semi-pro scouts. Henry had received some attention from a few college scouts, but his high school coach saw this as a great opportunity for Henry to get the exposure he deserved.

But it meant that Henry would be on the road for most of the summer. His road trips would last up to two weeks at a time with little more than a weekend at home in between. Henry was excited about the idea of long bus rides, staying in cheap hotels, and playing ball five to six days a week. But Molly Jacobs wasn't thrilled about the idea. Next summer, after they graduated, Molly would join her older siblings on staff at a summer camp down in the Mark Twain National Forest. And then it was off to college in the fall. So, in Molly's eyes, this summer was their last chance to make great memories... until travel ball came up. Henry was leaving after the Fourth of July.

Henry and Molly decided to go out on a date a few days before Henry left town. They went to Billy's BBQ & Burgers for dinner, home of the best burgers and chocolate malts in Gladstone. Then they went to see A *League of their Own*, a movie about the women's professional baseball league that was started during World War II. Molly was misty-eyed at the end of the film when the two sisters say their goodbyes after the championship game. This was the perfect film for them: a chick-flick about baseball. They walked out of the theater hand-in-hand to Henry's car, and then decided to go to the park near Molly's house. It was beautiful and clear, and there was supposed to be a meteor shower that night. They had spent many an evening hanging out - and sometimes making out - on their favorite bench in that park.

Henry and Molly arrived at their favorite bench in the park. Aside from suggesting they go there, Molly had been unusually quiet since they left the theater. Henry, who was still caught up in the joy he felt watching the movie, took a while to notice that Molly wasn't saying anything.

"You're awfully quiet," Henry said, "I mean, I know it was a good film, but I didn't expect it to leave you speechless."

Henry did not handle Molly's silence well. He usually tried to break the silence with a dumb joke, which typically just annoyed Molly and made things more awkward.

"It really was a good film," Molly said hesitantly. "But that's not it... Henry, we need to talk."

The five most terrifying words in the English language. Molly had never said those words to him before, something for which Henry thanked the good Lord every single day. His mind kicked into overdrive. *Is this it? Is she going to break up with me? Is there some other guy?* Henry's brain ran through all these thoughts and about a dozen more before she began to speak again.

"Look," Molly said.

Oh no. First "we need to talk," and then a "look." Is she trying to kill me?

"I think we need to talk about... us," Molly continued. "I mean, you're going to be gone practically the entire summer..."

Henry interrupted because he didn't like where this was headed, "I'll be home plenty... I mean, my first road trip is only two weeks, but after that..."

"Yeah, but you'll need to do laundry and spend time with your parents and... I guess what I'm trying to say is that I'm really... sad... that you'll be gone... *most* of the summer."

"Yeah, but this is an amazing opportunity... I mean, like 95% of guys who play on these teams either get offered a scholarship or sign a semi-pro contract," Ok, maybe he was making up that number. But his point was that this was not an opportunity that he could pass up.

Molly could see that Henry's leg was shaking and his hands were getting all fidgety. She needed to act fast if she wanted to salvage this conversation before Henry's anxiety really started its downward spiral.

"Look, Henry..." she took his hands in hers and could feel the slight tremble in them. "Henry, look at me... I am not breaking up with you. I love you..."

"I... I love you too," Henry said reflexively.

"All I'm trying to say is..." Molly took a deep breath and squeezed his hands a little tighter. "is that I think we need to start thinking about our futures. Senior year starts in a couple of months. Next summer, you'll probably be off playing ball somewhere, and I'll be at Camp Twain with my brothers... I guess what I'm trying to say is..."

Molly took another deep breath and then continued, "What I'm trying to say is, I had really hoped that we would have had this summer to spend together before... before all the craziness of senior year and next summer and..."

Her voice began to taper off a bit before another breath. She went on, "I mean, I'm just bummed that instead of figuring out our futures... our future... here, together... we have to do it while we're apart."

There was silence between them. Henry didn't know what to say. He couldn't even think of a dumb joke to break the silence. They just sat there for a while. The meteor shower was kind of disappointing, but they weren't really paying attention anyway.

Chapter 22

September 7, 1992
Molly Jacobs's House
Gladstone, MO

Labor Day in Gladstone, Missouri, meant barbeques and pool parties. And this year, it also meant that Henry Aaron Mitchell was officially home from his summer on the road playing travel baseball. From July 5 on, he had not been home for more than about thirty-six hours at a time. That time was typically spent at home, eating his mom's home cooking, doing laundry, and watching Royals games if they happened to be on television.

On a few of these short stays at home, Henry and Molly went out, usually to the movies. This gave them a chance to spend time together without having to spend a lot of time talking, which Henry was thankful for. After their conversation in the park before Henry went on the road, Henry had no idea what he should say to Molly Jacobs. He was too busy working on his breaking ball to think about their future together. Why did they have to decide that now? They were only 17 years old, for heaven's sake. But she wanted him to think about it. So, when he was on the road and had trouble sleeping, you better believe he was thinking about it.

What did she want? What sort of future did she imagine for them? Why was she worried about it now?

Going to the movies with her was the perfect escape from dealing with all this for Henry. It allowed him to spend time with Molly, whom he missed dearly, but he was able to avoid the inevitable serious conversation he felt awaited them.

But now Henry was home for good, and on his way to Molly Jacobs's house for a Labor Day barbeque. On the one hand, he had been looking forward to this day since he received the invitation a month ago. But on the other hand, his heart rate elevated every time he thought about going to that party. There would be no movies to fill the time with silence. He would have to talk to her.

She greeted him at the front door with a big hug and a quick kiss. She took him by the hand and rushed him into the house. "Come on, Henry," she said. "my dad can't wait to hear about your summer playing ball."

Molly's dad was in the backyard at the grill with a stainless-steel spatula in one hand and a can of Coors Light in the other. Molly and Henry were stopped in the kitchen by Molly's mom and older brother, who gave him a hug and a firm handshake, respectively. When they reached Molly's dad, he put down his beer to give Henry one of those half-handshake-half-hugs that guys sometimes give each other.

"Drinks are in the cooler," Mr. Jacobs said, pointing with his spatula hand. "Help yourself."

Henry grabbed a soda, cracked it open, and clinked his can with Mr. Jacobs's beer can. Molly went back into the kitchen to help her mother finish preparations for the meal.

"Really good to see you," Mr. Jacobs said.

"Thanks, it's good to be seen," Henry responded.

"So, tell me about your summer," Mr. Jacobs said. "I mean, livin' the dream, am I right?"

Henry took a sip of soda, then said, "It was amazing, truly amazing."

"I bet," Mr. Jacobs said. "So, what were some of the highlights? I mean, tell me all about it."

"Well, the highlight had to be the week we spent in Wichita," Henry paused to take a drink. "Eight games in six days. Not to brag, but I was lights out on the mound. I gave up three hits and only one run in six innings. Nine strikeouts, two walks."

"Impressive. What about at the plate? Are these guys harder to hit?"

"Yeah, I definitely faced some of the best high school pitchers around. These guys were pitching a good ten miles-an-hour faster than what I'm used to facing. It took some getting used to, but I managed."

Henry took another sip of soda, giving himself something to do as he thought about how to say what he wanted to tell his girlfriend's father.

"So... uh... I haven't told Molly this yet," Henry's tone shifted considerably. "But... uh... there's a single-A... uh... single-A team that made me an offer..."

Henry had a big smile on his face. So did Mr. Jacobs. Henry continued. "They're in Wichita, actually... They... they said that... uh... I can join the team after I graduate."

Mr. Jacobs put down his beer and offered his hand to Henry. Henry reached out and shook it.

"My dad and I are going out there in two weeks to negotiate the contract," Henry took another drink. "I mean there's not much to negotiate, but my dad wants to be there to look over the contract before I sign it."

"That's really amazing, Henry," Mr. Jacobs said. "Congratulations. I'm really proud of you."

"Thanks, Mr. Jacobs. That really means a lot."

Mr. Jacobs lifted the lid to the grill and started flipping burgers. Flames shot up as grease dripped down onto the burners.

"You know," Mr. Jacobs said, changing the subject. "My sister's son is going to start playing Little League in a few weeks and I volunteered to coach his team."

"That sounds fun."

"Yeah, I know you're busy - senior year and all - but I was hoping you might be my assistant coach."

Henry had never even considered such a thing. Then he thought back to his own days in Little League and his own coaches. A smile came across his face.

Molly's dad could see that Henry was thinking about it. "Practice is only an hour a week. Still haven't decided what day... we can probably work around your schedule, even."

It didn't take long for Henry to warm up to the idea.

"I can get you the details later," Mr. Jacobs said. "But think about it. I think you'd be great with those kids."

"Thank you, sir," Henry said. "I will definitely think about it."

Mr. Jacobs looked over Henry's shoulder toward the kitchen door. Henry followed his gaze and turned around to see Molly walking out of the kitchen with a tray of devilled eggs.

"You'd better go talk to Molly," Mr. Jacobs said, giving Henry a pat on the shoulder. Henry's pulse began to accelerate as he slowly walked toward Molly. She set down the tray of devilled eggs and jogged over to Henry.

"I missed you so much this summer," Molly.

"I missed you too," Henry said. "Hey, let's go sit down."

Henry took her hand, and they walked over to a couple of chairs under the large apricot tree, away from the others congregating around the food. After Molly sat, Henry moved his chair closer to hers, setting his soda on the ground. He took her hand in his, intertwining their fingers.

"So, I've got some news for you," Henry said with a long exhale. "When we were playing in... uh... Wichita... uh... a few weeks ago..."

Henry took another deep breath and shifted in his seat. His hand was getting very sweaty, but he was not about to pull away from Molly's grip.

"So, when we were in Wichita... uh... I had a *really* good series, and... uh... there were some scouts there at the games and... uh... they came up to me after the final game..."

Another deep breath and shifting in his chair.

"They came up to me after the game and said they... uh... they were really impressed with me and... uh..."

Still another deep breath.

"Long story short," Henry paused. "They want to... uh... sign me to play next season."

Molly's jaw literally dropped. Henry reached down and grabbed his can of soda and took a big drink. Henry could see the gears working behind Molly's eyes. He braced himself for a thousand and one questions.

"Oh my god," she said. "That's amazing! I mean, seriously, that's incredible."

She leaned over and gave him a great big kiss. She was typically pretty modest about such things when they were around friends and family, but she didn't care about that at the moment. Her boyfriend was going to play professional baseball.

And then the questions came.

"So, have you signed a contract or anything like that? And how's that going to work since, I mean, I assume their season starts before school ends?"

Henry answered, "No, I haven't signed anything yet. My dad and I are driving out there in a couple of weeks to work out the details. If everything looks good, then I'll sign the contract."

He paused again and took a drink from his nearly empty can of soda.

"They know I'm still in school... I guess... uh... they sign a lot of guys right out of high school. I'll join the team in June after graduation."

"So, I guess you're not applying to college this fall..." Molly said hesitantly, not sure how to bring up the subject.

"Well, I mean, I can... uh... take classes during the off-season at Metro," Henry said. Metropolitan Community College is a community college in the suburbs of Kansas City, a few miles north of Gladstone.

"Oh, ok," Molly said. She looked down at the grass at their feet.

Henry began to panic. Was that not the answer she was hoping for? Did he say something wrong?

"I... I mean, I could apply to college... I mean... uh... there are a few schools interested in me..."

No response from Molly.

"But they're all out west... like Arizona and New Mexico..."

Molly looked up at him. Henry's sense of panic prevented him from knowing how to read her expression.

"What are you talking about?" Molly asked.

Henry didn't know what to say.

"You would really consider going out to Arizona or New Mexico for school when you could play ball just over in Wichita?"

Again, Henry didn't know what to say.

"I... I... uh... I don't know... I..."

"Henry. Henry, look at me," Molly said, coaxing him back from the brink. "I think you should play ball in Wichita."

She briefly let go of his hands so that she could scoot her chair closer to his. He took the opportunity to finish off his soda. He instinctively crumpled the aluminum can, a habit he picked up from his teammates during the summer.

"Henry Aaron Mitchell," Henry knew that when Molly middle-named him that she meant business. "This is an opportunity you can't pass up. I want nothing more than for you to go to Wichita... They want to pay you to play baseball."

Henry looked in her eyes and smiled.

"They want to *pay* you to play baseball," Molly repeated. "They freakin' want to pay you to play baseball."

They both chuckled for a moment. Their eyes met, then they leaned in to kiss. They lingered on that kiss for a moment, only to be interrupted by her father.

"Knock that off, you two," Mr. Jacobs hollered from the other end of the yard. The lovebirds blushed.

After a second, Henry got a puzzled look on his face. "If you think I should sign with Wichita, then why were you asking me about college?"

Molly was surprised by his question. "I... I don't know... I guess your news just took me by surprise, that's all. The last time we talked, I thought you said there were some schools in Iowa that were interested in you..."

"Yeah, they seem to have lost interest. It might have helped if they had shown up to that series in Wichita," Henry answered.

Molly thought for a second then said, "Well, it's their loss."

Henry smiled.

"I think you're making the right decision to play ball now," Molly said. "You've got a great thing going here, and I think you'd be stupid to pass up this opportunity. I mean, college can wait."

Molly's last statement took Henry by surprise. "Wait, what did you just say, Miss-Going-To-Grinnell-College-On-A-Legacy-Scholarship?"

It was true; Molly Jacob's father and grandfather both graduated from the rather prestigious Grinnell College in Grinnell, Iowa. Between that and Molly's straight A's throughout high school, she not only received automatic acceptance, but a full-ride scholarship. Henry was surprised she could even put those words - "college can wait" - together in the same sentence.

"I said," Molly replied. "that college can wait... for now. Look, I've got my future all mapped out. Grinnell College. Then law school. Then working at my uncle's law firm. Then political office..." Molly just beamed with delight as she recited this to Henry, even though he knew it all by heart already. Most teenage girls in the mid-1990s would run away screaming from such a detailed plan of their future, but not Molly Jacobs. She reveled in it all.

"But you've got this amazing chance… to get *paid* to play baseball," she nearly shook with glee as she said this. "You've got to do it."

She paused a moment then continued, "I mean, you've gotta ride this train as far as you can. Think about it… what if you go to some school on a baseball scholarship and you mess up your ankle again…"

Henry instinctively turned his foot in a big circle to stretch his ankle; it was a Pavlovian response every time someone said something about his injury from freshman year.

"You could not only lose the chance to play ball, but lose your scholarship… and then what?"

Henry had not considered that before. If he went to college on an athletic scholarship, and then got injured, could he lose his scholarship? Would they do that? What would he do? No matter what happened to him physically, he could always go to college, get a degree, and make a life for himself. This might be his only chance to play baseball professionally.

After eating way too much dinner and dessert, Henry and Molly went back to their spot under the apricot tree. They sat in silence as the summer sun set. The sounds of nearby birds and crickets surrounded them. After their conversation earlier about him playing baseball after graduating, Henry knew that he had to now answer the questions Molly asked him at the beginning of summer: what were his feelings about their future together? Would this relationship last beyond graduation? Honestly, he had no idea what to say to her. He had thought about it plenty during the summer; he just had not come to any conclusions about it.

But he owed her an answer. He decided to bite the bullet and break the silence.

"So… uh… Molly," Henry said as he watched a bird flit around the tree in the neighbor's yard. "I spent a lot of time thinking… uh… thinking about your question…"

Molly turned to look at him, but Henry continued to keep his eyes on the bird. He didn't like to make eye contact while having important conversations, no matter how rude his mother said that was.

Henry continued, "Your… uh… question about… us."

Henry wished he had a can of soda nearby because all of a sudden, his mouth felt very dry.

"And... uh... I mean," the wheels were spinning, but Molly could see that he was having trouble getting any traction. She decided to give the guy a break and jump in.

"I've been thinking, too," she said.

Now Henry started getting really nervous. What had she been thinking? Did she want to end it now, so they could go through senior year with no strings attached? Had she met someone else during the summer and was just waiting to move Henry out of the way? So many panicked thoughts running through his head, he almost didn't hear what she was going to say.

"And what I was thinking," she continued slowly, seeing - even in the dark - that Henry was getting anxious. "that we've got a really great thing going, don't you think?"

"Yeah... yeah, of course," Henry answered.

"We've been together, what, like four years... off and on," she said.

"Uh... yeah, something like that," Henry answered.

"And, I mean, I don't think that we should just throw that away because, you know, we're headed in different directions next June."

Henry liked what he was hearing so far, but was still waiting for the hammer to drop. He was sure there was a big old "but" that she was building toward.

"But," - and there it was - "I don't think we should make any long term plans right now, either."

"Uh huh," was about all Henry could say.

"So, I guess what I'm trying to say is... that for now, I think we should just enjoy what we have and just see where it takes us."

Henry thought for a moment about what she said. So basically, he thought, she wants to shelve the conversation for another six to nine months. That was sort of what he was thinking during the summer; he just hadn't been able to articulate it... at all.

"Yeah, that's kind of what I was thinking, too," Henry said. Molly reached out and took his hand and gave it a squeeze. They sat there in silence, enjoying the last few moments of their summer vacation. After all, they had school in the morning.

Chapter 23

April 30, 1993
Winnetonka High School
Gladstone, MO

Henry hollered at the team of six-year-olds to join him on the pitcher's mound. Fifteen boys sprinted from all corners of the field and Mr. Jacobs walked in from the dugout bench. It was the Cardinals' last practice before the final game of the season. At this level of Little League - one step above tee ball - they kept score during the games, but did not keep track of teams' season record. Everyone got a trophy at the end-of-the-season pizza party. But Henry was keeping track and, by his estimation, if his Cardinals won their game on Saturday, then they would have the best record in the league. The league may not have acknowledged it, but he did.

Mr. Jacobs gave them a few words of encouragement, then turned to Henry. "Coach Henry, why don't you tell the boys one last baseball story. It is our last practice, after all."

All season long, Henry would end practice with one of his favorite baseball stories; stories he grew up hearing from his dad. He'd told them about the Great Bambino calling his shot, and about Jackie Robinson standing tall against the racism he faced. But his favorite stories were about the amazing feats of Satchel Paige. And he decided to save his favorite story for last.

"Alright boys, gather round," Henry said. "I'm going to tell you another story about... Satchel Paige."

The boys all cheered.

"It was the 1942 Negro League World Series, the ultimate matchup between the best pitcher around and the best hitter around... Satchel Paige versus Josh Gibson," Jack Mitchell's flair for dramatic storytelling had certainly rubbed off on his son. The boys were absolutely captivated.

"Satchel Paige was on the mound and the game was on the line. And he knew that he would be facing Josh Gibson if anyone got on base. So, with a man already on base, Satchel Paige walked one batter..."

Oohs and ahhs came from the boys circled round Henry.

"Then he walked *another* batter."

More oohs and ahhs.

"So, with bases loaded, Josh Gibson stepped up to the plate. And Satchel Paige kept his cool. He was so calm and cool and confident that he even told Gibson where he was throwing his pitches..."

There was an audible gasp from one of the boys, causing the others to break out in giggles.

"And even though the bases were loaded... and even though he was facing the greatest hitter in the game... and even though he told Gibson where he was throwing the ball... the great Satchel Paige struck... out... Josh... Gibson... with... only... three... pitches!"

The boys all clapped and cheered. Mr. Jacobs stepped into the middle of the circle.

"Alright boys," Coach Jacobs said. "Saturday is our last game..."

The boys moaned in disappointment.

Coach Jacobs continued, "And you guys have improved so much. So, I want you to go out there on Saturday, play hard, and have fun!"

The moans and groans quickly turned to cheers and applause.

"Alright, hands in the middle," the boys followed Henry's cue. "Cardinals on three! One... two... three..."

"Cardinals!" they all yelled together as they threw their hands into the air. The boys ran toward the bleachers where their parents were waiting to take them home. Henry and Mr. Jacobs walked over to the dugout to clean up the equipment. In addition to the team equipment - a bucket of balls, a few bats, and some batting helmets - at least one or two kids inevitably left behind a mitt or a hat. If they were lucky, the kid would have written their name on their stuff so that they could return the lost items to their rightful owners. But today the two coaches struck the jackpot; everybody took all their things home with them. It only took all season, but they managed to finally take home all their stuff.

"So, when's your next playoff game?" Mr. Jacobs asked Henry.

Once again, Henry Aaron Mitchell was leading his high school baseball team to a successful season. They took the league championship outright, and were making a run for the school's first-ever state championship.

"Uhh… tomorrow actually," Henry said. "It's a home game against… uh… Frederick Douglass High School in Columbia."

"Frederick Douglass?" Mr. Jacobs knew that name sounded familiar, and not just because he'd read Douglass's narrative in college. It took him a second to figure it out, and Henry just smiled watching Mr. Jacobs wrack his brain to remember why he should be familiar with Frederick Douglass High School in Columbia, Missouri. Then it clicked.

"Is that where…?" Mr. Jacobs began to say.

"Where Jackie goes?" Henry finished the question for him. "Yes, yes, it is."

Going into the top of the seventh inning in the regional playoff game between the Frederick Douglass High School Bulldogs and the Winnetonka High School Griffins, the score was tied 4-4. Henry Aaron Mitchell was on the mound, trying to keep the Bulldogs from scoring so that the Griffins would have a chance to win the game in the bottom of the inning. But the heart of the Bulldogs' lineup was not going to make that easy for him.

Henry took the mound in relief in the fifth inning after the previous pitcher gave up the tying run to the Bulldogs. He struck out four of the six batters he faced in the fifth and sixth innings, and the two hitters who made contact didn't hit the ball out of the infield. But to get through the seventh and final inning, he was going to have to face two hitters who would be playing college ball next year. But the hitter Henry was most concerned about also happened to be his best friend, Jackie Roosevelt Marcus, sandwiched between the two Bulldog sluggers.

The first Douglass hitter stepped into the batter's box. He worked the count to 2-2 before hitting a high fly ball to left field, but the left fielder ran it down and made the catch look easy.

The next batter was Jackie Marcus, who had started the Bulldogs' rally back in the fourth inning to tie the game. But that was a different pitcher. He had never faced his best friend in a real game, only in practices. The two of them stood there, sixty feet, six inches apart with the game on the line.

In this match-up, it's hard to say who had the advantage. Henry knew that Jackie liked to swing at high, outside fastballs, but that he rarely made contact with them. A seemingly easy way to strike him out. But Jackie knew that when Henry got nervous - which he was bound to be in this situation - he had trouble with his release point and would sometimes end up pitching right down the middle of the plate. All Jackie had to do was get into Henry's head and then wait for him to make a mistake.

As expected, the first pitch was letter-high and on the outside corner of the plate. Jackie couldn't resist. He took a huge swing, as if trying to win the game right then and there, but he was very clearly underneath the ball that found its way right into the catcher's glove. Henry smirked at his friend as the catcher threw the ball back to him. Henry circled the mound, rubbing the ball between his bare hands, then took his place back atop the pitcher's mound.

Henry gazed in to get the sign from the catcher, who called for the exact same pitch he'd just thrown. Henry shook it off; Jackie would be expecting it. The catcher then called for an inside curveball. Henry nodded and adjusted his grip on the ball in his glove. He went into his windup and, right in the middle of his pitching motion, Jackie caught his eye and gave him a wink followed by a big cheesy smile. Flustered, Henry released the ball too late, causing the ball to break too far inside, hitting Jackie squarely in the right calf muscle.

Both benches jumped to their feet, ready to rush onto the field if necessary. The home plate umpire removed his mask and took a few steps toward the mound to make sure that Henry and Jackie kept their distance. Jackie dropped his bat and hopped around home plate. He was bound to end up with a nice bruise, but it was the adrenaline of getting beaned causing him to jump around more than anything else. But he was also on the verge of laughter; he couldn't believe his best friend beaned him in the leg.

Henry stood there in shock about what transpired over the course of the past six seconds. He started to walk toward Jackie. The umpire, not knowing the two boys had been best friends since the third grade, hustled to intercept the boys. The crowds got louder, certain that they were about to see a brawl.

When Henry realized why the umpire was headed toward him, he held up his hands as if being confronted by a cop. He said repeatedly, "I'm sorry, I'm sorry," as Jackie jogged down to first base. Jackie tipped the brim of his helmet toward Henry and shook his head and laughed. The umpire saw that he wasn't going to have to play referee in a professional wrestling match on the infield. He gave each head coach a stern warning that there had better not be any further inside pitches.

Jackie got to first base and handed his batting gloves to the base coach. He rubbed his calf, trying to prevent it from cramping up. Henry looked to see that his friend was ok, then took his place back atop the mound. The next batter stepped into the box and play was ready to resume.

The batter worked Henry to a 3-1 count, mostly due to Jackie taking up residency in Henry's head. Jackie kept threatening to steal second by taking a huge lead off first. He drew at least three throws from Henry, but dove back to the bag safely each time. On the 3-1 pitch - a changeup on the inside half of the plate after two consecutive curveballs - Jackie took off toward second.

"Going!" the Winnetonka infielders yelled. After delivering the pitch, Henry went into a crouch to get out of the way of the throw from the catcher. The shortstop ran over to cover second base. The batter took a huge swing, purposely missing to distract the catcher and delay the throw to second, which seemed to work. The catcher, worried about the swinging bat, had trouble getting the ball out of his glove, and made a bad throw to second. But even if it had been a good throw, Jackie had clearly beat the ball to the bag.

The ball hit a clump of dirt about six inches in front of the shortstop's glove and took a bad bounce into shallow center field. Jackie popped up from his foot-first slide and took off toward third. The center fielder, who was rushing in to back up the throw to second, scooped up the wayward ball and made the long throw to third base. It was a close play, but Jackie

229

dove head first on the home plate side of the bag, extending his right arm to hug it as he slid to avoid the throw.

"Safe!" the infield umpire yelled, throwing his arms out to his sides. Jackie asked for a timeout to stand up and brush the dirt off his shirt and out of the waistline of his pants. He high-fived the third base coach, then adjusted his protective cup as he stepped onto third base. Henry stared him down, more upset at himself for letting Jackie get to him than he was at Jackie for taking advantage of knowing Henry's weaknesses.

The visiting crowd from FDHS cheered on Jackie, who was egging them on by throwing his hands up in the air and pumping his fists. Henry took a few slow laps around the pitcher's mound massaging the brand-new ball he received from the home plate umpire. His catcher came out and put his hand on Henry's shoulder, trying to calm him down. He'd seen Henry pitch his way out of other sticky situations; he just had to get Henry refocused.

The home plate umpire walked toward the mound to get the game going again. Henry removed his cap to wipe the sweat from his forehead while the catcher returned to his spot behind home plate. Henry put his hat back on and rubbed the baseball a few times as he took his place at the pitching rubber. The Griffins' coach yelled from the dugout, "You've got this Hammer!"

The home team on the bench joined in cheering for their star pitcher, which got the home crowd cheering as well. The visiting crowd took this as a challenge and started cheering on Jackie and the Bulldogs. And in the midst of the pandemonium, right behind the backstop, sat Molly Jacobs. If she believed in the power of telepathy, she would have used it right now to calm down her boyfriend so that he could get his team out of this jam.

Henry set himself on the mound, working from the windup with the runner on third. Yes, the windup was maybe a half second slower than pitching from the stretch, but he did not dare turn his back to the speedy Jackie Roosevelt Marcus on third base. The batter stepped back into the batter's box, and the umpire pointed at Henry to give him the go-ahead to resume the game. With a full count, the catcher called for a low, outside fastball; a pitch almost guaranteed to produce a ground ball to the left side of the infield. If Jackie broke for the plate, the shortstop could easily throw him out. If Jackie stayed put, it was an easy play at first.

Henry pitched the low, outside fastball. The right-handed batter was slow getting his bat around and hit a soft line drive right at the second baseman, freezing Jackie in his tracks. Henry breathed a deep sigh of relief as the second baseman recorded the second out of the inning, as did Molly Jacobs now on her feet in the stands. Henry felt a lot better about keeping Jackie from scoring now that there were two outs. Jackie attempting to steal home was no longer on the table.

The next Bulldog batter stepped into the box, and let's just say that this guy wouldn't be anyone's first choice of batters in this particular situation: game tied in the top of the seventh with the winning run ninety feet from home plate. It was this player's skills in the field that earned him a starting position, not his bat. Henry felt an extra boost of confidence when he saw this guy step up to the plate knowing that it should be an easy out.

However, the Bulldogs' left fielder was not going to go down without a fight. Before Henry knew it, he'd thrown at least eight pitches to the guy, all hard fastballs. The batter did have a keen eye and did not swing at any pitches outside the strike zone, and those in or near the zone, he managed to foul off. The count was now 2-2, and this guy had fouled off four straight pitches.

And Henry's arm was getting tired. For a split second, he thought about those diet pills that Eric had given him last season. He'd still be throwing some serious heat if he had taken a few before taking the mound. But those thoughts offered no help or consolation; he had to rely on his own strength and adrenaline to get this guy out.

Henry looked to his catcher for the sign. Inside curveball. Henry nodded in agreement. This guy had faced eight straight fastballs and was likely expecting another one. A breaking ball was just the thing to catch him off guard. He'd likely swing ahead of the off-speed pitch and Henry could end the inning with a strikeout. Henry, still working from the windup, reared back to throw the curveball. But he overcompensated for his fatigue and overthrew the ball. What was supposed to be an inside curveball ended up in dirt a few inches off the outside edge of the plate. The catcher lunged to his right, but the ball bounced under his glove and started rolling toward the backstop.

Fortunately, the backstop was not far behind home plate and the catcher had cat-like reflexes. He tossed his mask to the side and twisted around to find the ball. Henry noticed that Jackie saw the ball go in the dirt and past the catcher. Jackie broke for home plate and was at full speed in about three steps. Henry charged the plate to take the throw from the catcher and cut off the runner.

The catcher fielded the loose ball and shoveled it to Henry, who was in a lineman's stance straddling home plate. He was ready for impact.

And so was Jackie.

Jackie lowered his shoulder to plow through Henry on his way to scoring the winning run. Henry braced for the hit, but Jackie proved to be more than Henry could handle. Henry had not been hit that hard in a long time. He went from on his feet to on his ass before he knew what had happened. And as he tried to regain his bearings, he realized the ball was no longer in his mitt. Jackie had scored the go-ahead run.

Henry saw a batting glove in his face, offering to help him back to his feet. It was Jackie.

Chapter 24

July 10, 1993
Jackson's BBQ
Wichita, KS

If Henry could choose the opponent who would end the Winnetonka Griffins' pursuit of a state championship, he would have chosen Jackie Roosevelt Marcus and the Frederick Douglass Bulldogs. After Jackie stole home on the wild pitch, Henry finished off the batter at the plate to end the top of the inning. And unfortunately, the Griffins were not able to answer in the bottom half of the inning. Henry's senior season was over.

The final weeks of Henry's senior year went exactly how he would have hoped. The second weekend of May was the senior prom, which proved to be a magical evening for Henry and Molly Jacobs. Three weeks later was graduation. Henry walked across the stage, shook the principal's hand, and received his diploma. Jackie, who graduated two days earlier, was in the audience to see his friend graduate. After family celebrations at Henry's house and at Molly Jacobs's house, Henry, Molly, and Jackie went to Denny's for late-night burgers and milkshakes. But looming over their evening was the unspoken fact that they would be going their separate ways very shortly. Molly was off to work at a summer camp with her older siblings, while Jackie was starting his college career early at Central Methodist University in St. Louis during their summer session. Thanks to a really dynamic youth group director, Jackie had "found Jesus" during his senior year in Columbia and decided to follow in his father's footsteps into the ministry. But Henry was the first to actually leave; his parents were helping him move to Wichita in the morning.

After saying goodbye to Jackie and driving Molly home, Henry finally got to bed at around 2:15am. And his dad was standing in his doorway a mere four hours later to drag him out of bed. They had to pack the car and then make the nearly four-hour drive from Gladstone to Wichita. Henry needed to be on the field at 1:00pm for his first workout.

Before Henry's parents said their goodbyes after helping Henry bring his things into his motel room, Mr. Mitchell took an envelope out of his back pocket and handed it to Henry. "It's just a little graduation gift," he said.

Henry opened the envelope with a surprised look on his face. Some kids get new cars - or in parts of the Midwest, sometimes a new horse - for graduation; Henry got tickets to the 1993 MLB All-Star Game in Baltimore. He gave his parents extra big hugs and watched them leave his motel room.

On the afternoon of July 10, Jack Mitchell once again made the nearly four-hour drive to Wichita. He was going to stay the night with Henry in his motel room, then the two of them would fly out of Eisenhower Airport, with a connection in Louisville on their way to Baltimore for the 64th Major League Baseball All-Star Game. But first, dinner.

It had been less than a month since his parents had helped move Henry into a room at a motel down the street from the Wichita Wingnuts home stadium. Most of the players stayed there when the team was in town. Two blocks away was a greasy spoon barbeque joint called Jackson's BBQ where the Wingnuts always went to celebrate a win. Unfortunately, the team hadn't enjoyed the smoky goodness at Jackson's in over a week.

Since Henry had joined the Wingnuts, he had been working out with the team and was suiting up for games, but hadn't seen any action. But he had lots of stories to tell his dad over baby back ribs and smoked brisket.

The summer evening was cooler than normal that day, so Henry and his dad decided to walk to the restaurant. The dinner rush had ended, so they had their pick of booths in the dining room.

"So, what's it been like?" Jack asked his son. "It's not like you've been calling us every night."

It was true. Henry's mother had given him a calling card so that he could call home frequently, but Henry had called home maybe three times since he moved to Wichita. He knew his parents weren't happy about that. He hoped this trip with his dad would help smooth over any ruffled feathers.

Henry took a long sip of his Coke that the waitress had just brought to the table. "It's been amazing, Dad. Just... amazing."

Jack gave his son a big smile. Obviously, Jack was not upset about Henry's lack of communication, but he was anxious to hear all about his son's new adventures in professional baseball.

"Man, walking out onto that field for the first time... The grass is greener than any field I've ever played on. And it is perfectly cut... every blade of grass is exactly the same length," Henry said, beaming.

"And I've never seen an infield so smooth," Henry went on. "Hey... hey, remember that time in Little League? I think it was the championship game, and... and Jackie had that ground ball take a bad bounce... like Buckner... remember that?"

"Yeah, yeah. I remember," Jack said.

"Yeah... well if we had been playing on this field back then," Henry's voice was building toward a crescendo. "Jackie would have fielded that ball so clean... and... and we would have won that damn game."

The waitress brought them some garlic rolls and took their order.

"So, what about the team? How are practices and games and...?" Jack was eager to hear how Henry was fitting in with his teammates. Was he holding his own? Was he able to keep up? This was semi-pro ball, not just high school any more.

"Oh my god, I meant to call you..." Henry took a bite of one of the garlic rolls, chewed it a bit, then jumped into his story.

"The day I moved in was my first real practice. All the normal stuff... grounders... fly balls... all that stuff."

Henry finished his roll and his Coke. And it was like the waitress had a sixth sense or something because no sooner did he put his empty glass of Coke on the table, then she put a filled glass down in its place.

Henry continued, "So then, it's my turn to take a little BP. I grab my helmet and bat... I have to hit with a wooden bat now..."

Henry smiled when he said those words. Jack knew why. Several years ago, for a birthday present, Jack had brought Henry a personalized bat from the Louisville Slugger Factory and Museum. Jack was in Louisville for a regional salesmen convention and spent a free afternoon at the Museum. On his way out, he stopped in the gift shop to get Henry a souvenir, and he just couldn't resist the idea of bringing home a bat with Henry's name engraved on it. It became a token of faith in the dream that Henry would one day be playing in the Big Leagues. Of course, when it was time to pack up and move to Wichita, Henry wrapped it up nicely and stored it in his bedroom closet. There was no way in hell he was going to risk anything happening to it by bringing it with him.

"So, I step into the batter's box, and I guess there's this thing here in Wichita that they do to new guys," Henry took another sip of his drink. "Whenever a new guy signs with the team, he has to face the hardest-throwing pitcher on the team."

Henry paused to let that sink in for his dad.

"So, how'd you do?" Jack asked, dying to know.

"Oh my god," Henry said. "I've never faced a guy throwing so hard. I step into the box, and this guy winds up and lets it rip. All I could see was this little white and red blur. The radar gun said 93 miles an hour."

"Holy crap," Jack said.

"Yeah," Henry said. "The fastest pitch I ever saw in high school was that guy from Paige who topped out at like 78."

"So, how'd you handle this guy?"

"Well, before I knew what was happening, he threw his second pitch, another 93-mile-an-hour fastball, right down Main Street," Henry said, taking a sip of his soda to create a dramatic pause. "I took a swing, and I must have been like six seconds behind."

Jack shook his head in disbelief, and he was really hoping that this story wasn't going to end badly.

"So, I stepped out of the box and looked over at the guys in the dugout. Some of them were chuckling and the coaches were just shaking their heads."

Jack did not like where this was headed.

"But I knew this was all part of their... uh... welcoming party," Henry said. "But I wasn't going to let them get the best of me."

Henry smiled and winked at his dad, and then continued his story.

"So, I adjusted my batting gloves and choked up a little bit on the bat and stepped back into the box. I stared down that Hulk on the mound."

Another sip of soda. As much as Jack was on the edge of his seat to hear how this story was going to end, he was also quite impressed with Henry's storytelling abilities. A chip off the old block.

"He went into his windup, another hard fastball down the pipe... but this time I got a good read on it, and swung..." another bite of a garlic roll. "And man, you should have seen the look on everyone's faces when that ball went sailing into the gap in left-center."

"So, what's it like?" Jack asked. "What's it like to hit a 90+ mile-an-hour fastball?"

"Oh my god," Henry said. "Like nothing I've ever experienced before. I could feel the impact of the ball hitting the bat through my entire body... like an electric shock or something. I mean, I just stood there, shaking from head to toe... I mean, the shock... the adrenaline... like nothing I've ever experienced before. My heart was racing. My hands were shaking. It was... one of the most incredible feelings in the world."

Jack smiled big and reached across the table to give Henry a pat on the shoulder.

The next morning, they were up and out of Henry's motel room early to get to the airport to catch their flight to Baltimore.

Chapter 25

September 8, 1998
Henry Mitchell's Apartment
Binghamton, NY

Henry hung up his keys on the hook by the door as he entered his apartment.

"Honey, I'm home," he called out to see if his roommate and teammate, Billy Cordova, was home. There was no answer, but Henry could hear that a ball game was on the television in the other room.

It was nearly 8:00pm, and Henry had been gone for the past twelve hours. As he walked toward the bathroom of the small, one-bedroom apartment, he was debating internally whether to shower, eat, or watch the ball game first. He was hungry from not having eaten anything since those couple of McDonald's cheeseburgers at noon. But it sure would have been nice to wash of twelve hours of running all over town in preparation of moving home to Gladstone in a week. But the game. Tonight might be the night. Mark McGwire had tied Roger Maris's 27-year-old single-season home run record the night before, and he seemed primed to break the record tonight.

Why are such insignificant decisions sometimes the hardest ones to make?

It had been an unseasonably warm day in Binghamton, New York, so showering won the debate.

"Taking a shower," Henry hollered in the direction of the living room/dining room/baseball equipment storage room.

Henry closed the bathroom door, turned on the shower, undressed, and got in, letting the warm water rinse off the sweat and stress of the long day.

Henry had been in Binghamton for the past several months, playing for the Binghamton Mets, the AA affiliate of the New York Mets. After impressing the scouts during his time in Wichita, he was drafted in the late rounds of the 1995 Major League Baseball Draft by the Florida Marlins. He played the first half of the 1996 season in Single-A with the Batavia Muckdogs before moving on to play for the AA Jacksonville Jumbo Shrimp. Henry absolutely hated the hot, muggy weather of Florida, so he was thrilled to move 1,001 miles north to Binghamton when he was traded from the Marlins to the Mets in May of 1998. The trade had made headlines around the country, but not because of Henry. Henry had been included "for good measure" in the trade that sent future Hall of Famer Mike Piazza from Florida to New York only a week after the Los Angeles Dodgers sent Piazza to Florida.

During his time in the Minor Leagues, Henry had been moved from the pitcher's mound to the outfield. He had a great arm for a high school pitcher, but the standards are much higher in the Minor Leagues. But his arm strength and accuracy turned him into quite an asset in the outfield. He currently led his team in outfield assists. The Binghamton hitting coach had been working with Henry on his stance at the plate, which gave him a better look at the pitches he faced, as well as increased his bat speed. He was now hitting the ball more consistently and with greater power. If he kept up this kind of production, both at the plate and in the field, Henry would likely be moving up to AAA Syracuse at the start of the 2000 season.

Henry was fitting in well with his teammates in Binghamton. The team had good on-field chemistry and he had become good friends and roommates with the third baseman, Billy Cordova. Billy was a big dude, but surprisingly nimble on his feet and had some of the quickest hands in the division. And he was pretty laid back off the field, which made him an excellent roommate.

Even though Henry loved every minute of his time in the Minor Leagues, he did miss his home and his friends in Gladstone. He and Jackie talked on the phone every few weeks. Jackie had finished his undergrad degree and had moved on to seminary. The two of them would joke around about whether Henry would be in the Big Leagues first, or if Jackie would receive his ordination first.

And then there was Molly Jacobs. Over the past five years, they had drifted off in their own directions. She spent four years at Grinnell College, graduating with honors with a degree in political science, then spent the last year interning for her uncle's law firm in Chicago with the plan of going to law school the following year.

Henry had spent a lot of time thinking about Molly Jacobs, wondering what she was doing, wondering if she was also thinking of him. He still cared about her; he just wasn't sure if they would ever get back together again. Maybe it just wasn't meant to be. Maybe what they had was just meant to be a really great high school romance.

Playing ball full time made it difficult for almost anyone to have a steady girlfriend. Several of the guys liked to "play the field," so to speak and had a girl in every city. Some of his teammates tried to set Henry up on dates, both for one-night stands and for more serious relationships, but he always had some reason why he couldn't. Usually a dumb reason, but deep down - even though he wouldn't actually admit it - it was because of Molly Jacobs.

The hot water continued to wash Henry's long day out of his mind and body. His mind was almost completely blank - something not very common for his often-anxious brain - when he heard the pounding of Billy's large hand on the bathroom door. Henry's moment of tranquility vanished with the first thud.

"Yo, Hammer," Billy said from the other side of the door. "Get out here."

Henry breathed out very loudly, even though the sound of the shower drowned out his sigh. "Dude, I'm in the shower."

"Man, come on. Big Mac is up," Billy continued. "He's gonna hit number 62."

"Ah, shit," Henry muttered. He had finally reached a point of relaxation for the first time that day. He was at total peace after a long, busy, and sometimes stressful day. And he was dripping wet and only halfway through his shower. But he had the opportunity to witness baseball history, albeit on their 32-inch television set.

"Man, hurry up. You don't want to miss this," Billy said.

Henry reached down and turned off the shower. As he pulled back the shower curtain, Billy had flung open the bathroom door. Henry, dripping wet and completely naked couldn't help but smile at the giddiness on Billy's face.

"They're announcing his name right now," Billy said. He had turned up the volume on the TV before coming down the hallway to get his roommate, not wanting to miss any of the action. He snatched Henry's towel from the rack and scampered back into the living room, laughing loudly as he went.

"Bastard!" Henry shouted. As he got out of the shower, he grabbed Billy's hand towel out of spite. He dried his face, then used it to cover himself. He and Billy had been roommates for two seasons now, but he still felt uncomfortable walking around the apartment completely naked. The sound of the electrified crowd blasted from the television, and Henry couldn't help but smile. If Mark McGwire was actually about to make history, he'd have a damn good story to tell; if not, then his moment of Zen would have been interrupted for nothing.

It was the bottom of the fourth inning in the game being played in Busch Stadium in St. Louis. On the first pitch from Chicago Cubs pitcher Steve Traschel, Mark McGwire smacked a line drive that just barely cleared the left field fence and etched his name into the history books. The hometown crowd went wild as Big Mac circled the bases.

Billy jumped to his feet, nearly spilling the can of soda in his hand, arms outstretched in triumph. Henry joined in the celebration, jumping up and down and pumping his fists. Modesty be damned, this was history unfolding before their eyes. The two young men whooped and hollered, likely disturbing the peaceful evening for their neighbors in the apartment complex. Billy shouted, "Dude, we just witnessed history!" as he pointed at the screen.

The crowd in St. Louis was still cheering McGwire as he was mobbed at home plate by his teammates. His son, Matthew, was brought out onto the field to celebrate with his dad.

"History! Real baseball history!" It was obvious that Billy didn't know what to say, but was just spouting out words in his excitement.

"Yup, we witnessed history, Billy," Henry said. "And I was naked."

Chapter 26

August 15, 2002
Smith's Ballpark
Salt Lake City, Utah

Henry sat down in the chair in front of his locker in the Salt Lake Bees locker room and began unlacing his cleats. Several of his teammates patted him on the shoulder on the way to their lockers. Henry had had a good game that evening, going 2 for 4 and scoring the winning run in the bottom of the eighth inning. In fact, he'd had a very good past couple of weeks playing in his second full season for the Anaheim Angels' AAA affiliate team in Utah. Henry was traded from the New York Mets organization in December of 2001 to Anaheim as part of the deal that sent slugger Mo Vaughn to the Mets. The deal proved to be a major disappointment for the Mets, but the Angels fared pretty well with the help of their acquisition, pitcher Kevin Appier.

While all his teammates rushed to take showers so they could enjoy an evening out on the town, Henry took his time. Most of the guys planned to go to The Horny Hippo, a gentlemen's club about half an hour outside the city. One of the Bees, Luis Magana, was dating a girl who was a freelance exotic dancer who went by the stage name of Kitty McCune. She would follow the team when they were on the road and perform in clubs in whatever city the Bees were playing in; she also had a standing engagement at the Hippo when the Bees were at home. In some cities, she made more money from dancing in a weekend than some of the ballplayers made in a week. And even though most of the guys on the team had seen her show a couple dozen times, they never missed a performance.

Henry, however, was not much of a fan of the whole strip club scene for several reasons. He was not a fan of overpriced, watered-down drinks and outrageous cover charges. And he'd rather not spend an evening watching half-naked ladies prance around the stage then have to go back to the small two-bedroom apartment that he shared with one of his teammates. Not exactly his idea of a good time. So, it would be a long shower in the mostly empty locker room, then Chinese takeout and a movie on the couch for Henry. His roommate was going with the guys to the Hippo, so he'd have the place to himself for a few hours, something that Henry certainly didn't mind.

As the nearly too-hot water ran down Henry's back, he could hear his teammates finishing up at their lockers and heading out of the clubhouse. He stood there a few more minutes, waiting for the locker room to sound empty. He turned the water off, dripped dry for a moment, then grabbed his towel to dry off.

"Hey, Henry," Henry could hear someone calling for him from the locker room. The way the voice echoed through the hallway, it was hard to tell exactly who it was.

"Yo, Hammer. You still in the showers?" The voice called out. It sounded an awful lot like the General Manager of the team, John Blackwell.

"Mr. Blackwell, is that you?" Henry hollered toward the locker room as he wrapped one towel around his waist and flung his second towel over his shoulder. He saw Blackwell standing in the now empty locker room. Henry wiped the water from his face as he nodded in acknowledgement of his boss.

"How many times? Call me John," Blackwell said. "Get dressed and meet me in my office... and be quick about it."

"Y-yes sir... I mean, John," Henry said.

What could this be about? Am I being traded again? Being put on waivers? Blackwell left, and Henry immediately went into panic mode. He took several slow, deep breaths and focused his gaze on the torn baseball card that was pinned to the back of his locker. That Ken Griffey, Jr. card - the same one that he and Jackie had fought over as kids - had become not only a prized reminder of his friendship with Jackie, but also an object to focus on to help calm his anxiety attacks. This time, like most other times, it was helping him slow his breathing and heart rate, however his brain was running a mile a minute. Every worst-case scenario was running through his mind simultaneously.

Henry quickly got dressed and packed up his things into his backpack. He walked down the hallway to the management offices and saw Blackwell's office door open. He knocked lightly as he stepped in.

"Hey there, Henry," Blackwell said. "Take a seat."

Henry sat in the chair that Blackwell pointed to. He immediately began fidgeting with the baseball in his hand as he waited to hear what the GM had to say. He often carried around a baseball for this very purpose.

"I've got some news for you," Blackwell said. Henry hated those words, especially coming from an authority figure.

Blackwell continued, "As you know, the Bigs expand their rosters at the end of the month and they need two outfielders up in Anaheim."

Henry wasn't sure why Blackwell was explaining all of this; everyone in the clubhouse knew they wanted two outfielders in Anaheim. And it was obviously going to be Luis Magana and Jason Rockwell.

"Luis and Jason were slated to go," Blackwell went on. "But Jason is still nursing that pulled hamstring. We'd hoped he'd be in better shape by now."

It was true; Jason Rockwell had taken longer than expected to heal from a pulled hamstring. A spot on the Big-League roster was his for the taking, if he had healed the way he was supposed to. Instead, he'd seen very limited playing time in Salt Lake and a dip in his stats.

"So, we're going to keep Jason here, but they still need another outfielder," Blackwell paused a second, trying to be dramatic.

"You're next in line, my friend," Blackwell said with a big smile. He stood up and reached out to shake Henry's hand. "Congratulations, my boy. You're headed to the Big Leagues."

Six words. "You're headed to the Big Leagues." Words that Henry Aaron Mitchell had dreamed of hearing since his dad took him to his first Royals game. Mr. Blackwell went on to tell Henry when his last day with the Bees would be and tell him about flying out to Southern California and meeting with the Angels' front office. So many details, so few of which Henry actually heard. All Henry could hear, over and over in his head, were those six glorious words. "You're headed to the Big Leagues."

"Do you have any questions?" Blackwell was still talking. How long had he been talking just now? How much had Henry missed?

"Uh... Umm... no, sir," Henry was really hoping right about now that Blackwell would give him some sort of paper that had on it everything he had just said. But no such luck.

Blackwell shook Henry's hand again as he started to make his way around the desk. Henry only just now realized that he was standing as well. He must have instinctively stood when Blackwell did. Blackwell, who realized that Henry was in shock over the good news, gently guided him toward the office door as he let go of Henry's hand.

"Congratulations, son," Blackwell said. "I know you've worked really hard for this."

"Thank you, sir," Henry replied as he left the office. He paused for a moment to try to remember which direction to turn. Blackwell nudged him to the left.

"Have a good night, Henry. Oh, and don't forget to call your mother to tell her the good news."

Henry, who had finally begun to regain his bearings, began to think of all the people he would need to call. Of course, his parents and Jackie and a few of his old coaches from high school and when he played in Wichita. He still kept in touch with some of them. He would have to tell Mr. Jacobs. Even though Henry no longer helped him coach Little League, he owed it to Mr. Jacobs. After Henry's own parents, Mr. Jacobs was probably Henry's biggest fan.

But as he scrolled through the contacts on his cell phone, he saw her name: Molly Jacobs. He typically passed by her name in his phone on the way to another of his contacts without even giving it a second thought. But now, after hearing those six life-changing words, she was the first person he wanted to call.

Henry arrived at his car in the mostly empty players' and stadium staff parking lot. He had been staring at his phone nearly the entire time it took him to walk from Blackwell's office to the lot. On the screen, it still read "Molly Jacobs" and her phone number. His heart began pounding hard for the second time that evening. He had a sudden flashback to the first time he worked up the courage to call Molly Jacobs, that summer evening after she kissed him outside the community pool. But this time he was not afraid of her dad answering the phone, he was afraid of talking to her again. It had been months since their last phone conversation.

Henry unlocked his car door, got into the driver's seat, and stared at his phone as he put the keys into the ignition. "Ah, what the hell," he said as he hit the call button on his phone.

CHAPTER 27

September 26, 2002
The Ballpark in Arlington
Anaheim Angels (97-62) vs. Texas Rangers (72-87)

Molly Jacobs sat on the edge of her seat, staring at the jumbotron screen situated above the right field bleachers. They were showing a replay of the previous pitch in split screen. One side of the screen showed the typical shot you see on your television of the pitcher in the foreground with the batter and catcher also in the shot. The other side of the screen was a zoomed-in shot of Henry Aaron Mitchell's face as he stared down the pitcher. And sure enough, right as the pitcher went into his delivery, Henry winked at the pitcher, causing the pitcher to throw the ball high and outside. Most of the few thousand in their seats booed at the sight of it.

Molly couldn't help but laugh as she elbowed Jackie Marcus in the arm. They smiled at each other, remembering all the times that Henry insisted they watch *Field of Dreams* when they were in high school. In fact, Molly once bought Henry a new copy of the movie on VHS tape because he had worn out his first copy. The two old friends just shook their heads. Henry had actually gotten his lifelong wish.

The meager crowd settled down as play resumed on the field. Henry dug his back foot into the red clay of the batter's box as Alvarez dug his foot into the clay in front of the pitching rubber. Henry tapped his borrowed bat on the front corners of home plate then pinwheeled the bat around twice before getting into his stance. Alvarez peered in to the catcher to get the sign, shaking off the first two before agreeing on the third. Alvarez looked at the runners on first and second, then back at the plate. The Rangers catcher set up just off the inside corner of the plate.

Alvarez, again working from the stretch, reeled back and intended to deliver his fastball to the catcher's glove on the inside corner of the plate, hoping to either get Henry to swing at an unhittable pitch or to brush him back off the plate a bit after the stunt he had just pulled. But it was obvious before he even released the ball that Alvarez's adrenaline was still too high. The ball bounced about two inches in front of Henry's right foot, hitting a clump of clay and taking a bad bounce under the catcher's glove. Henry reflexively jumped back out of the batter's box as he watched the catcher toss aside his face mask and scurry after the loose ball. The baserunners easily advanced to second and third without even a throw to either base.

Up in the stands, Molly and Jackie cheered loudly, drawing dirty looks from the home team fans two rows in front of them. The tying run was now ninety feet from home plate; the go-ahead run just ninety feet behind him. And Henry was at the plate with a 2-2 count. This was Henry's big opportunity to prove to the General Manager that they had made the right choice in calling him up from Salt Lake.

The wild pitch triggered a visit to the mound by the catcher. Henry took a few steps back from the batter's box and took a couple practice swings. He looked down the third base line to the base coach. Through a series of hand signals, the coach told him, "if you get a good pitch, swing away." Henry nodded. The umpire took a few steps toward the mound to break up the little chat between the pitcher and catcher. The catcher walked back to his spot behind the plate, and Henry stepped back into the batter's box. Tap the plate twice, two pinwheels, and Henry was ready to go.

Alvarez took his spot on the mound. Jackie sat back in his chair, took a drink of his root beer, and muttered, "Why's he working from the stretch? With runners on second and third, he should go back to the windup."

Molly looked over at Jackie. It was just like old times; all those hours she spent watching games with Henry and Jackie and listening to them nitpick the players and coaches.

Alvarez went into his delivery, and in the briefest of moments, Henry recognized the look on his face: the same look he had as he delivered the previous pitch. *That mound visit sure did a lot of good.* Henry knew exactly what was coming his way: another fastball in the dirt.

Sure enough. Same release point. Same rotation of the ball. Same trajectory.

Henry took a running swing at the ball, intending to miss the ball and block the catcher's view as the ball hit the dirt. And his plan worked perfectly. Henry was ten feet down the first base line before the catcher realized the ball got past him. Henry never looked back to see what happened to the ball.

The catcher finally grabbed the ball about ten feet behind home plate. He first looked at the runner on third, who had taken a few steps down the line, but was not a threat to try to steal home on the wild pitch. The baserunner was too close to third to warrant a pick-off throw. But he didn't want his pitcher to face another batter with bases loaded, so he set himself to make what should have been an easy throw to first base to complete the strike out and end the inning. But he had to rush the throw if he wanted a chance of throwing out Henry.

Rushing the throw proved to be a mistake. The ball sailed at least six feet over the first baseman's head. As soon as the runner on third saw the throw go to first, he broke for home and easily scored the tying run. The runner on second followed his teammate's lead and took off for third.

Henry saw the first baseman jump straight up in the air and off the bag. He glanced to his right and saw the ball flying into foul territory. A quick stutter step and, instead of running straight through the bag, he was rounding first and starting toward second base.

The crowd in the stands rose to their feet as they witnessed the melee unfolding down on the field. Molly was jumping up and down, holding tightly onto Jackie's arm. Jackie was clapping and cheering, and doing his best to keep Molly from losing her balance.

The right fielder did not back up the throw, so the first baseman had to run down the loose ball. By the time he did, the runner who had started out on second base was now halfway down the third base line and about sixty feet from home plate. The first baseman threw the ball to the catcher, who was in the perfect spot to take the throw and block the plate.

But the throw was off-line, largely because the Angels' first base coach was in the first baseman's line of sight. The bad throw forced the catcher over to the first base side of the plate. The catcher fielded the ball cleanly off a short hop, but had to dive across the plate to try to tag out the sliding baserunner. The collision knocked the ball loose and the umpire called the runner safe, putting the Angels ahead by one run.

The off-line throw, the collision at the plate, and the now-loose ball gave Henry Aaron Mitchell the chance to stretch his wild pitch strikeout into the equivalent of a triple. He took off from second base and began sprinting toward third. However, his foot slipped as he stepped on the bag, and he felt a twinge of pain in his ankle. A pain he had not felt since his freshman year of high school. But the adrenaline coursing through his veins and the greedy determination to get one more base on the play were not going to let an old ankle injury slow him down.

Molly Jacobs could see the ever-so-slightest bit of a limp in Henry's stride as he ran past the shortstop on his way to third base. She gave a quick worried look to Jackie, who just shrugged his shoulders. They turned back to watch the action on the field and continued cheering for their friend.

The third baseman was yelling at the catcher to throw him the ball. The catcher, still on his knees, fired an off-balanced throw to the third baseman. But it was a bad throw.

Henry slid feet first into third base, trying to avoid the glove of the defender. But there was no ball in that glove because the wide throw bounced about a foot or two behind Henry and continued to roll into shallow left field.

Henry jumped up from his slide, again twisting his ankle as he scrambled to his feet and was running - actually limping is more like it - toward home plate. Both Henry and the third baseman could hear the popping sound that came from Henry's ankle as he pivoted toward home.

It was obvious to all in the Ballpark in Arlington that Henry was injured but that he was determined to turn his strike out into a Little League home run. The crowd, even the Rangers fans, were now cheering for him. Henry was like the Little Engine That Could; nothing was going to stop him.

As Henry limped down the third base line, searing pain shot up his leg with each step. His teammates were half cheering and half cringing. He could barely put any weight on that foot and his teammates could see the anguish on his face.

The left fielder, who was in place to back up the throw to third, scooped up the ball, and saw that he had plenty of time to make a clean throw to the plate. The catcher stood just inside the baseline and about two feet up the line in front of the plate. He had a firm stance, ready to take the throw and tag out the baserunner. The left fielder threw a strike to the catcher, who then held the ball firmly with both hands and waited for Henry to make his move. He wasn't going to get charged with another error on this play.

Henry realized he didn't stand a chance against the Rangers catcher. He could barely put any weight on the injured foot; there was no way in hell he was going to be able to plow through him, knock the ball out of his firm grip, and tag home plate. From the stands, it appeared that he was trying to do just that. His shoulder lowered as he was about to make contact. But in reality, Henry just couldn't take another step and practically collapsed into the arms of the opposing catcher. The umpire called him out as the catcher broke his fall.

The Rangers retreated to their dugout as the Angels' manager and trainer ran out onto the field to attend to Henry's injured ankle. It took the official scorekeeper as long to sort out what had just happened on the field as it did to load Henry onto a gurney and cart him off the field. And it took even longer for Rex Hudler and Steve Physioc to break down the play for the home viewing audience. Both used the phrase "like nothing I've ever seen before" about half a dozen times. Because Henry's strikeout had not been completed by the force out at first base, the two runs scored on the play counted and put the Angels in the lead. They would hold onto that lead and win the game, thanks to Henry Aaron Mitchell.

The team physician examined Henry and found that he had ruptured his Achilles' tendon on the play during that hard slide into third base. The injury would require surgery, so they loaded Henry into a stadium van and drove him to Memorial Hospital to be examined by an orthopedic surgeon. Luckily, the driver had the game on the radio in the van so that Henry could keep listening to the play-by-play.

Henry lay in his hospital bed with his leg elevated and enough morphine in his system to take away every care in the world. He was watching *SportsCenter*, whose lead story was his own play in the top of the seventh inning. The talking heads on the screen admired Henry's tenacity as well as laughed at the trainwreck that was the Rangers' defense on the play.

During the commercial break, there was a tapping on the door of his room as it swung open. Henry was expecting to see his nurse walking in with the chocolate pudding cups he had requested, but instead it was a face he had not seen in months: Molly Jacobs.

"Can I come in?" she asked as she stopped a few steps into the room. Had it not been for all the painkillers in Henry's system, he would have probably required a dose of Xanax to fight off the anxious feelings he would have had seeing Molly Jacobs again under normal circumstances.

He sort of mumbled and waved her into the room. She picked up his Angels uniform from the chair next to his bed and moved it to a nearby shelf before sitting down. She smiled that same crooked smile that Henry couldn't resist and tucked a few loose hairs behind her ear. Neither really knew what to say; too much time had passed since they had last seen each other.

"That was a helluva play back there," Molly said over the sound of the television. Realizing that Henry was pretty doped up, she took the remote control and turned off the TV.

"Thanks," he said with a smile. "I'm glad you came."

"Me too," she said after a slightly awkward pause. She reached over and took hold of his hand, intertwining her fingers with his. It was late and they were both tired. So, they sat together in silence until Henry nodded off to sleep. Shortly after, the nurse came in to check on Henry and to tell Molly Jacobs that it was probably best for her to leave and come back in the morning. She could see him again before his surgery the following afternoon.

Epilogue

March 6, 2010
Kansas City, MO

Henry Aaron Mitchell's Major League Baseball career ended the same day it began. The ruptured Achilles' tendon proved to be an opponent he could not overcome. A few days after his surgery to repair the injury, he was able to travel back home to Gladstone, Missouri, to rehabilitate at his parents' house.

After his injury, he was placed on the disabled list, so technically he remained on the Angels' roster until the end of the season. Understandably, he did not remain on the roster as the Angels headed to the playoffs. Henry had to remain on his parent's living room sofa as he watched his Angels go on to win the first World Series championship in the franchise's history. He would not receive a World Champions ring, but he did have an authentic game-worn jersey with his name on it hanging in his closet.

Henry decided to retire at the end of the 2002 season. His doctor - one of the best orthopedists in the Kansas City area because his medical bills were still being paid for by the Anaheim Angels - said that his recovery would be long and his risk of reinjuring the ankle would be too great to consider playing professionally again. While his stats in all his time in the Minor Leagues were pretty impressive, his entire Major League career consisted of one at-bat, a strikeout, that resulted in three total bases and two runs batted in, including the game-winning run.

It just so happened that Molly was now living and working in the Kansas City area when Henry moved home to recover from his injury. Her hours at the law firm were long, but she came over to visit Henry more and more as the weeks went on. It didn't take long for the awkwardness between them to dissipate, and it was almost as if they hadn't spent the past eight years hardly ever seeing or talking to each other. Not long after they started dating again, Henry moved into Molly Jacobs's townhome in Overland Park, one of the other suburbs of Kansas City. They were married about a year later in the spring of 2004.

Molly stayed with her current law firm - they treated her very well there - and Henry finished up his bachelor's degree at the University of Missouri-Kansas City. Because Molly made a good salary at her job, she was the primary breadwinner for the Mitchell-Jacobs family. Henry worked as a regular substitute teacher in the local school district and assisted the baseball coach at Winnetonka High School, the same coach he played during his high school career. The head coach was grooming him to take over the program when he retired.

Jackie finished seminary and became an associate pastor at his father's church in Columbia, Missouri. He completed the ordination process just in time to take over as the lead pastor of the congregation when his father retired. Jackie's parents had kept their house in Gladstone and had rented it out during the time that Reverend Marcus worked in Columbia. So, they moved back to their old home shortly after he retired. This meant that Jackie came to Gladstone often to visit his parents and have Sunday evening dinners with them, as well as to see Henry and Molly if he could.

March 6 was Opening Day for the Greater Kansas City Area Little League, an event celebrated by the whole community. One of the local high school's band would play the National Anthem. There was a speech by the mayor and the Little League commissioner. There was a carnival in the park near the ballfields. And every year, they found a local celebrity - a term used very loosely because it was Kansas City, after all - to throw out the ceremonial first pitch. This year they asked former Major Leaguer and Winnetonka High School star player Henry Aaron Mitchell to do the honors. The high school also planned to retire Henry's jersey number at the ceremony.

Not only was Henry thrilled to participate in this event as an honored guest, an event that had grown exponentially since he was a kid playing Little League, but he was even more happy to share this event with his daughter who was finally old enough to play Little League t-ball herself.

Georgia Ruth Jacobs-Mitchell - her parents knew the moment that they saw her name on the birth certificate that they were guaranteeing her years of therapy - was born during Henry and Molly's first year of marriage, and Henry spent the last six years looking forward to this day: her first Little League game.

Molly insisted on taking lots of pictures of Gigi in her uniform before they left for the park, which was making Henry nervous about not getting to the ballfield on time. He finally got them both into the car and he drove off toward the park. In the backseat of the car, little Gigi was getting squirmy and anxious about playing her first baseball game. What if she doesn't know where to go or what to do? What if she's the only girl on the team? (Henry had contacted the coach ahead of time and confirmed that there was another girl on the team.)

Even though Henry didn't enjoy the whining, he was very sympathetic toward his daughter. After all, he had the same feelings of apprehension on the way to his first t-ball game. But he had an idea of what might calm little Gigi's nerves.

"Hey Gigi," Henry interrupted. "You know, I felt the same way you do when I went to my first t-ball game. And when I started to feel all funny inside, my dad - Grandpa Jack - would tell me a story about baseball. Do you want to hear a story about baseball?"

"Yeah!" she shouted from the back seat.

"Well, I'm going to tell you a story about a player named George Herman Ruth."

There was a brief pause. Henry looked in the rear-view mirror and could see the gears in Gigi's head spinning.

"Hey," she said. "George Ruth... that's like my name!"

"That's right," Molly said. "It is like your name."

"Well," Henry said. "Let me tell you about the time that George Herman Ruth - the Great Bambino - called his shot."

About the Author:

Ryan M Blanck went to his first Angels' game when he was about four years old and a love affair was born. He played baseball for two years in junior high and two years in high school. He was a decent outfielder, but was too afraid of getting hit by the ball (something that actually happened quite often) to be a good hitter. Later, as an adult, his love for the game was rekindled when the Anaheim Angels won the World Series in 2002. One of his life's goals is to visit all 30 Major League stadiums (he has been to five so far).

Ryan is a husband, father, high school English teacher, LEGO artist and writer. He lives in Southern California with his wife and two teenage daughters. *Two On Two Out* is the ninth book Ryan has written, and his first novel.

Made in the USA
Las Vegas, NV
15 April 2022

47524007R00152